STILL
LIVES

STILL LIVES

a novel

Maria Hummel

COUNTERPOINT

BERKELEY, CALIFORNIA

STILL LIVES

Library of Congress Cataloging-in-Publication Data
Names: Hummel, Maria, author.
Title: Still lives : a novel / Maria Hummel.
Description: Berkeley, CA : Counterpoint Press, [2018]
Identifiers: LCCN 2017055410 | ISBN 9781619021112
Subjects: | GSAFD: Suspense fiction.
Classification: LCC PS3608.U46 S75 2018 | DDC 813/.6—dc23
LC record available at https://lccn.loc.gov/2017055410

Jacket designed by Jaya Miceli
Book designed by Wah-Ming Chang

COUNTERPOINT
2560 Ninth Street, Suite 318
Berkeley, CA 94710
www.counterpointpress.com

Printed in the United States of America
Distributed by Publishers Group West

1 3 5 7 9 10 8 6 4 2

For Kyle

Don't rub the sleep out of your eyes. It's beautiful sleep.

A LINE FROM THE FILM *A YANK AT OXFORD*,
CONTRIBUTED BY F. SCOTT FITZGERALD

THURSDAY

1

For the four years I've lived in Los Angeles, the Rocque Museum has been my university and my workplace, offering me a degree in contemporary art and the cosmopolitan life—brilliant as the blues in a Sam Francis painting, decadent as a twenty-four-karat cast of a cat testicle. Most days pass in a pleasurable blur of words and pictures. Most nights I hate to leave my little office, especially on April evenings like this, when I can look over my mess of proofs, out to the greening city, and imagine I am still happy.

A couple of blocks down the avenue, a new concert hall is rising like a silver ship from a dirty parking lot. Just past it, I see a theater pavilion, a row of jacaranda trees floating their violet clouds. A mile beyond that, I know the city's river is still flooding its concrete throat, and I can remember why I came to this place, to live a new life, away from old ghosts.

I would love to stay late tonight in this tiny room, with space enough for my chrome desk and file cabinet, a shelf of art catalogs, and one extra chair for visitors. It's quiet here past six o'clock. I know where everything is, I have editing to do, and my glass door makes it impossible for people to surprise me. I could wait out the traffic, drive home late in the flowing lights of the 101. On my way, I might glance too many times behind me; I might rush the key in the lock of my peeling bungalow. But I would make it home fast, and there would be fewer silent, empty hours before sleep.

Horns bleat below my window. I look down to see two beverage trucks heading for the intersection that leads to the underpass beneath our avenue. They will take two more turns and disappear down a ramping street tunnel to reach the museum's loading dock. The party is arriving.

Within a few hours, this whole street will clog with limousines. I need to steal my chance now and leave the Rocque. The entire L.A. art world converges tonight for the museum's Gala opening of *Still Lives*, Kim Lord's latest exhibition. Three hundred guests will arrive to eat, guzzle champagne, and crowd the galleries until the rooms hum and buzz. Then they will parade back outside to make glowing speeches about the artist, and dance. A tangible excitement will push out through their noise, like a ball held underwater. It will be the party of the year. Every show of Kim Lord's is a moment. Every painting "is so powerful it makes your eyes bleed," according to her new boyfriend, that up-and-coming gallerist with the crooked grin, Greg Shaw Ferguson.

Nice line. I can guess how Greg said it, too. First he looked the *Los Angeles Times* interviewer deep in the eyes, as if he were suddenly just seeing her, human to human. Then he spoke the words with a little gravel in his voice, shook his dark blond head, and ignored the reporter to brood on some secret thought. And during that brooding, which lasts just one second too long, she fell for him. They always do.

A white TV news van roars below, heading toward the same intersection. Time to go. Ruminating on Greg's irritating allure won't erase my own five-year folly over him, and it might thwart my escape. I sling my bag over my shoulder and grab some proofs to drop off with Yegina, our exhibitions manager and my closest friend. I need a good dose of Yegina's undying loyalty to the Rocque to inoculate myself against more wallowing. So what if the man who moved to L.A. with me, the man I once thought I would marry, will be squeezing Kim Lord's hand all night? Phones are ringing off the hook at our membership desk. We might all keep our jobs tomorrow.

When I reach the staircase that winds down the center of the building, I allow myself one slow take of the party I'll be missing. Our offices rise in a windowed, four-story tower above the low-slung hulk of the museum itself, a 1920s police-car warehouse converted to galleries. The Rocque's concrete walls, broken by a single glassy, steel-girdered entrance, give us the look of a bygone industrial gem plopped among boring skyscrapers. Our members love the building, but I'm sure its size and design incite the ire of every greedy developer who drives by our footprint on downtown's best hill.

The museum's western side is a low gray expanse that flaunts its drabness against the mirroring blaze of bank towers. Tonight, it wears a white banner bearing Kim Lord's name and a dozen sponsor logos. A red carpet unfurls beside it, under spotlights. Men in vests set out cones to block the street. Here, the limos will drive up, guests pouring out until the sidewalk disappears beneath their gowns. There, people will pause in the glare of cameras, not quite smiling. Then they'll follow a velvet rope to a staircase half a block away that descends to the delivery underpass below, now transformed into a cocoon of cloth and flowers. No stale ballrooms for Kim Lord's Gala. I can already imagine all the rich, pleased, apprehensive faces. The way they will glide like souls pouring into Hades.

I tread my own humble path down a corridor of fading art posters to Yegina's office.

She's alone, blinking, as if someone just handed her a trophy. She's a catch, Yegina, not in the favored Angeleno way of being so thin you could double as a cocktail straw, but noteworthy for her inky hair and slyly arching cheekbones.

She waves me in, beaming. "Guess what?"

"You got engaged since lunch without telling me?"

Yegina divorced her white slacker husband last year and is searching for the perfect Asian match, preferably Vietnamese.

"Ha-ha. Guess again," she says.

"Don finally got in somewhere?" Yegina's younger brother has been receiving rejections from med schools for the second year in a row. The whole family is devastated.

"They're going to vote yea or nay on Bas," she says in a dreamy voice. "At the next board meeting."

Bas Terrant is the museum's new director. Yegina loathes his preppy blond zeal and his appeal-to-the-masses agenda to make the Rocque a "must-see destination" instead of a museum. Since Yegina has spent her whole life despising the masses, and ardently defining herself in opposition to them, she's nearly come to blows with Bas over the exhibition schedule and when she can squeeze in his "people-friendly" new idea, *Art of the Race Car.*

"I thought he had a three-year contract," I say.

"It gets crazier." Yegina shakes her head. "Kim Lord is AWOL. She was supposed to be here this morning for press photos, and she still hasn't shown up."

I put my hand on the door. I don't care if Kim Lord has gone to Pluto. If I leave the Rocque in the next ten minutes, I can beat rush hour home to Hollywood.

"She sent a couple of texts, but she's not answering her phone." Yegina pauses dramatically. "PR's got major interviews lined up before the Gala." Her eyes catch me sideways and her lashes dip.

I know that look.

"Oh no," I say, opening the door. "I'm not calling Greg."

"Just dial and let me talk," Yegina says. "He's got to know where she is."

"It's too humiliating," I croak.

"Do you understand that the entire Development department will spontaneously combust if their Gala honoree doesn't appear on time?" She smiles at me brightly.

It's true. Our fund-raising team gets increasingly flammable the week before the Gala, and they go off like firecrackers at the slightest provocation. The museum depends on the money they raise, and this year's party has gotten more buzz than in decades. Art lovers know Kim Lord's name. They have seen the blood-red banners popping up all over town, and they want to be the first to view her shocking paintings.

"Please," says Yegina. "I'll go with you to that stupid pony party this weekend."

This is serious payback. I've been begging her for weeks.

I sigh and open my bag. "It's horses. In the hills at sunset."

"Fiery stallions?" she says hopefully as I claw through receipts and wrappers. "Oh, and Jayme is looking for you," she adds. "PR needs help."

"She promised I didn't have to work tonight."

At home is the F. Scott Fitzgerald biography I've been reading. And a glass of dry white wine. And the remains of a cherry pie I baked from scratch. It's a dull life these days, and not the one I thought I'd be signing up for when I first pored over maps of Los Angeles with Greg, tracing the vast quilt of neighborhoods with my finger, imagining our hikes in the Palisades, concerts at the Pantages, breakfasts at Los Feliz cafés, and me making my way writing for magazines. But it's an unpretentious life, and it's mine.

Yegina holds out her hand for my phone, a beat-up old flip that makes it difficult to text. I can't look as I offer it to her. Greg's number is still the first on my list of contacts, above my parents.

Just as Yegina presses dial, there's a knock on the door.

"Come in," she says, putting the phone to her ear.

"Could we talk?" says a hearty, patronizing voice that could only belong to our dear director, Bas Terrant, an East Coast silver-spoon scion layered under a sheen of Hollywood. Bas's suit and hair always seem to enter a room before him, and they are immaculate, his fabrics so pastel they melt in your mouth, his blond locks tapered to fall boyishly across his forehead. He is at the age where he should be showing wrinkles and gray hair, yet some aggressively shiny blend of treatments keeps both at bay. Tonight, however, sweat has darkened his temples and his eyes look crimped, as if someone tried unsuccessfully to button them shut. "Pressing problem with sponsor recognition," he says. "Among other things."

"Of course. Speak with me." Yegina's face morphs into a pleasant mask. She hangs up the phone and holds it out. It slides cool and solid into my palm. *Call to Greg disconnected.* He'll see that I tried to call him. Two months of rigid self-control for nothing.

Bas gives me a strained smile. "And do check in with Jayme. All hands on deck tonight," he says, and shuts the door.

2

I do not go straight to Jayme. I go back up to my office and stare at the Cy Twombly drawing on my wall, willing my nerves to settle before I allow myself to be dragged into this train wreck of an evening.

In every office at the Rocque hangs a real artwork from the museum's permanent collection. I wouldn't have picked Twombly, but his sketch has grown on me over time. Gray marks cover the paper, a storm of lines. I try to follow one with my eyes; it breaks. I follow another. It breaks, too. If you had asked me at twenty-seven about my life, I would have predicted marriage soon, children after that, a logical and contented unfolding of decades not unlike my parents'. But at twenty-eight, I can't see how anything connects.

I met Greg Shaw Ferguson almost six years ago, when we were both on a program teaching English in Thailand. A month's orientation in Bangkok threw us together with about twenty others to learn Thai. The program attracted a core group of the usual naïve, adventurous college grads; one constantly bickering married couple; one guy who wore his bike helmet at all times; and me, who was trying very hard to belong with the college kids. And then there was Greg. He was the same age as most of us, but his mother had just survived her first bout of ovarian cancer, and he had spent the two months prior meditating in a monastery. His head was shaved to a dark fuzz and his silences could pulse like strobes. Most people regarded him with a glum awe. I decided to woo him to our flock.

I should make it clear: I had no romantic stake in this. It was purely sympathy, fueled by my journalistic training in social fearlessness. Fifteen pounds too skinny and without his shaggy hair, Greg had a surly, reptilian look. He didn't grin or joke like he does now. I coerced him out with our merry crew to ride the canals, to watch a Thai movie with no discernible plot but shrieking and hitting. I gave him my cast-off Kundera novels to read. Yet I had no idea that I sparked any feelings in him until he wrote me after orientation, from his campus in southeastern Thailand, and invited me to visit. By then, his hair had grown, and obligatory drinking bouts with his Thai colleagues had forced him to abandon his hard-core Buddhist habits. The man who picked me up from the Chanthaburi bus station was a wry, warm, intelligent dreamboat, and strangest of all, he seemed to adore me.

That adoration is gone now, revoked by a toxic mix of grief and ambition. I know why Greg left me and whom he wants to become, and in the abstract I accept it. I even wish him well. He never once lied to me. But whenever I see him in person, it's like being in a room with an impostor: some creature who slunk out of L.A.'s giant billboards and gated studios and false hopes and took over my boyfriend's body. He goes by "Shaw" now: a slicker, smarter version of the old Greg. It's the name of his gallery, too: SHAW.

A shadow crosses my glass door, and Jayme West whips it open with one hand while talking on her cell with the other. Jayme spends most of her day attached to the device, and they both possess the same sleekness and utility—everything on my boss's gorgeous half-Norwegian, half-Eritrean body is exactly where it belongs, from her high, narrow hips to her low, smooth voice and the bright scent of tangerines that follows her everywhere. With her looks and poise, Jayme could make ten times her Rocque salary in Hollywood or politics, but she hates being on camera and always makes Bas take center stage. He adores her. We all do, because Jayme's hard work and behind-the-scenes orchestrating have helped the Rocque maintain its cultural reputation despite declining

MARIA HUMMEL

revenues. *Saved by Jayme* is a mantra, which is why her behavior around the Kim Lord exhibition has been especially puzzling to me.

"Yes, that's 'Rocque' as in 'lock.' *Still Lives* as in 'wives.'" Jayme hangs up the phone, rolling her eyes.

"Or crock," I say. "And hives."

Jayme doesn't smile. She is not a smiler by nature. It would interfere with the sixteen hundred other things she's doing at any given moment. "Got anything else to wear?"

Before I have a chance to answer, Jayme is marching me to her bigger, tidier office and pulling dresses from a closet, holding them under my chin. "You're the same size as I am, just shorter," she mutters. Her phone rings. She looks at the name and cringes, but her delivery is flawless. "Mr. Gillespie, we're going to need to move the interview again. The artist wants more time with you especially."

She waves the dress she is currently holding. When I take it from her, I'm surprised to see her arm is goose-bumped and shaking. I try to catch her eye, but she deliberately turns away and steadies herself on her desk. I carry the dress obediently down the hall to a bathroom stall, mesmerized by the shimmery green fabric, its leathery weight. I tend to choose demure grays and blues, the wardrobe of a Catholic schoolgirl. This dress feels otherworldly, like it was fished from some alien sea. I fear it will look terrible on me. To say Jayme and I are the same size is like comparing a Jaguar to a Yugo. Clothes don't fall on Jayme's lean torso. They float. She could attend the Gala tonight wearing a couple of crusty washcloths, and the fashion writers would fawn over the hot new trend.

I twist the stall lock and step out of my skirt and blouse. The cool air stings my bare skin, and I feel silly and guilty about the washcloth thought. I've seen Jayme anxious in recent weeks, but not like this. She and I usually work together on copyediting the exhibition catalogs—I check the text and she checks the images—yet for *Still Lives* she dumped the whole project on me. This was in January, just after Greg moved out, and only when Jayme found out that he was dating Kim Lord did she apologize for my extra workload.

"I wish I could help," Jayme said to me, or rather to the pen holder on my desk, because she would not meet my eyes. "But I'm still out on this one. Bas has got too many new irons in the fire, and I can't keep up."

And so, while seething at Kim Lord, I had the additional stomach-churning task of proofing the captions for the photos of the famous female murder victims featured in her show. I tried not to let my eye stray to the disturbing spectacle of Judy Ann Dull, sitting in an arm-chair, wearing a neat 1950s wool cardigan and flared skirt, her ankles and mouth bound by white rope. I tried not to see the chair's ratty upholstery, or Dull's wary, regretful expression at being taken in by a dopey television repairman who promised to help her with her modeling career. I didn't want to see Judy Ann Dull alive and well, because I knew that later she would be dressed in long black gloves and black thigh-high stockings, trussed topless to an X of wood, raped repeatedly, and strangled in the desert by Harvey Glatman, the Glamour Girl Slayer. Dull was only nineteen years old.

If I had trouble looking at one victim and her story, I couldn't imagine how Kim Lord had deeply inhabited eleven of these lives and deaths to make her paintings.

Despite her claims, I wasn't sure she had.

Still Lives street-pole banners hang all over town now, displaying the least graphic of Kim's works, a depiction of herself as a living Roseann Quinn, a 1973 stabbing victim with long ringlets and a toothy, innocent smile. The curators had insisted on an image without gore, but the banners have a crimson background. When I drove under a block of them on Fairfax yesterday, the color kept tearing my eyes from the road up into the sky. Kim Lord's face looked back at me, disguised in paint and the features of a murdered woman.

"I've been having terrible dreams about the victims," she recently told a reporter. "I'm just . . . haunted. Write this down: I, Kim Lord, solemnly swear my next show is going to be about bunny rabbits."

But Kim Lord's next show is always more dramatic than her last, she who started her career with *The Flesh*, a reconstruction of a dingy brothel, hung with paintings of herself costumed as both pimps and sex workers.

"By turning every viewer into a john, Kim Lord asked her audiences to question the ethics of their own gaze," I wrote for our press release. "Viewers paid an admission fee after seeing *The Flesh*, unusual for a gallery exhibition, and Lord became the youngest contemporary artist to sell her entire first show at a Catesby's auction."

Catesby's auctions are usually reserved for established artists, and Kim Lord could have been humiliated by lackluster bids, but instead she made an enormous pile of cash. She is no dummy, which is why I suspect her absence at the moment is just another of her "groundbreaking" moves to escalate her press coverage and drive more people to the museum.

A sudden vain hope bubbles up: maybe neither Kim nor Greg will show up tonight. And I'll get to attend the best party of 2003 without them.

I shake the dress until I find an opening. The garment slides over my head and tumbles to midthigh. Jayme's citrus smell floods my nose. I zip up the side and feel the cloth tighten over my hips, snug but not straining. So far so good. Except that the shoulder straps barely cover my bra, and the front of the dress poufs like overalls. The word *lederhosen* slinks into my mind.

A creak, the bathroom door opens, and someone enters the stall next to me. I check the shoes. Absurdly small blue pumps. Evie from the registrar's office. I've felt bad around Evie since I let our friendship drift a couple of years ago, and even worse lately. When I became overwhelmed by the *Still Lives* catalog this winter, she was the one who finally stepped in to help me. Registrars are better than anyone at fact-finding on artworks and images, and Evie took a whole chunk of captions off my plate. I promised to repay her by taking her out to dinner at our old haunt in Little Tokyo, but I haven't. Evie always wants to ridicule Greg's new name and ambition, or complain about how fattening our tempura is when she's as tightly muscled as a gazelle. Secretly I fear that she only needs me to feel better about herself.

I race past the mirror, trying not to see the vaguely Germanic oaf flashing across it, and am almost out the door when I hear Evie speak.

"Your clothes."

"Hi, Evie." I bend to grab my castoffs. The leather dress constricts like a snake around my abs. "What brings you up here?" The registrar's office is off the loading dock.

Her blue pumps twitch. "The crew's having a party on the roof," she says. "Watching people arrive and such."

This would be the opportune moment for Evie to invite me to join the party later, but she doesn't. The exhibition crew is the coolest club in the museum, mostly young artists who work part-time constructing the shows and part-time on their own projects. They hang out in their cavernous carpentry room near Evie's office and bust jokes in low, bitter voices about how broke they are. There's a distinct social disconnect between them and the upstairs office crowd.

"Fun for you," I say finally. "I got coerced into working."

"That's too bad."

"I just hope Kim Lord actually shows up," I add. "She's blowing all her interviews."

"Fashionably late," Evie says in a tone of fake cheer.

The toilet roll rattles. At this point I realize I am harassing someone having a private anatomical moment and apologetically take my leave. Jayme's in the hall, waiting for me, a paper in her hand. She looks calmer now, but she grimaces at the lederhosen.

"Here. Proof this while I fix you," she says. "And then I'll tell you your assignment." She shoves a press release in my face and starts digging in her closet again. "What size shoe?" she says, her voice muffled.

"Ten. With a sizable bunion on the right foot."

Jayme groans but keeps digging. I read.

Artist Offers Unprecedented Gift

Bas Terrant, director of the Rocque Museum, is pleased to announce that artist Kim Lord is donating the entire exhibition Still Lives *to the museum's permanent collection. The exhibition comprises eleven paintings of Kim Lord impersonating murdered females, including Roseann Quinn, Bonnie Lee Bakley, Gwen Araujo, Chandra Levy, Lita McClinton, Nicole Brown Simpson,* *and Elizabeth Short (the Black Dahlia), as well as one monumental still life. Before undertaking the portraits, the artist spent years studying the lives and deaths of the victims. The combined value of the paintings is estimated at more than $5 million.* [Here someone had scribbled $7 million?]

When asked about the reasons behind her munificent gift, Lord cited the Rocque's demonstrated support of female artists and her wish not to profit from these particular paintings. She said she sees Still Lives *as a tribute to the victims and as an indictment of America's obsession with sensationalized female murders.*

"I don't want these paintings ever to be associated with monetary value," she said. "No one should profit from them. No one should profit from the deaths of any of these women. They are not pinups—they were daughters, mothers, sisters, and wives torn from their lives and their families."

Terrant expressed his deep admiration for Lord and her work, saying, "An artist of Kim Lord's talent and generosity comes along once or twice a century."

"Looks correct, but is this for real?" I say. "Nelson must be livid." Gallerists like Nelson de Wilde earn a standard fifty percent from art sales, which means he will be out millions if he is not allowed to sell Kim's work to collectors. He shelled out seventy grand for the exhibition costs, too, covering the publication of the catalog and the gallery guide. It's not uncommon for gallerists to chip in on exhibitions (one of the many ethically murky practices of the art world), but in return they expect a reputation bump in their artist's prices.

"It's real." Jayme produces a green-blue scarf and a pair of tall brown boots. Her hands flit over my shoulders, tightening a strap here, tugging the leather there, flowing the scarf. Gusts of tangerine drift over me.

"Too bad we can't sell the paintings," I say. "It would completely fix the hole in our budget."

Something flashes in Jayme's face. "Too bad we can't send the release out if she doesn't approve it," she says after a moment, "and she can't approve it if she doesn't show up." She points to the floor. "Step into the boots."

I grip her desk to slide into them; they're too tight, but Jayme bends and zips them up anyway.

"Maybe she's already here, but in disguise. She loves costumes so much," I say, unable to suppress my annoyance. Every time Kim Lord has visited the museum in the past couple of weeks, she's arrived in a different camouflaging getup, complete with wig, sunglasses, retro dress, or boxy 1980s suit.

Jayme gives me an evaluating look.

"I'm a disaster, aren't I?" I say. "I should wear my own clothes. Should I take out the earrings?" I touch the studs, tiny gold butterflies that used to belong to my grandmother.

"Can't even see them. And you actually look almost fabulous," she says shortly. "But you have no idea." She unzips a bag on her desk, pulls out powder. "Close your eyes. I'm going to do your face."

Something swipes my brows, dusts my cheeks.

The strokes tickle but feel tender, too. No one has touched me for months.

"No idea about what?" I say.

No answer. Jayme's fingers grab my jaw, rub my cheekbones, but beneath their quick movements, I can feel her trembling. I have to struggle not to open my eyes.

"She thought she was being stalked," she says. "Last week she called me three times to check the names on my media list." Jayme's words burn with emotion. "She says he sometimes sneaks into the openings through PR."

"She told you that?" I didn't know Jayme and Kim Lord had gotten so intimate. I'd thought Jayme had had too many irons in the fire.

"She said she was close to nailing who it was." I hear Jayme sigh. "And now she's missing."

"Wouldn't she have told the police, too? Or did she just tell you?"

Jayme dabs my lips.

"You're done," she says gently.

When I open my eyes, Jayme has already swiveled away, her slender back to me, her straightened hair falling to the tops of her shoulder blades. "I've got to get ready myself," she says, zipping her makeup bag.

Jayme rarely divulges anything from her private life. I know she adores Prince and fish tacos, but boyfriends? Never introduced. Childhood? Nothing happened, apparently, before her halcyon years at UCLA. And her age? Late thirties? Hard to say. But after tonight's worries and Jayme's avoidance of the *Still Lives* catalog, I'm starting to think there's a reason she never tells anyone about her past. There's a memory of violence inside her. We might have more in common than I thought.

3

B as hired big-time Hollywood event designers for the Gala. Their first proposal for the decor included red-spattered walls and body outlines chalked on the pavement. This caused a near apocalypse in Curatorial, where scholarly types organize the exhibitions and define the art of our time. Stranded in a city of endless boob jobs and crumbling adobe, our curators take to their jobs with special piety. You would have thought their skin was melting off from the howls that went up.

"Nothing squalid. Nothing cop-show. This is supposed to be high art," snapped Lynne Feldman, our chief curator, earning her the nickname "High Art" among our fund-raising folks, as in "Hey, let's tell High Art we're serving Bloody Marys." "Stiff ones, ha-ha!"

When Kim Lord heard of the controversy, she suggested moving the Gala out of the museum entirely and into the subterranean underpass used for truck deliveries to the skyscrapers: a street party literally in the street. There's a good patch of the underpass behind the Rocque's loading dock—a vaulting asphalt cavern that also connects to a staircase to the upper avenue.

Everyone agreed that Kim's suggestion was the kind of brilliant and superbly impractical idea for which the Rocque was known, and the designers got to work. It's turned out to be an amazing space for a party—fifty-foot-high concrete columns soar to the giant girders that hold the avenue above. Instead of gazing at L.A.'s orange night sky, patrons will look up into the beams that hold a living road. The usual white dinner tent, gargantuan florals, cocktail stations, and dance stage will intersperse with real-life street signs and dented guardrails. Thursday-night rush hour will roar above the DJs, and the muted odors of tar and spray paint will mingle with champagne in the mouth.

I tried hard to avoid this occasion on account of my post-breakup bitterness, but now that I'm here, clad in my cutoff Nazi mermaid garb, I'm fearful and glad at once. I didn't expect how the late-afternoon glow would spill down the staircase to the upper avenue, making a grotto of the Gala's lower entrance. A small gauntlet of paparazzi flanks a second red carpet at the bottom. Mostly doughy, bearded men, they squint into the intense last half hour of sun, when L.A. seems to get the whole country's light in one concentrated dose before it fades. As the first guests descend past them, the paparazzi take a few shots, then lounge, cameras dangling loose on their chests. No one from Hollywood has arrived yet. Neither has Kim Lord.

In the black-carpeted cocktail area, vestiges of the old murder theme linger, making my stomach twist into its third or fourth knot tonight. A stalker would be right at home here. Bare lights, resembling those in interrogation rooms, hang from poles above the tables. The centerpieces blister with lilies and scarlet roses. Even the appetizers have a corpse-like color scheme: caprese salad with its red tomatoes and white cheese, rare beef toasts, some smeary fig-paste chèvre concoction that resembles an infected wound.

Unable to eat any of it, I chug two glasses of sparkling champagne, trying to pick out my PR assignment. Five years ago, I wouldn't have been caught dead playing the pleasant media escort; I would have expected to be the young, aggressive reporter nosing out the story. But here I am, balancing in Jayme's high boots with a fake smile on my face.

I need to find a fellow named Kevin Rhys from *ArtNoise*.

"Artwhat?" I'd asked Jayme.

"Doesn't matter," Jayme said. Kevin is writing a cover story for a new magazine funded by Mindy Allen, the daughter of a wealthy New York collector. "Development wants to hook them as a sponsor. Be nice to the guy. Just got here from the East Coast. He wants to meet all the players."

All the players? Our annual Gala draws hundreds of elite taste-makers: the people who make art, the people who buy and sell it, the people who opine about it, and the people who long to belong, which includes most of the museum staff, and random rich people, actors, scuzz-balls, and politicians. The cocktail area is filling with well-dressed folks, but I don't recognize any. So many of them look cut from the same mold: the men trim and spectacled, the women like forty-year-olds from the front and sixty-year-olds from the back, their faces feline and taut, their hands spotted and wrinkled. No suspicious figures that I can see, though I doubt Kim Lord's supposed stalker resembles the gaunt, goofy male I've constructed in my mind, an amalgam of the killers who stabbed, strangled, shot, and beat the victims of *Still Lives*.

My eyes stop on a familiar huddle: Yegina standing with Brent Patrick, leader of the exhibitions crew, and Lynne Feldman, our chief curator.

Lynne's gothic good looks always stand out in our crowd, as if she alone among us has never stepped foot from our cool white galleries into the abrasive L.A. sun. She is showing her cell phone to the others with a reprimanding look. Reprimanding is one of Lynne's three signature expressions (enraged and reverent are the others), and it usually indicates that she is politely and heroically restraining herself from pitching a fit. No other curator on the West Coast has organized more significant solo exhibitions than Lynne Feldman, and no one at the museum is more difficult to work with. Artists tend to regard Lynne as a figure of almost godlike generosity and vision, while coworkers go to such extremes to avoid her that some (okay, mostly Yegina) walk up the stairs and take the elevator down to bypass Lynne's office on the way to the coffee machine.

Lynne's crimson lips shape the words *seven o'clock*. I'm guessing that she has heard from the artist. Seven. Kim Lord will be here in time for the end of dinner, then. So why are the others shaking their heads?

Just as I'm stepping closer to eavesdrop, I see a tall, stocky guy weaving through the crowd with a notebook in his hand. He is wearing tweed. He is wearing tweed, leather loafers, and a full beard, and I have a sneaking suspicion that the tiny black stem poking from his breast pocket belongs to a tobacco pipe. The Angelenos glide apart for his passing like aquatic creatures in the presence of a clumping land animal. I have a hunch that he is my Kevin, and I go to rescue him.

He surprises me by shaking my hand warmly when I introduce myself. "You *work* here?" he says. "Doing what?"

As I tell him briefly about my role as the museum's writer/editor, he yanks out his notebook and scribbles. "Sweet job."

I'd gladly trade, I think. Even as I do, I feel the grief and the inertia that have kept me from trying to be a journalist, pitching editors, gathering clips.

"What do you think of the show?" he says.

"I haven't seen the actual paintings yet," I admit. "The crew doesn't like to be ogled when they're hanging them. But some of the reproductions are . . . intense."

Kevin pauses his note-taking to regard me. In an interested and possibly flirtatious manner. I don't experience this often in my day-to-day existence. Less than fifty percent of the museum employees are men; of those, half are gay and a quarter are married. The other quarter tend to date cocktail straws.

"I saw the Black Dahlia one," Kevin says. "Is *intense* a highbrow euphemism for freaking disgusting?"

"Highbrow euphemisms are my stock-in-trade," I say. I ask Kevin about his own gig, and he tells me he's here from New York for a week to get the inside scoop on *Still Lives*. He hasn't done much art writing; he's more of a rock critic. But he knows the magazine publisher, and she likes his style.

"Lowbrow euphemisms abound," he says.

As we banter, Kevin's tweediness recedes, and I am more aware of his height, his broad shoulders. If we were dancing partners, the top of my head would rest right under his chin.

"So where is the queen of art?" he says.

"Not here yet. That's her gallerist, though. Nelson de Wilde." I point out a lithe, silvery man as he joins a cluster of the Rocque's board members.

Nelson de Wilde's relationship with Kim Lord is historic—after *The Flesh*, when she was only twenty-one and he was an unknown gallerist, he paid her a significant monthly stipend to complete *Noir,* a group of paintings in which she depicted herself as fifteen different black-and-white film stars. Despite the poor critical reception, the show sold out at huge prices. Nelson must have been holding the same financial expectations for *Still Lives.* He is wearing gray tonight, which makes his close-shorn hair look more metallic than ever, but his mouth hangs down and both his hands are plunged deep in his pockets. Mine would be, too, if I were about to watch millions of dollars in commissions disappear.

Kevin asks me why Nelson looks perturbed.

I tell him it must be preshow jitters.

"How'd you get this job?" he says. "You have an art history degree?"

"Not exactly," I say.

"Communications? Journalism?"

I don't want to talk about my past, so I cast about quickly for someone else to identify. I gesture at Brent Patrick, striding from the bar in steel-toed boots. "He builds the shows. You should talk to him. He used to be a big set designer on Broadway."

I don't add that Brent quit his New York life because his wife, Barbara, suffers from schizophrenia and they moved to L.A. for a new treatment program. Unfortunately, Barbara's condition worsened in the program, and she had to be institutionalized. It's a tragic story, and almost justifies Brent's bullying condescension toward everyone upstairs, even the curators. ("Because they don't actually *make* things," Yegina explained once. "Neither do half of the artists we show," I said. "Well, he hates them, too," she said.)

But Kevin should meet Brent because Brent is unbelievable at his job. He can take an artist's flimsiest idea and transform it into a real experience—it is Brent who envisions the lighting, the path the viewer takes, and even sometimes the artwork's actual construction. "You know the *Executed* show we did last year? Jason Rains?"

Kevin nods vaguely.

"Brent was the genius behind it," I say, watching Brent slug a shot beneath a battered stop sign. The sign looks absurdly red and shiny now that it is surrounded by white linens and lilies, and I wonder if some lowly production assistant had to soap it clean for tonight. Some of the graffiti on the nearby tunnel also looks fresh and bright, and, is it me, or did someone fill those glass vases with broken windshield pieces? This kind of stagy urban decadence is Brent's legacy on Broadway; his set for *Rent* was nominated for a Tony. But I bet it rubs him the wrong way here. This party isn't art. It's commerce.

As if on cue, Brent glances up at the stop sign, then shakes his head grimly and clomps away.

"He created the whole set," I say. "Jason Rains just watched."

"You think I can interview Kim Lord?" asks Kevin, but just as I'm about to struggle with a lie, one of Hollywood's highest-paid actresses arrives on the red carpet and everyone stops breathing.

The actress is wearing jeans and a yellow blouse, platform sandals, a gauzy gold scarf in her hair. She is blond, willowy, and tall, and on anyone else this outfit would look suitable for a picnic. Yet as the actress gently spins for the flashing cameras, she rewrites the entire occasion around her. She's showing up for a real party, not another stuffy fund-raising affair. When she smiles the gleaming, genuine smile we've all adored on giant screens, people start talking again, louder, chattier, leaning into one another.

"That's—" I say.

"I know," Kevin mutters, and writes something in his notebook.

The last sun lifts from the staircase, and the real crowds start pouring down, a happy, upbeat mob: TV sitcom stars, famous architects, young sculptors looking gawky in their finery—and, far back at the line, Greg. Lean as a fox, in a dark-blue suit. Alone. Seeing him hits me like a punch to my sternum and I swallow the last sip in my glass. I tried so hard not to be here. Greg's face looks different, but it always looks different to me now, with its thin fringe of stubble and keen expression. This isn't the Greg who lounged in the hammock next to me peeling a purple mangosteen, or the Greg who helped me lug a secondhand couch into our new Hollywood apartment and hugged me as we surveyed its ruined gold grandeur. Nor is it the Greg who sobbed at our kitchen table when his mother died. He is no longer any of those people. He is Kim Lord's boyfriend. She sent him ahead. Or he came ahead of her, to have more time hobnobbing with the rich patrons he hopes to woo to his gallery.

"I take that as a no," says Kevin.

"Huh?"

"Kim Lord's probably booked for interviews."

"Probably," I say.

I see Greg make his way to one of the cocktail stations. A server, a skinny brunette, passes him and thrusts out a tray of crackers heaped with rare beef. Greg stares at the red offering, then shakes his head. The server's eyes stay on him after he walks away.

"Might wander around, then," Kevin says.

As if he senses my own gaze, Greg spots me and waves.

"No. Wait," I say, turning and taking a step closer to Kevin. "Stick with me. I'll take you to a party with the crew that built the show."

"Right on," he says eagerly.

Now the crowd is spilling past every guardrail and curb of the decorated urban cave with their leather and perfume and expectations. The guests are milling and staring, holding red cards with their assigned dinner seats. The more people who enter, the bigger this space feels, the higher the girdered ceiling, like we'll never be enough to fill it. The vast scale reminds me of old cathedrals—the architecture made to dwarf us, to remind us of our insignificance, no matter how many we are. This will be the party everyone dreamed of. The guests will start to notice the smaller touches—the trails of scarlet rose petals over every folded napkin, the Hitchcockian soundtrack the DJ is playing. They'll line up for snapshots around the stop sign. But soon the novelty of the space will wear off. They've come to see Kim Lord and her new show, and to be seen seeing it. So where is she? Where is *she*?

I keep my head turned from Greg. I should be saying something clever to hold Kevin's attention, I should be taking his arm and leading him around, but suddenly I'm struck by the fear that everything we've made tonight—everything Kim Lord made—is spinning on the same sick fascination that she spoke against in her press release. That beneath all these layers of pleasure and provocation are women who were slaughtered.

4

K e-*vin!*" shrieks a voice. "Kevin *Rhys*! What on earth are you doing here?"

I have never been so glad to see Thalia Thalberg in my life. Actually, I've never been glad to see her at all. She's the chair of the Rocque's Young Collectors Club, and her life's work—being rich and spending her money in elegant but fussy ways—puts her in a caste of people who bear as much resemblance to ordinary human beings as fur coats to the animals from which they were flayed. Nevertheless, to my relief she grabs Kevin's arm and twirls him toward her and her formidable attire, which looks like a tutu made from shredded sandwich bags.

"Just here on assignment," mumbles Kevin.

"Mindy's new magazine?"

"Yeah," Kevin says with a sheepish glance at me.

"Fantastic." Thalia's eyes rake up and down my torso. "How is Mindy?"

"Busy," says Kevin. "Have you met Maggie?"

Of course she has. But she won't remember.

"I work in Communications." I extend my hand and shake Thalia's. Her fingers are the texture of thawing shrimp. "I'm showing Kevin around. How do you two know each other?"

"We went to school together in New York," Thalia says, and mentions some expensive-sounding academy. "And Kevin's father was my history teacher."

"Faculty brat, that's me," Kevin says wearily.

Thalia wants to know what Kevin thinks of the Gala, and I'm expecting some glib version of the observations we've been hearing all around us, how cool it is to see the gritty street and the glamorous party together at once, but Kevin seems to take her question seriously. He knits his brow and scans the scene as if he just noticed it.

I wait awkwardly beside Thalia, trying to think of one thin sentence of small talk to screw into the impassable social wall between us.

Thalia touches her brunette bob. "Oh, come on, Kevin. It's not an exam."

"Well," he says finally, "I've seen the lions and the otters, and the panda was cool. But I can't find the aye-aye house, and I've heard they've got this creepy long finger for picking out fruit. I really want to see that."

"You are too funny," Thalia says in a blank tone, then waves at someone over my shoulder. "I've got to introduce someone to Lynne," she says. "I'll see you later, okay? Nice to meet you, Mary."

Kevin squints after her, shaking his head.

"Non sequiturs are the only way to get rid of her," he mutters, but he sounds bothered by the exchange.

I'm about to ask why when I see Greg. Alone again, walking the rim of the cocktail area, where the wall breaks for the museum's loading dock. Greg's never alone at parties. He instantly finds a group and joins, hands in his pockets, head bucked back for a ready guffaw. A camera flashes near him and he cringes.

"Ladies and gentlemen!" Bas booms from the stage in the middle of the dinner tent. "Please take your seats for dinner."

Around us, conversation ceases, and people start cutting and weaving toward the tent, talking about their table numbers. Greg starts heading our way, and Kevin looks lost in the swirl of pushy, ageless ladies desperate to know their social standing. So I grab Kevin's hand.

"Follow me," I say. "You'll want to get your seat before all the paparazzi take them."

His fingers, surprisingly dry and strong, grip mine back. Suddenly we're not doing that light-steering social touch—we're actually holding hands, the gesture more intimate than I intended. My heart starts thumping, and I try not to trip in the boots that have been squeezing my feet to throbbing hooves. Kevin hunches forward as if he's ready to tackle anyone who impedes us.

I drop Kevin's fingers when we reach the dinner tent and it gets too tight to move in tandem. We pass Janis Rocque—affectionately known in-house as J. Ro—heir to the Rocque fortune and her father's floundering private museum. Tonight she looks distinctly uncomfortable in her sea-green suit and coils of brown hair. J. Ro likes being at the center of things, but she hates the spotlight and she must be getting worried about our missing guest of honor by now. After her trails an expressionless Nelson de Wilde, and Lynne after him, checking the watch on her slender wrist. It's six o'clock. The caterers have lined up with the salad plates.

On the other side of the tables, the crowd opens and I turn back for Kevin. I don't know what expression I'm wearing, but it seems to silence him.

"You can find a seat over there," I blurt, showing him the tables reserved for the media, where photographers are now sitting with their cameras and peering around like meerkats. "I'll be nearby if you need me."

I point to the back entrance of the dinner tent, where Jayme and I will perch at an unbouqueted white table with other Rocque staff members and our laptops, pretending we don't need to eat. I can feel Kevin's eyes on me as I limp away.

"Ladies and gentlemen," Bas repeats, "I'd like to welcome you to the Rocque's Gala for 2003, a street party literally in the street. Any traffic violations will be prosecuted by the board . . ." He pauses for some faint, forced laughter. "Before we tuck into this delicious dinner and begin the extraordinary evening we have planned, I have a brief announcement. Our Gala honoree and the star of the evening, Kim Lord, has been delayed."

A murmur of concern rises from the crowd.

Bas holds up his hands. "She will arrive quite soon, and I can assure you that her paintings are already here, and they are devastating. Here's some advance praise from the *New York Times*, just in: 'Kim Lord's eleven portraits and one monumental still life are the product of years of examining the lives, deaths, and media coverage of murdered women, but they are also a statement about painting, how alive it is, how it can still challenge the dominion of photography in our age.'"

Clapping interrupts him.

He smiles. "Thank you all for coming out to celebrate Kim Lord, the Rocque, and the gift"—he lurches and grips the podium, as if he has for a moment lost his balance—"we are bringing to Los Angeles for the next three months."

He hasn't announced the real gift. The millions-of-dollars gift from Kim Lord, courtesy of her donation of *Still Lives* to the Rocque's permanent collection. I search for Kim's gallerist again and spot him holding his fork, about to spear his frisée and beets. For some reason, Nelson's tan, metallic look always makes me think of prosthetic limbs, things that are made to look natural but are creepy instead, and also more durable. He sneers and shakes his head, briefly, as if disgusted. It's an odd expression for someone whose prize artist just got heaped with critical praise.

Bas returns to his seat in a storm of applause. His wife pats him on the shoulder. She is a predictably pale blonde with a talent for smiling without seeming friendly at all. I've heard a rumor of divorce. Does she know Bas may lose his job?

I reach the PR table and relieve Jayme so she can ply the most impatient reporters with extra bottles of champagne. Yegina comes over in a tight blue dress and combat boots and sinks down beside me.

"What was that?" she asks in an impressed voice.

"What?"

"Maggie Richter grabs handsome stranger's hand just as ex Greg approaches," says Yegina. She can't bear to call him by his new moniker either. ("*Shaw*," she said scornfully. "It's like a cross between a soap opera name and a tractor brand.")

"Handsome stranger is called Kevin. I was afraid we were about to be devoured by Thalia Thalberg," I say. "Clearly she hasn't eaten since 2001."

"I wish you were edible," says Yegina. "I'm starving."

I laugh. She waits, gazing at me with her gray-brown eyes. Yegina has carried me through my breakup, as I bolstered her last year during her divorce from Chad, the bitter end of a long string of white surfers, skaters, and Tibetan Buddhism majors that she has been rescuing since age sixteen.

Now Yegina has given herself over entirely to Asian speed dating and singles nights at her parents' church, but every fellow she meets has some fatal flaw. Humming when he drives. Absolutely silent in bed. Never heard of the Dead Milkmen. Mispronounces Ed Ruscha's last name. Bad teeth. Too-perfect teeth. Doesn't know the meaning of *ennui*. Yegina needs a guy who gets her, and that's hard to find. There's a large class of men who can't endure humor in a woman.

"Anyway, what did our beloved chief curator show you on her phone?" I ask.

Yegina confirms that Lynne got a text from the artist announcing her arrival at seven o'clock. I tell her what Jayme told me about a possible stalker.

"That's creepy. No wonder she's been showing up in disguise," says Yegina.

"Though why can't she disguise herself as Margaret Thatcher or something?" I ask. "Why only dress as starlets? She's practically forty."

Yegina shrugs but doesn't reply.

My fingers find my little butterfly earrings and twist them. I wish I could rid myself of this poisonous jealousy. At the head table, Kim Lord's absence looms at Greg's left elbow, and Greg himself is looking worse and worse, his cheeks rough and red, as if he shaved them with a dull razor. In times of stress, he forgets to take care of himself. He was a stubbly, hollowed wreck the month after his mother died.

I watch Janis Rocque lean across the table and start interrogating him, which is the conversational equivalent of being whipped around in the locked jaw of a pit bull. I have witnessed Bas being berated by her through the glass door of his office, and Greg now has the same eye bulge, as if he is forgetting, second by second, how to breathe. Dark-haired J. Ro—with her masculine suits, enormous cash flow, and abrupt, decisive manner—is CEO, patron saint, and mercurial monarch of the L.A. art world. She is greatly beloved by many and feared by more. Although the Rocque is just one of her projects, it's been the core of her vision since the 1980s—that L.A. will not play second fiddle to New York, with its entrenched and historic art scene, but will seize the future by taking risks, supporting art that surprises people and forces them to self-examine. Those of us who love the Rocque believe that if we fail, it's not just the museum that will go under but also the potential of our city and what it could become.

Regardless of the Rocque's fate, J. Ro's public censure could be a big blow to Greg's gallery. Before I feel sorry for him, however, I remind myself that he chose this fate, this attempt at life among the ultrarich. You can't succeed in art dealing without such effort.

After a few minutes, Greg stares down at the table, silent and rigid. J. Ro yanks out her phone and wanders away to make a call.

"You guys hungry?"

I look up to see Kevin standing over us, holding three dinner plates. Why am I blushing? I duck my chin and stare at the ink stain on one of my fingers.

"Half the paparazzi are heading out," he says. "Apparently there's a premiere in Hollywood."

"Thank God," Yegina says. "Sit down."

I don't think I am hungry, but when Kevin slides the plate in front of me, I eat the salmon and asparagus gratefully, ignoring Yegina's raised eyebrow.

"Hey, so have you met the artist?" I hear him ask. "What's she really like?"

5

The first time I saw Kim Lord, she was a picture in a New York magazine. My mother had sent me the magazine in a care package to Thailand, and, even more than the little jar of crunchy peanut butter and packets of Oreos, the glossy pages made me miss America. I missed our messy, mixed-up country, and I missed our media, the blustery way we talked about one another, our constant cultural introspection. I must have read the issue twenty times: the brief newsy dispatches about Dolly the Sheep and *The English Patient*'s odds for Best Picture, the music and book reviews, and four long articles, full of a bustling culture far away from my decrepit teak house in the Thai countryside. One of the long pieces was a profile of Kim Lord. It featured a photo of one of her paintings—which was actually the painting of a photo she had destroyed. The writer made much of this esoteric process from photograph to self-portrait, which I found mostly befuddling at the time. Instead, I was moved by the figure: a young man smirking in a cutoff T-shirt, tattoos, his neck hung with chains, a cold, evaluating look in his eye. "Pimp #1," he was called. He was also Kim Lord.

The article said that Kim Lord was born to a wealthy Toronto family, a child of private schooling, piano lessons, and high teas. She spoke perfect French. She won a poetry recitation contest for performing Portia's mercy speech from memory. Then she broke away from bourgeois life in her teens and went hitchhiking and train-hopping around the United States, and was accepted to art school at the Cooper Union. She spent a year among New York prostitutes and pimps, and then moved into a studio for two weeks and wore disguises and took photos of herself until she got the exact poses she wanted.

With her own self-portraits as subjects, she started the paintings, sometimes capturing herself with exacting realism, sometimes with expressionistic techniques that washed her blurry and indistinct. The day all the paintings were done, she destroyed the studio photos, erasing the only record of herself as a living subject. In the early years, she burned her films and negatives, but once photography went digital, she put all the images on a flash drive and smashed it with a hammer. She emphasized the importance of this last ritual, likening it to a kind of honor sacrifice.

"I don't want that record to exist," she said in the article. "It links the work to me, and I am not painting myself."

This statement lodged in my mind when I first read it, riding an air-conditioned bus through durian plantations to visit Greg. *I am not painting myself*. It was a curious thing to say when your entire oeuvre was some variation on the self-portrait. I talked about it with Greg on our lazy vacation in Ko Samui. We were side by side on beach towels, me on my belly, Greg sitting up, reading the magazine. Beyond us, turquoise water lapped white sand and boats droned, carrying tourists to snorkel over dying coral reefs. The heat was making my bones melt. I loved it, yet I still missed America. Greg flipped a page.

"Doesn't it make you homesick?" I mumbled into my bare arm.

"Some of it," he said. "Kim Lord's painting is the best thing in here."

His admiration rankled me. I propped myself up on my elbows. "She claims she's not painting herself. But isn't she?"

"No. She's painting a subject."

"A gorgeous subject." I gestured at Kim's narrow, girlish body, visible somehow through the male clothes, the posture. "Would her art be so famous if she was ugly? Or poor?"

Greg shrugged, brushing the sand off his legs. But he kept reading.

"She also says that unless women artists simultaneously inhabit the roles of artist and subject, the art world will never escape the prison of the male gaze," he said. "I don't know why you'd be jealous of her. She's on your team."

My team. I'd told Greg that my Thailand adventure was "a break" from pursuing a career in investigative journalism, that I wanted to apply to J-school once I'd sorted out my feelings about Nikki Bolio's death.

"I am not jealous of her," I said. "I just don't see why she needs to keep justifying herself."

Greg backed up a page, peered at the image again.

I dropped my head to my towel. Beneath the cloth, the sand made a grainy static in my left ear until it settled into a hard, unstable pillow. I closed my eyes and let the sun drape its flame across half my face. I hadn't sorted out any of my feelings about Nikki except one: I didn't want to return to Vermont. I wanted to go back to my own country but live far away from my home state, anonymous, starting over.

"We should move to a big city when we get home," I said. "A big warm city."

Something soft and light touched the back of my neck. It was Greg, kissing me.

"We should," he murmured, and then withdrew. "I'm going swimming."

There it was, in that moment on the white sand. I said it first; I claimed a future with Greg, the one that led us to Los Angeles. The one that led him to Kim. What happened between us still mystifies me: how two lovers can move to a city, and the city itself wraps around them like vines, pulling them apart, pushing them toward others, until they become so entwined in their separate lives that they no longer recognize what they once felt, or even who they once were.

I sound so young in that memory. So full of sunlight and glittering beach. The only clock the distant *tock-tock-tock* of the cook cracking coconuts for dinner.

•

The second time I saw Kim Lord, she and another woman were racing each other on two large mechanical sperm in a wall-to-wall crowd at a gallery opening in Silver Lake. Greg and I stood on the street, too shy to do anything but gawk through the gallery's big windows. Players at two video game consoles controlled each sperm, aiming them around curving red foam pieces to a dais where a glowing egg waited. The sperm moved with the lurching glide of automatons, but each was covered in chrome that reminded me of 1950s cars. Each also bore a tiny vanity license plate: FINISH and FETISH.

Greg and I knew only two people there: Phil and Spike, the tall, big-headed identical twin designers that I worked with at the Rocque. The twins were easy to spot: they usually towered over crowds, and as if to further fool with their eerie likeness, they routinely costumed themselves as conquistadors of dork. That night, it didn't take me long to find them, wearing matching striped one-piece vintage swimsuits and hunched behind the video game console. Together they watched impatiently as a bearded hipster fiddled with the joystick. Judging by their expressions, the console was wired to Kim's sperm, which was nosing futilely into a wall of uterine foam.

It wasn't Kim Lord's show. It was a recent MFA grad's, and it astonished both Greg and me to see Kim there, like a movie star showing up at your favorite breakfast place (a frequent occurrence in our new L.A. life). But we tried to play it cool, somehow striking up a conversation with the smokers beside us, making dumb puns about being "pro-creative" and speculating about what sort of "donors" had given to this show.

"Think she'll beat the other sperm?" I said.

"Not if Spike and Phil start driving," said Greg.

And then, I don't know exactly how it happened, Greg pulled me inside, got us icy cans of beer from a plastic tub, and suddenly he was next to Phil and Spike, joysticking Kim Lord to victory while I drank my cheap brew in the corner alone. As Greg jolted Kim through the gallery on her sleek chrome tadpole, I watched his face sharpen with something that looked like lust, but wasn't quite. It was the savage desire to win. To win this crowd of people in their post-punk leather, their trousers and embroidery and heavy black glasses, to be one of them and the best of them at the same time. It happened fast, and then other things happened: a guy came up to hit on me, aggressive and insistent; Greg returned with Phil; Kim came over to meet Greg.

She was smaller in person and not as pretty as I'd imagined, but she had this long, scrutinizing way of looking at you that made you feel noticed. She remembered my name after hearing it once, and when Phil told her I'd just gotten a job with him at the Rocque, she said we should all have a drink sometime, she loved a museum that said screw you to mediocrity. She uttered it in a humorless tone that brooked no laughter or clever retort. Perhaps she was already preoccupied with *Still Lives* then. She must have started on the work by that point—it was about four years ago—and she must have been poring over the killing of Nicole Brown Simpson, who became the subject of her first painting and the reason Kim eventually wanted to open the exhibition in Los Angeles.

"This city is the magic looking glass to North American culture— it shows us what is most beautiful and passionate about ourselves, and what is most monstrous," she said later in an interview. "Nicole Brown Simpson's murder was all three. Her bloody death speaks as much to the obsessions of our society as it does to the violence in one man."

The second time I saw Kim Lord was the second time I wanted to dislike her but couldn't. Instead, we became the kind of provisional pals you only meet at parties, always nodding and acknowledging each other, but never really talking. Why would we? What Kim Lord and I have in common could be measured by the teaspoon: a childhood in the North, a tendency to stay quiet while everyone else chatters. Yet sometimes I think I'm the only one in L.A. who understands her: she is not a genius, but she knows how to package herself, how to make it sound like she matters. She looks the part, too—a gaunt, darkening blonde, size four in jeans. She has a neat little way of licking her lips before she speaks. It makes her seem younger, though she never acts eager to please.

Here, at the Gala tonight, I can't tell Kevin-the-rock-critic any of this, so I just listen to Yegina say that Kim Lord is pretty easy to deal with for an artist who finishes paintings six months later than she says she will. And who refuses to do educational events of any kind because her work is "not for children." And who always arrives dressed in elaborate disguises and insists on entering the museum through the loading dock.

Then Kevin asks how we decide which artists get the green light for shows at the Rocque, and Yegina goes into another long-winded answer.

"It's a pretty collaborative process, except when your director forces something down your throat," Yegina finishes, loathing in her voice. "As in *Art of the Race Car*. Next year, September 2004. I kid you not. George W. Bush will be running for reelection, and Bas wants to park a Corvette in front of the museum."

For years, the brilliant shows at the Rocque have made up for other failures in Yegina's life: the museum's failure to promote her, Chad's failure at staying faithful to her, and, most of all, her parents' failure to understand any of her artsy, leftist, cash-poor choices. I half wish that her brother gets rejected by med schools again so that he can share the burden of disappointing them.

"And then Bas wants to tear down this building and make something huge," she adds. "He doesn't understand that people actually *find* us because we're a break in the skyline. We're at a human scale."

A break in the skyline.

I remember the last time I saw Kim Lord. It was yesterday, almost lunchtime, and I was heading downstairs to grab Yegina for our toning class at the gym. As I held the rail, gazing out on my favorite view of the avenue below us, I caught sight of a woman in a platinum wig and trench coat, hurrying downhill, away from the museum and toward Pershing Square. She jumped as if something had startled her, patted herself, and then kept hustling west. In that moment, I didn't register what I was seeing. Scarcely a day goes by in Los Angeles when I don't witness something odd on the streets. But the woman was Kim Lord. And she was fleeing the Rocque.

I excuse myself to use the restroom, which is inside the building. As I totter through the increasingly younger outer circles of the dinner tent, I catch sight of manicured hands cupping glasses, smooth bare legs extending from slitted dresses, unbuttoned tux collars, gleaming watches. I hear snatches of conversation.

"Her shows are never worth the hype, but I still want to see it."

"When was her last one, when Reagan was president?"

Kim Lord's *Noir* exhibition had bombed so badly that it shadows her reputation almost as much as her early success brightens it, and there are some, possibly many, here who expect to be underwhelmed again. Another night, their derision might privately cheer me, but now I'm glad when I make it out of the humid clouds of talk to the cooler, grittier open air of the underpass.

The dock looms like a tomb. It used to be the basement for the police-car garage. The architect retrofitted the walls and beams to be earthquake-safe and extended the museum's underground level two stories so that we could use the same delivery underpass as our neighboring skyscrapers. The Rocque's remodel is considered a subterranean masterpiece, because the architect retained the drama of the old walls and arches while making the space much larger and more modern. Our garage door is forty feet tall, and when it's up, as it is tonight, you see a dark cathedral of art crates and shelving, the thresholds that lead to the registrar's office and the carpentry room, and another massive door at the back, where much of our permanent collection is stored.

Security guys in white shirts stand, arms folded, all over the dock, but they don't recognize me and I don't have my badge or an official wristband for the evening. I bob along them like a horse looking for a break in the fence until I find Fritz, our main daytime dock guard, a short, robust, close-shaven guy who sports tinted glasses and a friendly air. Fritz likes me because I helped his daughter with her college essays last year and she got into UCLA. He beckons me in with a smile, and I pass into the underground vault of the Rocque, with its smells of fresh carpentry and old paint. I cross the hard cement floor and hide in the restroom, unzipping my boots down to the ankle to pop out my complaining feet.

My toes flex, prickling. They feel like little knobs pounded into the ends of my feet. Kim Lord should be at the Gala by now. Her absence is a wind, invisibly touching everything. The last time I felt this sensation was six years ago, the cold spring day when Nikki Bolio, my source, was found dead on the shore of Lake Champlain.

I hear the bathroom door swing open, and two guests talking.

"Hurry, okay?" says one. "I don't want to get stuck behind a massive crowd. I hate craning my neck."

It must be seven already. *Still Lives* is open for viewing. Starting with tables one and two, guests may take the freight elevator up to the galleries, or they can take the long way, walking up the staircase and coming in through the museum's front doors.

I shove my boots back on and hobble from the restroom and into the shadows by the staff elevator. Moments later, Janis Rocque and the rest of the head-table guests flood the loading dock.

Is Kim Lord finally among them? No. Neither is Greg. I hang back to watch, trying to imagine which group a stalker would infiltrate.

First come the wild gray heads of the renegade artists who once carved out studio space among the oil derricks of Venice Beach. They built their art from junk piles and car paint and light. One got arrested for obscenity and some died, but a surviving few have become rich old men. They chuckle and nudge each other, and their eyes have a sharp brightness; they know they are the youngest people here.

A more proper, more resplendent group follows. These are the male board members: CEOs, bankers, music industry magnates who have spent their lives leading meetings and driving up profits. Although their looks range from svelte to plump, they all have the same restless gleam, as if they can't help jockeying for power, even now.

The last cluster comprises the women on the board and the wives of the men. Mostly platinum-haired, graceful, and over forty, they fall into two categories, the born rich and the born beautiful, rarely both at the same time. An occasional young, foxy girlfriend dots the landscape of older bodies, and she trips along self-consciously in high heels, smiling hard. Of the three groups, only this last one shows any anxiety at Kim Lord's absence; I catch sight of a couple of ladies glancing back over their shoulders at the glare of the party, and another tightening her silky wrap as if chilled.

Tailing all these groups is one misfit, walking alone: a dark-haired guy, early thirties, with a mustard-colored corduroy suit jacket thrown over jeans. There's something familiar about him. Not familiar as in we've met before, but familiar in type. If I had to guess, I'd say he's from somewhere rural and East Coast. Overdressed for the warm night, underdressed for the occasion. No interest in fanciness except to flout everyone else's high opinion of it. His blue eyes look sleepy, as if someone just woke him up and dragged him here. He sees me staring and gives me a wink. I look down at my aching feet, first embarrassed by my scrutiny, then irritated by his cheek. He clearly didn't dress to blend in.

The massive doors of the freight elevator slide open. In its day, the freight elevator has carried paintings the size of pools and an entire crumpled Volkswagen. It's hallowed ground, this scuffed metal box; along with thousands of artworks, this freight elevator has lifted L.A.'s reputation, putting our city on the map of critics and collectors. But the cabled mechanism also rattles and lurches, and the interior panels are in dire need of replacement. The guests file in, dwarfed by the elevator's size. In its silvery light, their faces and bodies are suddenly blank and interchangeable, except for their leader, Janis Rocque. She wears the stoic scowl of a human about to enter an alien spaceship.

Where is Greg? I'm surprised he isn't keeping up with his crowd.

There's a flash of blue and tweed beside me: Yegina and Kevin, looking breathless.

"Come on, we can take the staff elevator. Everyone's walking up the staircase way. They don't want to wait," says Yegina, waving her all-access badge on the security pad. "It's going to be mobbed."

6

When the staff elevator doors open, Yegina, Kevin, and I rush through the permanent collection to reach *Still Lives*. All the galleries feel large and cold and secretive tonight, even as I pass familiar white slabs and cubes of light, the red flower of a smashed car hood that's always on view. The air smells like nothing—not disinfectant, not paint, not wood or plastic, just pure absence. I look over at Kevin, and he's a wash of fluorescence and shadow, patting his tweed pockets like he forgot something. Beyond him, Yegina wears the cool, keen look of a cat about to be fed.

"Not mobbed yet," I say, but neither of them answer. Our footfalls are the only sounds, fast and ominous, as they approach the black-painted rooms of *Still Lives*.

I've read the hyperbole about Kim Lord's talent. Heck, I've been writing it for months, ripping adjectives like *stunning, harrowing, shocking, edgy,* and *stark* from reviews of prior shows, and coupling those words with the gory stories of the eleven murdered women depicted in *Still Lives*. The more praise I penned, the more it rang false to me—to be so stagy in your subject matter, to take another woman's victimization and make it your material. Not until today's undisclosed press release about her gift has Kim Lord ever acknowledged that she, too, might be capitalizing on these horrific crimes. She seems to think it is her right to depict the victims, to paint herself into their lives and stories, just as she—a well-heeled Canadian—feels it is okay to toss out damning statistics about Los Angeles and its murder rates, and the way Hollywood sensationalizes female homicide. "I picked this city deliberately," she said. "I want this city to see what it is doing."

Fine. Let's see it.

I am wary when I step inside the first black room.

Stabbing victim Roseann Quinn hovers over me with her curls and her wistful grin. Lord based her painting on a well-known photo of Quinn in a loosely tied head scarf and round librarian glasses, grinning at something beyond the camera. In the original photo, Quinn looks as if she's strolling down a suburban street, past a white house and a yard, the photo snapped just when she's spotted a friend and beams in recognition. Kim Lord painted as Quinn has the same clothes and sweet expression, but the background to her face is old newspaper clips, their headlines: "Teacher Found Nude and Slain," "Teacher Victim of Sex Slaying," "Drifter Held in Roseann's Slaying."

Roseann Quinn's 1973 murder exploded in the national news because it was a timely I-told-you-so to the new generation of women choosing sexually liberated lives. Quinn was a New York City teacher who lived alone and allegedly went out to bars at night and brought home men. One evening she made the wrong choice. *She* made the wrong choice. The words in the headlines: *Nude* and *Slain*, *Sex* and *Slaying.* How important it was to use both words, in that order.

Their message is so loud that I almost miss that the painted Roseann Quinn has thin red stab wounds all over her throat.

I move on to the next female face: close-lipped smile, head tilted, her pretty eyes lined in black, her blond-streaked hair arrowing beneath her chin. Everything about this subject's posture suggests a readiness to be viewed: she is posing; she is composed; she has practiced for this picture. Lord captures this preparedness in precise paint that blurs only once, smudging a high elegant cheekbone all the way to the frame of the canvas. This is Gwen Araujo, one of Lord's last subjects, a transgender

California teen who was allegedly beaten and strangled by four men last October, after two had had sex with her and then discovered she was biologically male. The perpetrators are awaiting trial. I study the long smudge again, its slight red tinge. It works. The distortion makes the face's calm beauty hurt.

On the far wall, a monumental Kitty Genovese sprawls in a hallway, bloodied, her face turned to the viewer. Genovese was stabbed outside her Queens apartment at three in the morning in March 1964. She cried for help, loud enough for many to hear; someone in the building shouted back. But no one emerged. Her attacker left the scene. She crawled to the apartment's back entrance but could not get in. Her attacker returned, raped her, and robbed her, and still no one came to her aid. Later, reporters estimated that thirty-eight people had heard Genovese but failed to save her. She died that night.

This painting is the first time in *Still Lives* that real gore appears, and at the same time it draws my eye, I find my resistance rising. I've seen too many lurid photographs of the victims in our exhibition catalog. I was expecting blood, its cheap horror.

I look dispassionately at the crumpled body of Genovese. Unlike the other two works in the room, this is a depiction of a slaying. Her back is bleeding; her hands are crossed with red slashes. The dull light in the hallway bleaches her panicked face into a ghastly mask.

Ghastly, but familiar. I look back at Araujo and Quinn, and it feels like someone shot a bolt into both of my knees.

The paint thickens and thins differently around each of the figures, but the women's expressions all have the same eerie clarity, like they've been rinsed clean. They stare back into the galleries. Hard. The likeness flashes out—the way Kitty is also Gwen is also Roseann is also Kim. All are Kim. In each of the paintings exists a dead woman—identified by her hair, her eye color, her clothes and gestures—and also, inexplicably, Kim Lord, wearing that death, the way the shamans of old donned the masks and cloaks of spirits.

I am not painting myself.

No. I'm starting to see that now.

I am aware of Kevin and Yegina behind me, also looking, but they seem far away. We don't speak as we move into the next dim room to-gether: Bonnie Lee Bakley, the Black Dahlia, Nicole Brown Simpson. All Los Angeles murders. Our city's murders.

Bonnie Lee Bakley, blond, doll-like, is painted in multiple, a half dozen times, her expression shifting from young and perky to fearful and sagging, but always smiling. Two years ago, Bakley was shot in a parked car outside a restaurant. Her murder doesn't have the same vis-ceral brutality as many of the exhibition's other deaths, but the leading suspect, her actor-husband Robert Blake, played a famous killer in the movie *In Cold Blood*, and this has magnified the story's impact in the media. Robert Blake is on house arrest now.

In Kim Lord's painting, Bakley's murder is not acknowledged at all, only her aging face and fading confidence. Bakley's dark, perfect arch-ing brows and bared teeth never change, but her cheeks swell and sag. Her curled yellow hair straightens and darkens. Before meeting Blake, Bonnie Lee Bakley made her living with a mail-order business, send-ing nude pictures of women, including herself, to men. She also asked her male correspondents to support her. With her proceeds, she bought several homes, but she dreamed of a celebrity life. Bakley was forty-four when she married Blake. It was her tenth marriage, and a loveless one, arranged so that Blake could have legal access to their child.

I don't understand this artwork yet, but I have some idea of what Kim was after. Bonnie Lee Bakley had traded on her face all her life, and the progression of the images reminds me that growing old must have terrified her. I remember something Kim Lord said about paint, her chosen medium: "The Lonely Hearts Killer, the Original Night Stalker, the Grim Sleeper—Los Angeles serial killers get these profoundly cool names. Meanwhile, their victims look like models. There's this glamour that glosses their suffering and their humanity," she said. "Photography is partly to blame, I think. It's an instant medium and only captures the flash of surfaces. Which is why I wanted to paint these women."

I move on reluctantly, not wanting to see the next painting.

"The Black Dahlia" scarcely has a single patch unsplashed by red. The woman's figure, severed in half, is almost indiscernible in the chaos of impastoed color, yet her exposed leg resembles Kitty Genovese's and connects to her in the most disquieting of ways. I've seen a reproduction of "The Black Dahlia" already. I knew it was graphic. Disgusting, as Kevin said. As everyone would expect it to be. Elizabeth Short's killer had mutilated her body so badly that the woman who first discovered it thought she'd come across the strewn pieces of a department-store mannequin. The pale scoop of Short's pelvis, with its puff of pubic hair and bent legs, is sliced and set apart from her bare torso, her raised arms, her head. Yet the catalog reproduction flattened this painting's singular effect—the way Kim's thick, active brushstrokes make the remains vibrate with life, as if they seek reconnection. The pieces lie separate in the green grass, but they also reach toward each other, as if trying to reunite.

Elizabeth Short was found in Leimert Park. That patch of grass is not two miles from here.

Before I entered these galleries, I was sure Kim Lord would make me feel something—maybe sadness, maybe anger, maybe awe or jealousy. But whatever is flooding me right now, I can't name it—it's like the feeling you get when your car starts hydroplaning on a rainy road and you don't know where the pavement is anymore or when the sickening glide will end.

There's one more picture to see before I leave this room.

Nicole Brown Simpson lies at the bottom of a staircase, face hidden, her blond hair soaked in so much blood that it glistens like wet clay. Her blood also runs down the tile, filling its cracks. This is the first painting where Kim Lord isn't looking out at me, and for a moment I struggle to see what she's done to make the image different from a terrifying photograph of the murder's aftermath. After all, Nicole Brown Simpson's 1994 killing is probably our city's most famous, both for its high-profile suspect and the media circus that followed the trial. O. J. Simpson and the clues to the homicide became so much the focus of the news that it's easy to forget the savagery of the actual attack. Nicole Brown Simpson was knifed so many times that her head was almost separated from her body. Quarts of blood spilled from her.

I can't grasp what the painting has made of this. Then I spot it, how Nicole's blood in the tile cracks extends and extends until it forms a dark, shiny inverted tree. From the upside-down branches, hundreds of tiny orbs hang like drops. Like fruits. The meticulous delicacy of each. I look back to her collapsed body. The black walls draw closer.

Behind me, voices amplify in the first room; people are starting to arrive in droves. Below me, the cold floor. There's another gallery to this exhibition, but I don't move.

I never viewed Nikki Bolio's body, but I read the autopsy report: the raw skin at her wrists and ankles, the water in her lungs. Death from hypothermia and drowning. The likely scenario: the murderer towed her behind his boat at night. Her flesh would have burned at the touch of the icy lake, and she would have sunk because she could not kick or paddle. She must have struggled in the water; she must have screamed. So he sped up until her head whipped and body bounced, turning his boat until the wake washed over her and black waves flooded her mouth. Then he threw her toward the shore to be found.

She must have struggled; she must have screamed. Her thrashing must have been ugly and violent. Her cries must have ripped the night over the lake, ripped into the cold, inky New England sky, into the pines lining the shore. How long did it take for him to kill her, his hand pushing the throttle, steering the wheel? What made her finally give up and breathe water?

No matter the power of the paintings around me, the violation of homicide is so terrible, so unknowable, that it exists beyond any meaning we might make from it. And once the horror touches you, as Nikki's murder touched me, you're aware of it, all the time. It's like having an abyss next door. Just beyond your ordinary patio and fence: a giant, sticky hole to nowhere. It makes you sick. It makes your skin crawl. It makes your eyelids feel like they are blinking over dry glass.

I feel a tap on my shoulder.

"You okay?" says Kevin.

"Come on, you'll miss it," says Yegina.

I tell them to go ahead.

"You need me to get you some water?" says Yegina.

I shake my head. "I'm fine. Go."

After a hesitation, she squeezes my arm and heads into the next room. Kevin waits by the threshold, pulling out his notebook. In my peripheral vision I can see the last series, among them Chandra Levy, Lita McClinton, Judy Ann Dull, and a giant still life of objects honoring the thousands of other female victims of abduction and murder. I close my eyes. Open them again.

Printed on the wall beside me is a square of text about still lifes. I've read it before. I copyedited it. But I read it again because Lynne's stuffy, informative voice calms me:

> *A still life is a work of art depicting mostly inanimate subject matter, including both natural and manufactured objects. In prior eras, it was considered an ideal art form for women artists, who would not have been allowed to learn life drawing from nudes.*
>
> *The typical still life gives the artist more freedom of arrangement than landscapes or portraits do. Early European paintings often incorporated moral lessons through the placement of objects that were also symbols, such as an apple suggesting temptation or a snuffed candle being synonymous with death.*

Black letters on a clean white background. Black wall behind it. Nearby, the doorway to the next gallery. I push my eyes through the threshold, where Yegina stands with Hiro, our new grant writer, gazing silently at a painting I can only see the edge of, but I know it is Judy Ann Dull by the sharp-heeled foot, the ankle bound to a board by wire. A solid, warm bulk materializes beside me, and I get a whiff of overheated wool. I turn to Kevin, relieved.

"I thought still lifes were grapes and dead hares and stuff," he says. "Aren't these portraits?" he asks.

"Not according to the artist," I say. "She says that these paintings are still lifes because the subjects are inanimate and positioned to relay a meaning."

"Kim Lord is inanimate?"

"Her photos of herself are. And the victims are."

Kevin looks dubious.

"Also, because still lifes were often a display of opulence or wealth," I explain. "Some rich person showing off the luxuries they own. Well, what if the liberated woman is one of our society's luxuries? And what if she's something hunted and killed, too?" I can't keep the edge from my voice. I can't get Roseann Quinn's headlines from my brain, or the staring eyes of Kitty Genovese. I won't forget Jayme leaving an early *Still Lives* planning meeting, a queasy look on her face; or Evie's confession that she couldn't sleep after checking all the captions for the catalog's graphic photos. I suppose we knew what was coming with *Still Lives*— it would expose us, it would expose most women's oppressive anxiety about our ultimate vulnerability, a fear both rational and irrational, like the fear of the footsteps behind you at night, magnified a hundred times. But we suppressed our dread in the excitement of a successful show.

Kevin doesn't ask me to explain. Instead, he scribbles in his notebook. I get a sick sense that someone is watching us, and I search the growing crowd for Greg. The faces of dozens of strangers drift past me before I spot the guy with the mustard jacket, loitering across the gallery, his gaze on me. My discomfort returns. What if he's the stalker Jayme mentioned? It makes sense—he obviously sneaked in late, and he doesn't belong to an event like this. He isn't talking to anyone. He's just staring.

Suddenly, more than anything, I want to be home, safe in my own bed.

"Didn't you say there was a crew party somewhere?" says Kevin. "Maybe Kim's there? Has anyone checked?"

I tell him I doubt it, but a ray of hope splits my dread. It would be just like Kim Lord to favor the crew, to be standing high on the roof of her party while the rest of us parade through the dark, bloody cave she's made.

I need to get away from the paintings, so Kevin and I grab Yegina's badge and take the elevator up to the top floor of the staff offices, which houses our boardroom and the rooftop patio. We can hear the crew party before the door opens, a low hum of chatter and Brent's voice above it, declaring drunkenly that this is the best goddamn exhibition the Rocque has ever shown and the crew had nothing to do with it.

"It was all her," he says in a voice soaked with astonishment and booze. "It was all her."

At the last elevator stop in our office tower, the doors open on a small crowd in T-shirts and jeans scattered around the low walls of the patio. The shadeless square of cement gets so hot during the day that no one uses it, but the night and the cooling dark transform it to the kind of spot trendy bargoers would line up to visit. It's raised just enough to give a bird's-eye view of the avenue, but it's only knee-high to the looming skyscrapers, so you feel both elevated to the California sky and shielded from its vast emptiness. Scattered offices and hotel rooms glow in the sheer, giant buildings beyond, revealing strangely intimate but anonymous views: a parted curtain, a single lamp shining on an otherwise darkened floor. Even more than in the daytime, you realize how many thousands of people occupy this same square mile.

But few crew members are gazing outward tonight. Most of them are clutching red plastic keg cups and watching Brent with mounting concern. Brent is the god of this crowd; everywhere he goes at the Rocque, a certain coterie of scruffy MFA grads follows, slumping and lurking as if hoping no one will notice their efforts to steep in his brilliance. Brent rewards them by making one or two inscrutable utterances under his breath or by ignoring them completely. Tonight is different, and it could be the booze, but I've seen Brent drink at every opening. Alcohol tends to increase his dark taciturnity until it pools around him.

Tonight, he's taken off his suit jacket, pushed his white sleeves up to his large biceps, and is actually broadcasting his thoughts to our twin designers, Phil and Spike. They lean back on their elbows, their broad foreheads glowing. They are nodding, agreeing with Brent. *It was all her.* It was all Kim. Although I've never seen Phil and Spike roused out of their cool torpor to admire anyone, they stayed up all night to design the print materials for *Still Lives*. I know, because I had to sit in their unwashed radius the next morning when they presented the materials to the exhibition team.

Kevin follows me out of the elevator. I scan the crowd. No Kim Lord here. Not many people I recognize.

Aside from Brent's outburst, a morose quiet pervades this scene. Evie, the registrar, is smoking in the corner with a crew member and trying ineptly to slouch in a blue blazer that matches her pumps. With her blow-dried bangs and perpetual business casual, Evie has the air of a lost bank teller who stumbled into a college party. I wave at her, but she's focused on Brent and fighting a scowl. Evie worships Brent as much as his devoted crew does. She must not like seeing her idol unravel. She stabs her cigarette out on the ground, then lights another.

Spike spots me and grins with his upper teeth, but Kevin is already punching the elevator's down button.

"I need to get back to the galleries. To those paintings," he says as the panels slide open again. "You sure you're all right? You're pretty pale."

I tell him I'm fine but I'm going home, if he doesn't mind. We return to the elevator and it hums earthward.

Kevin pulls out his notebook and jots something down.

"Can I take you to lunch tomorrow?" he says. "This is turning out to be a bigger story than I thought."

It's not a story to us, I think. But I am ready to say anything to be alone, so I give Kevin my work number and ride silently beside him as he scribbles his notes.

When I was twenty-two and struggling to get my first clips in dinky Vermont newspapers, a beloved university professor arranged for me a job interview with Jay Eastman. Eastman was a Pulitzer Prize–winning New York journalist, and he'd relocated to Vermont to work on pieces that would become a book on drug smuggling in the rural Northeast. He possessed a thundercloud of gray hair and fierce eyes that could strip through your layers like paint thinner. He wasn't unkind, but he was always right. He needed a research assistant who understood the local culture but would not insist on taking too much credit for it. When he gave me the assignment to talk to the teenage ex-girlfriend of a major drug dealer's son, it was because he knew that Nikki would open up to me—another girl, about her age, just someone to talk to. And I, young and inexperienced and eager to please, would report back everything she said.

Two days before Eastman's first story broke and Nikki officially disappeared, I was walking home in Burlington from my second job as a waitress. The spring sun was out, the lake melted, the lawns sodden, and crocuses were nudging up beside porches and stoops. Little throbs of yellow, the buds promised warmer days. Seeing them, I began fantasizing about my move to New York. In two more months, I'd have saved up enough to rent a room in Brooklyn while I took a bottom-rung job at a newspaper. I'd have the clout of a letter from Eastman, my experience from helping with his research, and my name in the back of his book. I'd find my own stories, one by one.

The fantasy had one glitch: Nikki. In two days, everyone she knew would be changed by Eastman's article on the backwoods winter drug routes and the ways locals were smuggling opiates into the smaller towns. Eastman had promised to protect her anonymity, despite the fact that local law enforcement might subpoena him. He'd taken Nikki personally into his cluttered office and spoken to her about how he would never betray her to the police or anyone else, but still she should be careful.

Nikki had looked bold in his presence, then self-conscious and blushing. She tugged at her tight blond ponytail, then pushed her hands deep in her jean-jacket pockets until the denim was as taut as a sail, and said, "I'm ready." But within months we would move on, Eastman and I, and with us would go Nikki's assurance that what she'd done had purpose and meaning. As I hurried home through the chapped Victorians of downtown Burlington, I imagined Nikki a year from now, five years, living with her betrayal. If the police cracked down, it wouldn't necessarily help the addicts. It might just mean jail time for the people she knew, while others took their place.

Eastman had made me promise not to contact Nikki, but I wished then that I could offer her a place to stay if she became afraid. The fragile sunshine around me faded and a chill made my cheeks burn. It hurt, that air, but it wasn't a wind. It was just coldness sinking into everything: the budding trees, the strips of yellowed grass between me and the wet, open street. The cold amplified the slam of a porch door, and the slushy whispers of cars passing. It aged the grand, turreted houses, made their ornate windows seem brittle in their frames. It reached into my coat and enclosed me. By the time I got home, I couldn't stop shivering.

Something is wrong tonight. I know it with a certainty so strong that it makes my skin prick, like the sting of that cold spring afternoon in Vermont. The light down here has darkened to orange-black. Stained napkins, empty cups, crackers smashed to circles of crumbs—everything that was laid out to delight us two hours ago has been violated by human touch. The caterers have hauled back the tables to create a dance floor, but hardly anyone is here to dance. They're still upstairs, or possibly they've already left, discomfited by a party that is still without its guest of honor. The DJ slowly turns up the beats. The music sounds thin and anxious.

Jayme and J. Ro are talking intensely by the stage, glancing over at the enormous fluffy white cake and a stack of plates that someone has rolled out to the center of the tent. The cake bears the name of the artist and the exhibition in bold red and black:

KIM LORD
STILL LIVES

Nodding at Jayme, Janis signals to a petite brunette caterer, who struggles to roll the cake away and bumps it over a curb, making the frosting slump and a plate fall from the top of the stack. The plate smashes on the tarmac beside our beleaguered museum director, Bas, who has just emerged from the loading dock. The caterer flies into apologetic motion, gathering the pieces with her bare fingers, and after a slight pause Bas reaches down an arm to stop her. She scurries off, presumably for a broom. Bas doesn't move. He stuffs his hands in his pants pockets, crumpling the front of his pale jacket. He seems to be staring exactly nowhere, not at the broken plate, not at the cake, not at the party, and not toward Jayme and J. Ro striding his way. He looks crushed and exhausted, but not surprised.

It hits me. He hasn't looked surprised all day.

FRIDAY

7

My neighbor's cough wakes me. Every morning, he goes out to the wet grass of his garden, turns on his fountain, coughs, and contemplates his mortality. At least this is how I imagine it. Maybe he's contemplating poetry or his property taxes. I've never spoken to my neighbor. I've never seen him or his fountain. The wet grass is a guess. His wall is too high. White and peeling, it runs all the way down the alley behind our courtyard apartments. It's a large lot for Hollywood.

My neighbor's cough has three sounds: the hack, the seizing breath, and then the rumble. The cough comes and goes, always in that order, though this morning his hack is harsh and deep, and the rumble lasts a long time. The noise of his discomfort disfigures the objects around me: my dresser bare of photographs; Jayme's scarf and dress, twisted on the floor; her boots flopping against each other like drunks. The single butterfly earring on my nightstand. I lost one last night. I've had the pair since the day my grandmother died. They went to Thailand in my ears, pricked my jawbone when Greg cupped my face to kiss me for the first time.

I hold the remaining butterfly for a moment, pressing the sharp stub into the pad of my thumb until the pain wakens me. Then I go downstairs to make my morning tea, filling the pot with water, twisting the knob to the burner.

I click the computer I left on last night: there are a couple of local news articles on Kim Lord's disappearance. No updates, except that Bas is quoted in one, saying that the museum is cooperating with the LAPD and that the exhibition will open to the public today as planned. By the gentle light of a Hollywood morning and the sound of squirrels chittering in my avocado tree outside, it seems possible that everything will be resolved. Kim Lord will reappear soon with some provocative message for us all, and an extra wave of press will drive more viewers to the Rocque.

Yet I wonder how much sleep Bas got last night, contemplating his missing Gala honoree and his potential firing all at once. Why did I see a weary acceptance in his face last night, while everyone else looked shocked? Maybe he's thinking of resigning. Maybe he's ready to give up on saving the museum. Come to think of it, he and I had a bizarre conversation on Monday, in the elevator to the fourth floor.

It was a busy day, a major exhibition looming, the museum like a hive with people hurrying in and out carrying folders and parcels and tools. I was happy to slip into the elevator alone.

"Hang on," said a voice as the doors closed, and Bas stepped in, giving me an overly friendly grin that suggested he'd once again forgotten my name.

As we stood in the rising box, he kept rubbing his arms and shifting from foot to foot. He looked awful, like his whole body itched. I felt awkward riding silently beside him, so I asked how many people were coming to the Gala.

"Don't know the exact figure, but it's sold out. First time in years." He gave me a pained smile. "Everything Kim Lord touches turns to gold."

The elevator door opened then, and Bas practically ran to his assistant Juanita's cube and asked her to get Nelson de Wilde on the phone.

"Isn't that good news?" I remember wanting to say. But it hadn't seemed like good news at all.

My teakettle shrieks. I pour the boiling water over a sachet of green and pink herbs that I bought at a fancy kitchen supply store, then head for my computer again. But I never get to read more news, because my mother calls me: the story of Kim Lord's vanishing has aired on National Public Radio.

"How's Greg?"

"I don't know," I tell her. My tea tastes like a marigold garden. I pour some maple syrup in it. Now it has the exact flavor of allergy medicine.

"How are you?" she asks.

"Fine. Thanks for asking," I say.

"I could fly out there if you need it."

"Why?" I say. "It's not like *I* was dating her."

"It's just . . ."

In my mother's pause, I hear her sadness that I am not married to Greg, not living on the East Coast, and not about to pop out a grand-child. It relieved her when I moved home after the Bolio case, but then I got my teaching job overseas and started "tramping all over the world." My serious relationship with Greg marked a new page, and she'd hoped that I might settle down in a nearby state, might even choose a long-term teaching career like she and my father had done.

Instead, Greg and I had moved to L.A., pulled by the siren song of California, its warmth and ease, the limitless possibilities.

As a consequence, my mother allocates the city a loathing she usually reserves for Karl Rove and tomato hornworms. She always pronounces the second letter in L.A. with vindictive force, as in *You're moving to el-AY? What could you possibly want to do in el-AY?* The one time she and my father visited us, she surveyed the palm trees and sun-bleached streets with hurt distaste and declared our movie-star-laden Hollywood neighborhood "a bit seedy." For Christmas and birthdays, she mails me a steady stream of Green Mountain mugs, T-shirts, and notepads, as if to remind me of my rightful surroundings.

"It's just . . . it sounds dangerous for you," she says.

"Nobody even notices me here," I say with a little laugh. I tell her how kind she is. How I need to get off the phone soon. "I've got to beat rush hour."

•

As soon as I drive up the freeway ramp, the traffic thickens to sludge, and I inch and dart from lane to lane, but it doesn't seem to bring me any closer to downtown until finally I'm there. I barely make it to the emergency meeting that Bas calls in the auditorium at 9:30 a.m.

The Rocque's auditorium is a large, dank room at the back of the warehouse, capped with skylights. No matter the time of year or grandness of the occasion, the auditorium lowers the same cranky gloom over its visitors. The texture of the painted concrete floors and walls remains perpetually clammy, and the fold-up wooden seats seem designed to simultaneously pinch and collapse beneath you. The low stage looks like it was stolen from a high school production. It's a horrible place for performances, or acoustics of any kind. Sound waves pile on each other, making voices and words linger and layer. As we settle into our creaking seats, I catch *show sold out* and *the cops* and *disappearances* and a tone, like a bass line, of deep uneasiness.

A clean-shaven Bas introduces two LAPD detectives who will be investigating the case, DeLong and Ruiz, a man and a woman, respectively, both black-haired and wearing gray suits. "We're not sure we even have a case yet," says Bas. He is blinking a lot. "But we're taking precautions. Kim Lord was last seen on Wednesday and, following a text Thursday evening, has stopped communicating completely."

Janis Rocque stands behind him in bold blue-and-white stripes, hands on her hips. She looks like a parent who's just come home to a trashed house and wants to know who is responsible.

Yegina shifts in her seat beside me. "Should we even have Craft Club today? My brother got another rejection, too," she whispers. "My heart's not in my knitting."

"Is it in organizing your inbox?" I whisper back. "Come on. We all need to decompress." Craft Club is where we hear most of our museum gossip. Our confederation of nine women, all from different departments, meets every other Friday to knit, embroider T-shirts, gripe, trade recipes, and gripe some more. I need that today.

"Please comply with the officers—they'll be coming around to interview many of you," Bas urges. "Any hints, any clues to where Kim Lord was going when she left on Wednesday. Any conversations you had with her. Tell the police, not the press."

Kim Lord was going toward Pershing Square. I saw her, I think. But what if it wasn't her? I don't want to get sucked into a police investigation, and I'm sure I'm not alone. I search the crowd and find my eyes jolting against the gazes of others. Most people look scared or lost. The entire education staff, all women, have their arms folded. Lynne has a scowl so severe that her dark-painted mouth has almost disappeared. Jayme has made her face completely immobile; if a fly landed on it, she would not twitch a muscle.

Phil and Spike, the twins and my closest department colleagues, are sinking deep in their seats like they're in the front row at a cinema and trying to avoid neckache. I wonder when their chairs will snap. I wonder how they're absorbing the news. There are lumpy people and smooth people, and the twins are smooth. Maybe the smoothest people I've ever met. It's as if two decades of constant interaction with an identical human has worn them each down to their essential contours. Like stones sanded by water, they tumble easily through their days, never laughing more than a chuckle, never complaining more than a whine, and never working without reminding the rest of us that they regard the Rocque's whole operation as kids' play. But an abduction? The cops? It's too abrupt and dark to mock.

Now Bas is talking about a new museum confidentiality policy and only speaking to the media through Jayme. The twins slide lower, as if some tide beneath the seats is tugging them under. They admired Kim, but were they friends? Who else at the museum knew her well?

In the third row, I recognize a silhouette with rumpled hair.

Ice threads my veins. There, also tipped back in his seat, is the stalker from last night.

"That's him," I hiss, bumping Yegina.

"Who?"

I tell her about the guy in the mustard-colored jacket, how he lurked in the galleries. "He's here again. How do you think he got in?"

She follows the line of my gaze. "He's not stalker material. He came with J. Ro. Maybe he's police, too."

He doesn't look like police to me. He doesn't have that stiffness and reticence. He looks, once again, like someone who would rather be taking a nap.

"On a positive note, the timed admissions for the first three weeks of *Still Lives* have sold out," Bas says almost eagerly.

Janis Rocque makes a noise like a soft bark. She muscles Bas aside to take the microphone. "We know you all have busy schedules," she blasts. "Meeting is over. Carry on with your days. We'll update you as we can."

The staff of the Rocque has never responded well to an order, but today we file out silently, somberly, except Yegina, who is already texting someone and treads on the back of my heel. I yelp. My voice carries through the hard room, and suddenly a hundred people are staring at me with visible curiosity and fear. In the dim room, they look like cave dwellers startled from a sleep.

"I'm okay," I say too loudly, and hurry along.

Across the rows of chairs, I catch Evie's eye and wave. She shakes her head sadly, as if to say, *What is happening to us?* I wonder if she's thinking that Kim has been kidnapped or thinking that she chose to disappear. Evie told me once that she herself ran away at eighteen to escape her stepfather.

"Miss," says a male voice behind me.

I stumble against a chair trying to step out of the way. Another crash.

"Excuse me, miss." A hand touches my elbow. I look back into the face of last night's outlier and flinch. His blue eyes ride slowly over my face.

"Hendricks," Janis Rocque calls out to him.

"Sorry," I say, though I don't know why.

He waves to her, then says to me, "You dropped this last night." He holds out my butterfly earring.

8

When I get back to my office, I set my earring down carefully, simultaneously bothered to have lost it and relieved to have it back. My maternal grandmother loved butterflies. She never learned their names or natural history, but she saw them everywhere as signs of good luck. Blind optimism was a lifelong calling for Grandma Margie, a petite, rich New York teenager whose father lost all their money in the Depression, whose brother lost his mind in the Second World War.

By the time I was her grandchild, Grandma Margie had evolved into a perpetually raven-haired beauty who liked to wear mint-colored suits and shoes "with a little heel" in them. She abhorred bad posture. Whenever we watched movies on television, she would chat her way through them if they bored or unsettled her, which was often in our house because my mother adores PBS. "Oh look, there's a Mercedes," my grandmother once murmured during a crowd scene in *Gandhi*. "You don't look like a monkey to me," she told me as I stared at *Inherit the Wind*. Even when we were kids, my brothers and I treated my grandmother with the kind of protective reverence one usually reserves for a child. Yet we all wanted—needed—her to take pride in us.

I bear my grandmother's name: Margaret. She was Margie and I'm

Maggie. My grandmother is with me at all times, yet, like the earrings, I don't feel her presence unless I press against it. Last night, it was Margie who stopped me from going into that third gallery, who felt I'd seen enough. Six years ago, it was Margie who refused to believe what would happen to my source, Nikki Bolio.

It was I, Maggie, however, who decided to flee overseas afterward, and then never to go back to the career I once dreamed of having, of recording people's stories, writing their difficult truths. I don't know what my grandmother would have decided in my shoes. She came from a different generation, with narrower ideas of what a woman could do.

A figure appears in my doorway. A woman with thick eyebrows, a high waist, hair that seems deliberately plain. One of the LAPD detectives.

"Got a minute?" she says, and introduces herself as Alicia Ruiz. She's carrying a notebook, but she doesn't uncap her pen as she sits down. "I hear you know Greg Shaw Ferguson?"

"We lived together." I hate the squeak in my voice.

"When was the last time you saw him?"

"At the Gala."

Her brows knit. "Before that?"

"Sometime in late February." Greg came then to pick up a few boxes he'd left in our garage. Summer clothes, books. I tell Ruiz this. She doesn't write it down. She glances over her shoulder, leans in. Her brown eyes are warm. She wants me to trust her.

"You ever feel threatened by him?" she asks.

"God, no."

"Did you ever threaten him?"

"Of course not."

She opens her notebook, uncaps the pen, and scribbles something. Even with her gaze averted, there's that deep absorbency about her, soaking me in. Me, the angry ex. The angry ex? I was the doormat ex.

"Where do you think Kim Lord is?"

I don't like this. It's a speculative question. Jay Eastman taught me to ask speculative questions if I thought my source was lying. Listen to the story, then ask something to try to get an opinion out of the witness. Opinions need justifications. Justifications lead back to facts.

"I have no idea. Am I supposed to guess? I last saw her leaving the museum on Wednesday."

She notes this. "What time?"

"Late morning? I saw her from the stairway when I was going down to the mailroom." I point toward the view, but Detective Ruiz is focused hard on me. I fumble to describe that little jump Kim had done, as if something had bitten her. "She looked like she was in a hurry," I say.

The detective nods, waiting. What else does she want me to say?

"She was going fast." I'm starting to sweat.

There's a clattering noise in the kitchenette near my office.

Detective Ruiz's attention suddenly breaks. She taps her pen against her notebook and rises. "Thank you for your time, miss," she says.

"I really hope you find her," I say. Only when she leaves do I realize that my face is sore from holding the same fake, worried expression.

My phone rings, Yegina's extension. "That guy you thought was a stalker? He's a private investigator, working for J. Ro," she says.

"What? How'd you find out so fast?"

"He wants to interview me." She sounds reluctantly intrigued.

"You?" Why am I surprised? "I just got interviewed by the LAPD."

"About what?"

My phone blinks with a second call.

"Nothing, really. I'll phone you back," I say, and click over to the other line.

"How much time can you get off for lunch?" says a deep voice. Kevin, the reporter from the Gala last night. It surprises me when my stomach flutters.

"Can't," I say. Development needs me to copyedit some fund-raising manual.

"Thirty minutes?" says Kevin. "I want to show you something."

"You can't get anywhere in L.A. in thirty minutes."

He asks if I know the order in which Kim Lord's paintings were made. Which one was last.

"The big still life. Why?"

"It could make a difference in finding her."

"You should tell the police, then."

"They don't have time to hear speculation. It's just a theory for a story, but I need your help. Please. I'll bring burritos."

I am not so different from you, I tell the departed Detective Ruiz and her curiosity, which coats my office like fingerprint dust, making even my stacked catalogs, my scuffed gym bag, the little Zen garden on my windowsill gleam with possible evidence. If Detective Ruiz suspects Greg, then she suspects me, at least as an outside player in whatever drama has ripped Kim Lord from her presently successful life. Detective Ruiz suspects, so she watches and waits.

I can watch, too, I think as I turn the pages of the Rocque's new membership brochure, letting the errors appear, as they always do, as tiny breaks in the patterns of punctuation, sentence, style. Copyediting bores most people to tears. This is why—before I got hired—the Rocque printed ten thousand copies of a gallery guide for a show before anyone caught the missing *l* in its title, *Public Offerings*. This is also why the Rocque hired me, even with no museum experience. I was the only candidate who aced their copyediting test.

Detective Ruiz watches me, Maggie Richter, known ex-girlfriend, but part of her dismisses me because I am female. Most violent perpetrators are male. Most killers of women are family members or intimate partners. The police went after Nikki Bolio's ex-boyfriend first, but he had a solid alibi, and evidence to arrest anyone else was insufficient. Local witnesses clammed up. Jay Eastman and I might have helped the case, except that Jay destroyed Nikki's tapes. He said he was doing it out of principle. He did not approve of the way that Vermont law coerced journalists into testifying in criminal cases. When he did speak to the cops, he left my name out of his statements. *You're my assistant,* he said. *That's the only responsibility you have in this. All right?* It wasn't all right. I couldn't sleep for fear of a break-in, so I moved in with my parents and then across the world.

Nikki appears often in my dreams: sitting on a bench by Lake Champlain, her arms folded, legs sprawled out in pale-blue skintight jeans. She sees me approach and buckles as if someone just kicked her lightly in the stomach. Then I'm right beside her, and she is looking over at me: long-jawed, slightly dopey, acne pitted, and solemn. Nikki is the type who hangs at the back of a room, the corner of a party, her blond hair thin and limp, pulled back hard in a barrette because she thinks it makes her eyes look exotic. She risks brown eyeliner. She keeps a small assortment of cheap jewelry but rarely wears it because she is embarrassed at longing to be beautiful. Vermont's long winter makes her skin lunar and her bones achy, but Nikki doesn't believe she can move elsewhere. Only women who seek their own importance leave her circle of family and friends. She is no one until she dates Keith, and then she is his, a figure at the center of a circle of new cars, huge TVs, and a four-hundred-dollar leather jacket for her birthday that makes her feel tough and as sexy as a Hollywood movie. Then Keith dumps her and she is no one again—until I find her and ask her to tell me her story.

In my dreams, we sit side by side, staring at the lake and its islands. Nikki opens her mouth and says *Maggie, wait.*

But she never says anything else.

At noon I am standing outside the Rocque when Kevin pulls up in a blue convertible. He has shed his tweed and pipe for a dark T-shirt and jeans, but he somehow retains the earnestness of an overgrown student. After several tries, he squeezes into an illegal spot beside a hydrant and waves to me. It's the only open space on the whole street. The line for *Still Lives* has been steady all day, from older men in biker jackets to pretty bankers in pressed suits on lunch break, all checking out their shadowy reflections in the Rocque's glass entrance as they wait for their timed entry.

I smell fresh leather as I climb into the car.

"You're living the dream," I say.

"I know, I know. I got a little spendy with the rental," he retorts. "But it's thirty degrees today in New York." He squeezes into the traffic behind a massive tour bus, and we follow the avenue past the new concert hall, its silvery billows catching the light, and under the jacaranda trees losing their sticky purple-blue flowers.

"How far are we going?" I ask, surprised when he cruises over the freeway to the end of the avenue, where it meets the start of Sunset Boulevard.

"How much L.A. history do you know?"

"Once upon a time, everything was orange groves," I say. "And some other stuff."

"Yeah?" he says, and looks at me in that warm, intent way of his and darts us forward through a yellow light.

I want to tell him that if we kept driving down Sunset we'd reach the Short Stop Bar, where Rampart cops celebrated their bloody shootings. We'd reach the faux Egyptian arches of the mall that was D. W. Griffith's movie studio. We'd pass the parking lot that was once the site of the Garden of Allah, with its discreet clay-roofed villas and Black Sea–shaped pool for the rich and famous, where F. Scott Fitzgerald drank away any possibility of succeeding in Hollywood. We'd coast by upscale storefronts that once were jitterbug clubs like the Trocadero, and Sherry's, a gin-swilling site with a long, ruffled awning that overlooked the 1949 attempted assassination of gangster Mickey Cohen. Glamour, corruption, violence, dust—this street is a trail of dreams twisted into might-have-beens. It is the mythic L.A. that people arrive from all over the world to see, and some to spend their lives in. But there's also another L.A., a city I didn't notice until I started working on the *Still Lives* catalog. It's the city where murderers come to hide—where the Black Dahlia's killer cut her mouth all the way up to her ears and slipped away, never to be found; where a figure once called the "Southside Slayer" turned out to be multiple serial killers murdering poor African American women in South Central for decades.

But it's all too much to say, so I just reply, "Yeah, I read some books on it."

Kevin looks disappointed, but he nods and we lapse into an awkward silence, staring at strip malls. He eventually turns off Sunset, glides a couple of blocks, and slows down before a large white building notable for its roundness and mass.

"Recognize this?" he says.

"Church?" I say doubtfully. The churches of my New England

childhood are narrow brick-and-wood affairs, built skyward, for small audiences. But this place runs the width of a block and looks vaguely governmental. Entrances and arches line the first stories. Flags from many different nations jut from poles above. Then come the stripes of smaller windows. A little cross perches on a lunar dome, almost like an afterthought.

"The Angelus Temple," he says, as if I should know the name.

"Are we going in?"

"You didn't see that third room in *Still Lives*, did you?" says Kevin. "Or did you go back later?"

"I didn't go back." I don't know why I feel defensive about this. I had a right to decide I'd had enough.

Kevin doesn't notice my scowl. "Well, you know the painting 'Disappearances'?"

"No." A week ago I proofed the wall labels for *Still Lives*. Each painting bore the name of its victim, except for the last, the largest still life, entitled "Anonymous." I tell this to Kevin.

He frowns. "Well, it was called 'Disappearances' last night, and it's full of objects. That's what's causing all the buzz. People think Kim was leaving clues to her vanishing."

No wonder Lynne had looked so furious at the press conference. She hates that sort of *Da Vinci Code* stuff—conspiracies and quests embedded in paintings.

"Kim Lord's only been gone forty-eight hours," I say. "It's hardly even a police case yet."

"She's a famous person and she didn't appear at her own party. That makes people very nosy." Kevin pulls out his notebook, reading, "'The typical still life gives the artist more freedom of arrangement than landscapes or portraits do.' Freedom of arrangement. Clues."

"Wow. Rock critic graduates to investigative reporter," I say sharply.

Kevin grabs a greasy brown bag from the back seat and offers me a foil-wrapped burrito. "Why not?" he says. "I know how to track down leads. But it'd be helpful to hear your take. You know a lot more about this world than I do."

I accept the burrito, but I'm bothered by his words. Tracking down leads. Like that's the job. Getting quotes and facts. *Never look for the what*, Jay Eastman told me. *Find the who. Who gets hurt. Who gains. Whose life will never be the same.*

I clutch the warm saggy package in my palm. "My take is this: A couple of years ago, an artist barricaded the entrances to his gallery on opening night. He wanted all the fancy insider guests to experience the exclusion of the art world," I say. "That's the kind of stagy thing they do these days. They don't make treasure maps."

"Maybe not." Kevin shows me his notebook, filled with small sketches. "But I counted twenty-seven objects in 'Disappearances.' Most of it is food: apples, lemons, that sort of thing. But she also included this." He flips a page to a drawing of a circular object with smaller circles on it. "Recognize it?"

I tell him no.

"It's an old-time microphone, the kind used by Aimee Semple McPherson. It's in many of McPherson's pictures. The artist even painted a faint cross on this one." He nods at the temple, and I finally connect the name with the female radio evangelist who amassed a huge following giving sermons here in the 1920s and '30s.

I scan the building. The small windows at the top unnerve me. They look like they belong on a prison. I can't remember McPherson's whole life, only that it didn't end well.

"Was she murdered, too?"

"Abducted. Take a bite and I'll tell you," says Kevin.

The burrito is tangy and delicious, and Kevin tells me the whole sordid story. The year is 1926 and Aimee Semple McPherson—in her midthirties, overworked, and embattled in local politics—goes for a swim at Venice Beach and disappears. Her followers flock to the coast to search for her body. One drowns. A diver dies of exposure. The media circus reaches a zenith when the *Los Angeles Times* hires a plane and a parachutist to search the ocean. A little over a month later, McPherson reappears in a small Mexican town, walking out of the desert, claiming she was drugged and kidnapped by an outlaw couple named Steve and Mexicali Rose. Not only is McPherson's story full of holes, but it also comes to light that a woman who looked very much like the evangelist spent several weeks in a Carmel hotel with McPherson's married radio engineer, Kenneth Ormiston.

"But the truth of her abduction was never proved," says Kevin.

"So the last painting is about abductions," I say. "But what would be Kim's motivation for faking her own?"

"When was her last major show?"

"Ten years ago."

"Isn't that a long time between big shows? Wouldn't she need this one to make a splash and drive her prices high?"

I would love to bust Kevin's theory by telling him about the press release that Jayme showed me, but I can't. It's too big a secret to share with a reporter, let alone one I hardly know. "What does your editor think of your angle?" I ask.

Kevin rubs his beard and gazes up at the temple. "I haven't told her yet. I need more time here." Then he holds out his hand for my crumpled burrito wrapper. "And, yes, I detect the subtle sarcasm in your voice. She is my fiancée. Of five years."

"More inquiry than sarcasm," I say. "Five years?"

"It's a long story." He glances at me. "You have one, too, I think."

"Had." It's my turn to avoid eye contact.

We both lapse into silence.

"I should get back to work," I say, brushing tortilla crumbs from my skirt.

Kevin sighs and taps the steering wheel, as if remembering some musical beat, then restarts the car.

"She'd have to have deceived everyone she knows, and risk the backlash when she reappears," I say. "It would be a huge price to pay."

A woman in a white dress enters the temple, her head bowed as if she's already starting to pray. The park and the lake beyond the building make a quiet oasis in the city, without the distracting parade of cars and ads for jeans. I wish I could stay in this pocket of calm.

"But it's enough of a theory for your story," I add. "You should write it."

"Yeah." Kevin sounds relieved to be back on topic. "There are some holes, I admit. What would you pitch to an editor?"

We pull out into traffic again.

"I wouldn't even know where to begin," I say before the silence gets too uncomfortable.

My phone pings and I open it to see a text from Greg.

I need to talk to you.

I close the phone and let the breeze wash over me.

"If she really is missing, your boy may end up needing a lawyer," Kevin says, driving us through panels of sunlight and shade. "My sister, Cherie, went to Loyola. She could help."

Failure: it never interested me before moving to Los Angeles. Yet after Greg moved out, I saw it everywhere, like dark matter, holding the city together. Ninety-nine out of a hundred people who come to L.A. eventually fail—at acting; at screenwriting; at modeling, painting, surfing, skating; at opening trendy restaurants, galleries, bars; at writing books; at finding love.

For a while after Greg moved out, I stopped reading for pleasure. I watched TV and went to movies. I listened to the radio. I fell asleep early. But I left all my novels and biographies alone, their covers closed and pages pressed against each other.

Only at the Rocque did I read, and because I was trying to keep the deadline for the *Still Lives* catalog, I spent weeks verifying facts about female homicides that the curators and critics quoted in their essays. It was grisly work, and I was glad when Evie took over checking the photograph captions. But something happened to me during that period when all I consumed was a horrifying assemblage of truths about men killing women. I decided I would never fall in love again. It wasn't just the rejection from Greg that had hurt me; it was how it became wound up with the cruelty of Nikki's murder and page after page of accounts of beatings, bloodshed, and dumping of women's bodies in shallow graves. I felt I could never again find a man to desire and trust. If I tried, I was sure I would fail.

When I finally returned to my books, I'd forgotten everything I'd read before. I had the uncanny feeling a stranger had randomly opened the pages and shoved a bookmark in. Novels now bothered me—too much invention in the narrative felt like a meal with too much sweetness.

In the Fitzgerald biography, I had to turn back to the spot where Scott meets Zelda and start all over, only this time their early fascination with each other—their late-night parties and jumping into fountains—didn't seem giddy and romantic but vain and silly, as if they refused to see the disaster of their lives ahead. So I skipped to Fitzgerald's waning years in Los Angeles, when he went to a young actors' gathering with his mistress, Sheilah Graham, and the partygoers were pleased and astonished to meet him. The author of *This Side of Paradise*! The Jazz Age superstar! They'd thought he was already dead.

As Kevin drives off and I pass a large line of people waiting to enter *Still Lives*, I remember that moment. What it must have meant to Fitzgerald to be greeted like a ghost, and how desperately the writer later poured himself into his final novel, *The Love of the Last Tycoon*, the book he thought would secure his literary reputation again. Kevin is right about one thing: With ten years since her last major show, Kim Lord, too, is starting to fall off the cultural map. She must realize how much of her future career rides on *Still Lives*. What would she trade to ensure its success? Would she give up her sanity, plunging herself into the stories of the tormented victims? Or would she drop Greg for a relationship with some bigger art-world star? Would she fake her own kidnapping? Or does she even care about her own success—she who, for the sake of a principle, wants to donate paintings worth potential millions?

I look back at the crowd that winds down the sidewalk to our nearest architectural neighbor, a mammoth insurance company tower that caps the hill before it starts to tumble toward Pershing Square. The line's now thirty people deep, and they're mostly hiding behind sunglasses in the April warmth, dressed in jeans or long pants, boots or heels. The occasional pair of khaki shorts and sandals mark a tourist. There are more of them than usual. Even visitors to L.A. have heard about the exhibition, then. Maybe Bas's efforts to attract them have worked, or maybe they've simply read the news.

These are the multitudes we all hoped for. The ones who would save the Rocque. And yet through them I see my last view of Kim: her trench-coated figure hurrying down this same sidewalk, running away.

9

formally call the Craft Club to order with a question," says Yegina, holding up the purple scarf she is knitting. "Who else wants to ban conversation about Kim Lord?"

Silence greets the announcement. We're in the swanky boardroom on the offices' top floor, the walls made of dark wood, slanted windows spilling light onto our needles and yarn. Jayme flips a page in the cookbook she's reading, Evie shrugs into her embroidery, and Lisa and MeiMei from Membership pick at the quilt they are sewing together. Dee, a skinny crew member who wears genderless compilations of T-shirts and jeans, prods the tiny cats she makes out of dryer lint.

"It's so sad," says Lisa finally, tugging a thread. "I mean, if something has actually happened to her."

"Something has," says Jayme.

"Because I just spent an *hour* with that investigator," Yegina barrels on. "And I suspect I'm not the only one tapped out on the subject, right, Maggie?"

A whole hour? "I guess."

In Craft Club we occasionally outlaw office gossip for the sake of having deeper conversations about our lives. Last month, the topic of watching our thirtysomething friends become mothers of babies evoked a passionate discussion and a few snarky anecdotes. We spent a long hour once debating the merits of MFAs and graduate school for artists. Post-9/11, we cried together and plotted our escape routes from L.A. Yegina is always the funny, bossy one; Lisa and MeiMei brim with gullible empathy; Evie has a passion for Hollywood gossip; Jayme warily steers us from too much cattiness; Dee makes spacey, sometimes careless remarks; and I—what do I do? I used to play the wide-eyed, eager new-comer, until I learned to hide it better.

"What did the investigator ask you?" Dee says to Yegina. "I missed everything. Out sick Wednesday and Thursday."

Dee sounds funny when she says it, and not just because she has an adorable British accent that coordinates well with her dryer-lint cats and her muscular handiness with carpentry tools. Dee is Brent's charismatic first mate, the longest-standing member on an often revolving crew. Without Dee's upbeat wrangling, Brent's ideas would not be so easily re-alized. But she must be feeling awkward. Wednesday and Thursday—the last two full installation days for *Still Lives*—were odd ones for her to be absent.

"He asked me not to tell." Yegina loops her yarn and begins to knit.

"Oh, come on," says Dee.

"It was nothing," Yegina says primly.

I struggle not to frown. I know Yegina is trying to protect me. After Greg moved out, I camped in her apartment—in a bed she made for me between her Pocky sticks and hard-core record collection—until I could bear to go home. If someone says the word *kindness*, I see a curvy silhouette like Yegina's bringing cookies and Valium on a tray. Yet Yegina protects by exerting control, even over other people's feel-ings. She saw me freeze last night in the galleries, and she doesn't want to see it again.

"We could talk about the 'I Survived Cancer' party that I invited you to tomorrow," I say. "On horseback."

I feel Evie's eyes flick to me. I could have invited Evie instead. I prob-ably should have.

"You survived cancer?" says Lisa. "I'm so sorry. I mean, I'm happy."

She's almost tearing up over her sewing needle, so I explain. My friend Kaye has survived throat cancer and she's throwing herself an official fete. *I Survived Cancer. Join Me on My Gallop Back to Health.*

"Her words," I say. "It's at some ranch in Griffith Park. We're supposed to ride over the hills at dusk, eat dinner at a Mexican restaurant, and then ride back." I'd debated about making an excuse not to go, since Greg is also friends with Kaye and a couple of weeks ago he RSVPed yes for two. I retaliated by RSVPing for two as well. I didn't have a date until I successfully coerced Yegina.

"Griffith Ranch? I've been on that ride," says MeiMei. "Make sure you get a mellow horse."

"Or what?" says Yegina. Her brows are furrowing.

"They have to have mellow horses," I say. "Or they'd be out of business."

MeiMei regards both of us before continuing. "It's just a long way in the dark," she says.

An awkward quiet falls. I know Yegina wants me to release her from her promise, but I need her tomorrow. I don't want to be out alone on winding roads.

"That private investigator guy's been watching the loading dock all afternoon," Evie says in her soft voice. "He just sits there. Maybe he thinks the stalker's going to show up."

And then we're sliding into the same conversation we've been having all day, all over the museum and outside it, too. About the rumor of the stalker. About Kim Lord's theatrical nature, how she often had some performance element to her exhibitions. About the large still life I didn't view last night, the one called "Disappearances." ("She changed the name on Monday," Yegina tells me. "I didn't want to bother you for one label.") Our voices grow hushed, and we are bending closer together like conspirators, knowing that beyond these walls the press and the world await the news of what will happen here, at our museum.

After a while, it grows clear that my friends are of two camps. While Jayme and Yegina believe something ominous has happened to Kim, the rest are hopeful that the disappearance is a stunt. It doesn't surprise me that the groups would divide this way, given Yegina's usual cynicism,

Jayme's anxiety about the show, and the others' tendency to hero-worship artists and invest them with intentions and capabilities far beyond a mere mortal. I am the only one on the fence. Kim Lord hasn't even been missing forty-eight hours, and given her oversize, confrontational approach, I agree with my pals and Kevin that she might have another performance up her sleeve. But it's hard to ignore the cold, blank fear that flooded me last night in the exhibition, or the tone of the artist's statements in the press release. She didn't sound like she was planning to vanish.

Evie thinks Kim Lord might be leading us to another set of paintings, somewhere beyond the museum, representing all the women murdered outside the media spotlight. "For all the Jane Does," she says with a smirk. Sometimes the way Evie contributes to discussion reminds me of Nikki Bolio—she speaks to the air in front of her, with a self-conscious twist of her lips, as if her utterances are aimed at some invisible, judgmental third party. Maybe it's how you learn to talk when you grow up afraid of the place that raised you—in Evie's case, a series of abusive homes in small-town Northern California. The few stories she's told me make me both sad and impressed by her current job, her loft across the river, her neat olive suit and chunky beads.

"I did see her leave the museum in a rush on Wednesday," I say, and tell about my view from the stairs.

"I wonder why," says MeiMei.

"She never made it to the galleries," Evie confirms. "She just got upset about something and left."

"I don't know how she handled it, frankly," says Jayme, looking surprised to be saying something.

"Handled what?" says Yegina.

Jayme turns a page in her Oaxacan cookbook, glares at a new recipe. "Making that whole show," she says.

No one knows how to respond to this comment, not coming from Jayme, whom we all admire, and who is so private that she works out at a different gym from the rest of us and never stays at happy hour for more than one gin gimlet. Even trickier, we do know what Jayme means— what it must have cost Kim Lord to inhabit these murders—yet saying it aloud strips away the safe armor of our own intellectualization, the same armor that got us through the Jason Rains show on capital punishment, when we each allowed ourselves to sit in a lethal injection chair and watch the syringes come closer. *Still Lives* is art. Art should shock us. We work at the Rocque.

Silence falls over the table, but we keep knitting and sewing, and the needles make tiny clicking and piercing sounds.

"I bet the police will turn up something soon," says Lisa.

"Motivation," says Yegina. "That's the first thing on my mind: Why would anyone want her missing?"

Motivations are misleading, I think. Only after all the evidence is in, after you unearth so many little hows, can you try to piece together the great why.

I'm about to say so, when Dee announces that boyfriends are the likeliest suspects, and that Shaw Ferguson looked shocked and miserable last night.

Here we go.

I feel everyone's eyes on me now. They all know he dumped me. For her. Their collective sympathy is the hardest to endure. I knit harder, the yarn scratching my fingers.

"I thought he looked awful, too," says Evie. "Like he hadn't slept a wink."

He did look awful.

"Greg Shaw Ferguson is too much of a narcissist to kill someone," Yegina says.

He also looked deeply afraid.

"Oh well. That leaves Maggie, right?" Dee says. "The jealous ex."

Dee clearly means it as a joke to clear the tension. I should have my own clever retort, but I don't. My mouth tastes stale and hollow. The dread I felt in the galleries is carving through me again. I stare down at my hands, shoving the needle, ripping a new loop.

"Low blow, Dee," Jayme says.

"This is what I was trying to avoid," Yegina mutters.

•

One warm winter day in our first year in Los Angeles, I was driving the 101 with the skyscrapers streaming past on my right, the hills on my left, when I felt the city—really felt it—for the first time.

I was en route to the Rocque, my radio tuned to indie twang, my skirt tight over my thighs, my sunglasses heavy on my nose and just starting to slide on the sweat, and it happened—the sensation of *metropolis*—expanding me like a balloon.

I passed a parking garage under construction. Out of the corner of my eye: giant steel girders, ramps, and levels. *When this is finished,* I thought, *two hundred people will come every day to slide their cars into these spots, and I will never know a single person by name or what troubles them, and they will not know me, and if two hundred more take their place, I won't know that either.*

I—who'd grown up in a Vermont village, who could identify every local family by name or habit—was now surrounded by so many thousands, millions, they could only be specters. Ever anonymous to me, and I to them. The isolation almost made me choke.

That was the painful part of my awakening.

After that, exhilaration. The road opened like a sea. I could be anyone speeding down it, not the daughter of my parents, the sister of my brothers. Not the girl who struck out at bat her entire first year of Little League. Not the teenager who sang a torturously earnest a cappella rendition of "This Land Is Your Land" in the school talent show. Not the Rocque newbie who brought maple-bran muffins to a cocktail potluck. And especially not the unknown young woman who sat outside Nikki Bolio's funeral in her car, weeping uncontrollably.

All those old, encumbering selves slid away, leaving me feeling exposed but light, too, as if it were suddenly possible to float.

When I'd reached my office, I'd called Greg. "What's wrong?" he said when he heard my husky voice. "Has something happened at work?"

"No, I just . . ." I paused. How could I explain the tingling in my skull, as if I had just hatched from a shell? "I could be anyone here. I just realized that. And it terrifies me."

"Why?"

"Because it's too huge—this city—"

"That's not the city. That's life. Life is huge. Isn't that what you wanted?" Greg sounded earnest and impatient.

I meekly agreed with him, but something inside me did not. Maybe that was the moment things started to fall apart between us. Maybe it was also the moment I started to realize how naïve I'd been about Los Angeles. I'd come here thinking that the sunny metropolis would catalyze me to a second start, but instead its staggering possibilities left me paralyzed.

Later that afternoon, I went downstairs to the galleries to check a wall label and ran into our exhibitions manager, Yegina, standing in the center of a room of hand-stitched photographs by a Cuban artist. Her dark head was cocked and her lips parted as her eyes followed the lines of red thread the artist had used to finish the Havana buildings that the Castro regime had left half constructed. Yegina looked more like she was listening than looking. Listening to a sublime symphony.

I'd heard that she and the curator had made a huge effort to get the artworks past the U.S. government embargo.

"It was worth it," I said, coming up beside Yegina. We didn't know each other well yet. I knew she'd just gotten married, but that was all.

"I hope so." There was a wistful tone in her voice. Though the museum had been open two hours, the galleries were nearly empty.

"It's going to get great reviews. Jayme told you, right?"

Yegina looked back at the photographs, the black-and-white images of the half-completed buildings, the delicate red stitching that suggested their final facades, their arches and roofs.

"Richard is leaving," she said, referring to our old director, who'd been with the museum for fifteen years. "He's resigning tomorrow. The fiscal-year reports came in yesterday, and we overspent by six million. Again. Janis told the board last night that this is the last time she'll bail out the Rocque." She nudged me. "You might want to keep your eyes out for another job."

I could tell by the way Yegina said it that she wasn't warning me of my own layoff, though layoffs were sure to come. Everyone on the staff knew that the Rocque was in trouble—various board members had stepped in over the years with big contributions, but we could never get our revenues up to meet the costs of our exhibitions.

"You, too," I said, trying to imagine the museum with our long-term director gone.

Yegina gave me a small, sad smile. "I can't leave this place. I don't want to be anywhere else. It'll have to leave me."

Maybe the best friendships begin with admiration. It's true of my feelings for Yegina. On the same day I panicked at my unknowable future in Los Angeles, Yegina reminded me of the value of being part of something greater than myself. She also had a deliciously subversive sense of humor and knew the best hole-in-the-wall restaurants downtown. We started to spend more time together, weathering the layoffs that came and the hiring of Bas Terrant over French café lunches in the fashion district and happy hours at Luster's Steakhouse before we stumbled home to our significant others, then later stumbled home alone.

Through all those close moments, I never told Yegina about Nikki Bolio. I could never tell her, because she'd want to analyze it, this place she'd never been and these people she'd never met. She'd want to break my big, heavy grief into smaller griefs, and then into dust so that I could stop hauling it around. But I want to haul it around, the whole clumsy story: Nikki's testimonial, our failure to protect her, her mysterious death, and the sad truth about small towns and how they can smash down the person who dares to stand up.

Besides, there have always been so many other things for Yegina and me to talk about, and for once, today, she asks my advice.

"What should I wear to the riding party?" she says as we're parting at my office after Craft Club.

I tell her boots, jeans, and a relentlessly positive attitude.

"Yuck," she says. "Do you even like this Kaye person?"

"I love her," I tell her truthfully. "But you'll see."

SATURDAY

10

Of all the creatures at Griffith Ranch, Uncle Bud is the most desirable. A great black gelding with a grizzled nose, he has aged into a melding of flora and fauna—an earthy slowness has crept into his limbs; his legs are like fence posts, and his gait like an Ent's. To ride Uncle Bud over the steep hills will be no more challenging than sitting on a sawhorse with a saddle slung over it. For the sixteen (of the nineteen total) people at Kaye's party who have never ridden a horse outside of a petting zoo, Uncle Bud is a dream come true. But alas, he is only one, and all the other horses have their defects: too much prancing energy, too much height, a mouth that flashes yellow teeth, ears that roll back. But the sun is slowly sinking toward the sea beyond Malibu and we have to choose. Or be chosen.

The second most desirable creature at Griffith Ranch is Rick, the ranch hand who is leading us to the paddock to claim our horses. Rick has the easy, loping grace and tawny skin of a man who spends most of his time outdoors. Under his shocks of shaggy blond, his smiles are inward and fleeting. He knows how to wear the admiring glances of women, and from all directions they fly at him like feathers and drift off again. Yegina has so far sent a whole peacock's tail his way, but she's not alone. It's mostly women in our party, except for two rather concerned-looking husbands, and Greg, whom I have so far avoided because he never returned my call back to him. Or my text with Kevin's sister's name and number. Or the dozen follow-up messages I've sent in my mind, alternately begging him to answer and telling him off.

Rick leads us past the gate to the paddock to a low mounting platform, and motions for us to climb. The extra two and a half feet give us a great view of the ranch: a red barn situated between jutting tan hills, the walls flanked by steel fences and three dozen milling horses. It's a sight I'd expect to find in rural Wyoming or Montana, but half a mile down this slope, clay-roofed mansions rise beside pools and bright-green gardens. Beyond them surge the giant apartment buildings that line the east-west streets of Los Angeles, and way off, there's downtown. The skyscrapers jut like tiny, sharp blocks, but the city doesn't end with them. It goes on far into the haze beyond: hundreds more streets, maybe thousands. Now they look like a chaotic mosaic, but by night they will become a smooth, endless tapestry of light.

A woman in jeans and chaps is throwing saddles on the horses who pass her, stepping forward to lightly cinch straps. Past her, another woman fixes their bridles, shoving bits in with quick fingers. Then she tightens the saddles and slaps the horses toward the gate. Everything and everyone wears freckles and splashes of dust. Everything and everyone is making noise—the women are clicking and shouting, the horses are whinnying, their hooves are thudding the earth, which is already dry and cracking, even in April. I find the hubbub as comforting as a cocoon—it reminds me of friends' farms back home. Then I hear, ever so faintly, the bleat of car horns from below, and I look out again at the thousands of buildings below me, their western walls ablaze.

"Beginner or intermediate?" Rick asks each person, then jabs his thumb at a line on either end of the platform. So far, Greg is the only intermediate. I'm not going there.

When it's Yegina's turn, Rick says "Beginner" without even asking her.

"What about her?" Yegina asks, nudging me. "Can you tell she used to own a horse?"

"You just told me," Rick says. He points to Greg and says to me, "Behind him, then."

"I haven't ridden in fifteen years," I protest, but Rick has already sauntered on.

Yegina squeezes my arm. "I'll be right next to you," she says. "In the pack."

"Herd," I say. "Do you know how much you're herding me?"

But Yegina is already brushing past Rick on the way to her line, and he looks befuddled first, then sly, then licks his lips.

Time-lapse cameras could not capture the negative speed at which I move toward Greg, who gives me a casual wave. He is wearing clothes I recognize—an old pair of jeans, a T-shirt for a Vermont reggae festival— and the sheepish expression he gets when he feels outnumbered by women. As I approach, I feel like I am walking into the past, into the era when he was still my boyfriend. I wave back, attempting nonchalance, but it looks like I'm swatting at gnats.

Kaye, cancer survivor and woman of the hour, throws her leg over Uncle Bud and gives a whoop.

Greg leans toward me. "Can you give me a lift home tonight? I need to talk."

"But I drove Yegina," I say.

"Can she get another ride?"

"Maybe. I don't know." Already I'm falling into my old pattern with Greg, almost unable to refuse him.

"I'm sorry I couldn't call you back," he says. There's an emotion in his voice that I can't read.

"Friends, Angelenos, and the cancer-free," a helmeted Kaye shouts from atop Uncle Bud. The horse ducks his head as if to put distance between himself and Kaye's vocal cords but otherwise remains motionless. "I am so touched and honored that you could be with me today."

A few cheers go up, and so do a couple of riders, awkwardly spraddling their mounts. One woman in pink flip-flops gets into a heated conversation with Rick, and then storms off to her car. Kaye blinks at the exchange and then soldiers on with her speech. Kaye excels in soldiering on. She is the classic beautiful girl from the Midwest who comes to

Los Angeles to break into TV and ends up as a personal assistant to a celebrity—in Kaye's case, to the same famous actor/collector duo who once hired Greg.

The sight of Kaye usually fills me with both admiration and despair, but tonight I'm just admiring. Tonight I need to sun myself in her blithe optimism. A blue-eyed honey brunette with fabulously long legs and the waist of an ant, Kaye could easily get through life without female friends, but instead she courts as many as possible. I have never known anyone else as warmly and successfully social as her. I have also never met anyone else with such cheerful self-love. When Kaye found out she had throat cancer, she transformed herself from a human being to a living campaign; she started a blog and a fund for cancer research; marketed a green-tea cookie line (Kaye's Anti-Cancer Snaps); and wrote daily updates on her radiation, surgery, and experiments in holistic treatments. "Don't let the 'meanies' rule your life," she posted. "The reins are in your hands." (Sixth-grade slang and horse metaphors abound in her prose.) The way Kaye talks about the disease, you'd think cancer was something she invented in her quest for self-improvement.

Yet within eight months, Kaye beat back her tumor. She looks radiant now.

"Saddle up," she says to me, to her life-coach friends Sara and Nelia, and to a new woman who has been introduced as Kaye's "personal acupuncture savior." "First round of margaritas is on me."

I click on my helmet and cheer with the others. If I didn't feel Greg's amused eyes on my face, I could fully enjoy being Kaye's eleventh or twelfth best friend. Instead of acknowledging him, I focus on the horses that Rick is leading our way: a tall cream-and-brown pied gelding and a slender black mare who keeps lunging sideways and tossing her head. I am not much of a horsewoman, but it's apparent to me that something is bothering the mare.

"Babe," says Rick, and mutters something low. The mare ducks her head, nostrils flaring. "Come on, Babe," he says.

He hands the gelding's bridle to Greg. "This is Cheyenne," he says. "You might need to give him a kick up the hills, but he's a good boy."

Then Rick appraises me again, holding Babe's bridle. "She'll be fine. She's never been out at night, so keep her with me and the others," he says. "S'okay?"

She's never been out at night? It's not okay. Yet under Rick's and Greg's gazes, my defiant little-sister self kicks in: I want a different horse, but I'm not going to admit it in front of the boys.

"Rick!" calls the ranch owner from across the swirl of horses and riders. "We need six more mounted over here."

"S'okay?" Rick says to me again.

"I'll switch with her," Greg calls from beside the giant shoulder of Cheyenne.

"I'm fine." I take Babe's reins. Greg once had a rich girlfriend who played polo, but I bet he's never ridden on a real trail in his life.

I swing into the saddle. The musty warm smell of horse, the way Babe's dark spine bobs beneath me, makes my Vermont childhood come back again in a rush of grassy memories. We did own a horse. He was old and hated going down hills, so mostly I curried him until the air in the barn shone with his red-gold hair.

Babe stomps and pulls at her bit, but I hold her back, waiting for others to rise into their saddles. Finally we all start moving, led by Rick, and I get absorbed in the business of steering a large creature. Greg leans across from his own mount and asks me if I'm sure I'm all right. It's then, in that weird swaying second as Babe lurches from Cheyenne, that I really regard Greg and see through his polite mask to the hollows gathering under his eyes and cheekbones. His skin is the color of cement.

"You need to eat," I say to him. "You're not eating."

He smiles remorsefully at this. "Maggie," he says.

But then Rick is whistling at us all to follow him out the ranch gate, and the whirl of horses distracts me again. By the time I reach the dirt road leading to the ridgeline, we're in the last throes of the sunset. I can't see the ocean yet—it's blocked by the rim of hills—but the sun must be close to the Pacific. Our faces are bathed in light, but the shadows have risen as high as our stirrups. The slope's shrubs are also sunk in shade, and the pebbles that spin from the horses' footsteps roll beneath their branches and vanish. Part of me can't believe that I am riding a horse here, in this dusty-green chaparral above sprawling Los Angeles, that this city and this wilderness can coexist, that I can exist on top of this massive uppity animal that carries me. According to Kaye, we'll be riding a total of five miles tonight, up through the treeless hills and down the other side to eat and drink, and then return.

"It'll be dark coming back," the ranch owner shouts, "but don't worry because the horses all want to get home." She slams the gate behind us. "Just keep them away from your margaritas."

Weak laughs scatter over our group, and we're off. The earth is still sun-warm now, but a damp cool is spreading. I wish I'd brought a jacket.

"Pull to the right to go right," Rick hollers. "Pull to the left to go left. Give them a little kick if they get slow. Let the horses lead. They know the way."

I steer Babe after Rick, but suddenly Rick is breaking away to retrieve Yegina, whose dull-eyed brown mare seems fixating on going back to the paddock. Yegina, ordinarily graceful, looks lumpy and lopsided, as if she can't find the right place to balance.

"No, no. No. Please," she entreats the mare. "Not that way."

"Susie, Susie," Rick clucks, grabbing the reins from Yegina, pulling the horse around. "You got to go out one more time."

Susie's slight reversal of course is all Babe needs to get the same idea in her head, and I have to wrench her around to follow the others, too. Her ears whip back and her gait hardens into a stiff, huffy trot, leaving Rick and Yegina in the dust. This is not going well. Up ahead, Kaye whoops again and circles an invisible lasso over her head. Uncle Bud plods beneath her, unaffected. The sun falls another degree, and out of the corner of my eye I spot Greg's horse coming up alongside me. I'm bracing myself when someone else speaks.

"You've had a rough week." It's Nelia or Sara, on Greg's other side. I can't tell them apart, especially in the fading light. They are both attractive red-haired life coaches, and they've cowritten a book that is made up entirely of bullet points.

He ducks his head. "Yeah. You could say that."

"Do the police have any leads?"

"Apparently I'm their lead," Greg says tensely.

"Oh, Shaw. As if . . ." Sara/Nelia trails off. "Do you have a lawyer?"

"Maggie sent me a good name, and I'm talking to her." He glances over at me. Cheyenne dances to the right, startling Babe, and I fall back before I can reply.

"I just wish they wouldn't waste their time on me, and would *find* her instead," I hear Greg add.

The road narrows to a steep trail that switchbacks up to the ridge. I pull on the reins to keep Babe from crashing into the horses ahead of us. One by one, they start to heave up the channel of dirt and stones. Babe prances from side to side, her ears flitting back. A cool wind starts to blow, and it smells like nightfall.

"It's just a little hill, Babe," I squeak.

She cranes her neck and looks longingly down toward the dim red barn now far below.

"You okay, Maggie?" Greg says, but Cheyenne is already carrying him upward.

Dust fills my mouth as Rick surges ahead of us, still holding Susie's reins, Yegina clinging to the pommel. She gives me a pained smile.

"Easy does it," Rick tells Yegina. "Give Babe a kick now," he says to me as he passes.

I dig my heels into the mare's ribs. She jolts a few steps up the trail. Behind me, the city is orange and velvet and glitter. Before me are silhouettes: horses and riders merged into massive creatures that all climb skyward except Babe, who stops again and snorts. I wonder if I'm sitting wrong. I lean my torso forward into her neck, but my pelvis slides back in the saddle, dragging her down.

"Give her another kick," Rick shouts again, twisting back. "She'll go."

So I kick. But because Babe is whipping her head around again, I also stupidly, fearfully, pull back on the reins at the same time. Her front legs rise into the air, her back legs skittering. We both hang, the whole thousand or so pounds of us about to tumble, me first, and then she will pin me. And then, just as suddenly, Babe regains her balance and starts to come down.

Greg's voice splits the dark: "Jump, Maggie! She's going to fall on you! Jump!"

I do what I'm told, throwing myself from the saddle, landing hard on my right hip and then rolling off the path into a prickly bush.

I don't feel the pain until after I see Babe's hooves smash the trail. She gives a full-body shiver and gallops giddily upslope. Rick leaps from his own horse, grabs her reins, and ties them to his saddle.

"You all right?" he yells to me. "Can you get back on?"

Sharpness stabs through my hip, but I feel more ridiculous and relieved than hurt. The horse would not have fallen on me. But for the panic in Greg's voice, I probably would have ridden it out, landing back down with Babe and holding on as she charged up the trail. I don't know what to think about this. I can't distinguish Greg from the rest. He's just another dark figure.

"Coming," I say.

I stand and limp up the hill, sliding on stones, until I reach Babe's warm flank. Her head jerks, but Rick holds her. I stick my boot in the stirrup and get back on.

11

I n 1935, F. Scott Fitzgerald gave a speech at a banquet honoring the work of Mark Twain. "Huckleberry Finn took the first journey *back*," said Fitzgerald. "He was the first to look *back* at the republic from the perspective of the west . . . And because he turned back we have him forever."

I read this speech aloud to Greg when I first stumbled across it in Fitzgerald's biography. It was last December, a couple of months after Greg's mother had died. He was booking a flight to Art Miami to do some consulting for his employers, two art collectors.

"Don't you love that last line?" I said. "'And because he turned back we have him forever.'"

"More Fitzgerald, huh?" said Greg, turning from the computer. "You should be reading James Ellroy or something."

"I will," I said, though I had promised this before. "But I want to imagine Hollywood in the 1930s, like when this bungalow was built— can you imagine how different it was?" I gestured at our living room ceiling, its cracking crown molding.

Greg snorted. "Sadly, no. I doubt they've updated anything."

"I mean the city."

Greg turned back to the computer screen.

"Nostalgia is an eastern preoccupation," he said. "Fitzgerald talks about it like it's a virtue. It doesn't have to be."

"Not all back-looking is nostalgia," I said. "Sometimes it's self-examination."

No answer. Red and purple panels flashed across Greg's screen.

"Those who ignore history are doomed to repeat it." It was a stupid cliché. But we didn't talk anymore. Not enough. Not about our ideas or feelings.

Greg sighed. His chair creaked as he swiveled again toward me. "Don't you feel freer out here?" he asked, searching my face. "I never realized how oppressed I was growing up in Europe and New York. Everyone important had already lived. Everything important had been done."

I recalled my drive on the 101, passing the parking garage, being flooded with metropolis. Was that freedom or exposure I'd felt? Or both?

"I just thought it was a beautiful quote," I said.

Greg kept facing me. "I'm moving out," he said quietly.

I wasn't sure I'd heard him correctly, but I couldn't find the voice to ask. I just stared.

"I found a space for a gallery," Greg said, his eyes sliding from mine. "I'm going to live there while I fix it up. It's going to take a lot of work."

His mother had left him an inheritance. A few weeks ago, Greg and I had discussed using it to buy a house. With an extra bedroom for our kids one day.

"I'm sorry," he said.

"You could still sleep here," I said.

"I'm really sorry," Greg said.

He slept on the couch that night, and the next day he left with his first bags of stuff. I assumed, in a self-protective way, that grief was overwhelming him. That he needed to cope with the loss of his mother by throwing himself into his new career. The next week, Greg presented me with a key to the gallery and his new apartment—"In case you need it for any reason," he said—and he kept his set to our bungalow, though he never slept there again. When we spoke on the phone, we spoke like lapsed friends who are pretending they still care. I wanted to yell at him, I wanted to cry; I just didn't feel allowed. Permission to suffer could only be granted to the most injured. So I kept my weeping to myself, where it festered and spread until I felt like I was two people: the serene, hardworking Maggie Richter everyone knew at the Rocque, and the private one who wanted to kick the young couple kissing on the street corner or set a big hot fire to the tiny sign that hung outside Greg's new gallery, announcing his evolution, man and gallery combined: SHAW.

After all, I was the one alone. Truly alone. Alone, for Greg, meant inviting Kim Lord to shack up with him weeks later. Apparently she "needed" a local studio space to complete her show for the Rocque. Apparently she stayed late one February night and they fell helplessly in love.

And apparently I have not gotten over the shame of all this, because here I am months later getting drunk in a turquoise Mexican restaurant until the heavy table corner stabs me every time I stumble to the bathroom. I get in a fight with Greg then Yegina then Greg *and* Yegina *and* Kaye about who will take me home. Greg has volunteered because he still wants to talk to me—about what? About his worries for his famous, beautiful missing girlfriend? Screw her and her death obsession! Not every woman fantasizes about being a sex slave or a starlet or a murder victim! Some of us just want to get sucked into a good novel and grow our own tomatoes one day when we have more time. When Rick asks me if I'd like to call a taxi instead of riding Babe over the hills again, I say with great dignity that I love Babe because she is a back-looking creature and I love the past, too, the past defines us and to ignore it is like putting down roots in a city that will one day fall into the sea and what is wrong with words anyway why is everyone here so obsessed with pictures I've got a picture for you what kind of person wears flip-flops to a riding party?

Greg's voice is far above me and spinning. It's farther than the ground, which is awfully close and spattered with wet, sour-smelling chunks. In the distance I hear neighs, hooves stamping. I didn't want to vomit in the taxi, so I held it in. Now, in the ranch parking lot, it's all coming out.

"Feel better?"

My stomach heaves again, and a pair of hands catches my hair.

"No," I say, wiping my mouth.

There's a blurry station wagon ride down through the hills. Then Greg walks me into our bungalow, through our old kitchen, with its still mismatched cups and plates and the knife his mother gave us, and out the back door, where he sits me down on the patio in our old hard chairs. I haven't swept the fallen leaves in a long time, and they crackle underfoot. Why is he here? I'm too tired to understand. The evening returns to me in flashes: Kaye's face wrinkles with concern as I tell her for the umpteenth time that, yes, my hip hurts but I'm fine, I know how to roll (as if leaping off horses is a hobby of mine). Then Rick the ranch hand says, "I might need to rope her horse."

Then Yegina tries to stop me from refilling my glass and gets a heavy splash of margarita on her blouse. "All yours, Greg," she says, throwing up her hands.

I'm not anyone's, but here we are, Greg and I, sitting side by side on our old patio in the dark. It's a small rectangle of concrete and brick between my house and the next bungalow, planted long ago with an avocado tree and a guava tree and a dark-green bush with glossy jagged leaves. A wooden fence blocks the view to the courtyard. The wood is so ancient, it has a soft gray texture and the nails have turned to circles of rust. A child could punch the whole thing down.

Greg shifts in his chair but doesn't speak. The cool air makes my sticky cheeks feel stickier.

If we were still a couple now, our silence would be the dull, smooth silence of two people who are so accustomed to each other that they don't need to talk.

This silence is different. Prickly and hesitant. Why doesn't Greg just go? We gaze up into the avocado tree, me sipping the sparkling water he has brought for me. I guess he's waiting to see if I'll be sick again. I try to stand, but the effort makes me dizzy so I subside into my chair.

"How did you get there anyway?" I say. My throat is acid, sore.

"Where?"

"I mean, why didn't you drive to the ranch?"

"I wanted to walk."

"You walked. From Echo Park."

"I walk a lot these days," he says.

"Hoping to run into her?" It comes out more harsh than funny.

"Kind of. I can't sit still and I can't sleep."

The avocados are ripe now, and they hang like dark jewels in the high branches. The squirrels around here are as fat as cows. They're smart, too. We used to call them the squirrels of NIMH. Last week I saw one using a fence post to cut through a peel.

"I'm sorry I hurt you, Maggie," Greg says quietly. "You never did anything to deserve this."

A stillness descends through me. My hip throbs, but otherwise I feel senseless, weightless. Even Greg seems distant, though I could touch his arm from here. His voice seems detached from him, too.

"After my mom died, it became frighteningly clear to me: you wanted to settle down and I didn't," his voice continues. "You were ready to have children whose father would be around for them. I wanted to do something that . . . changes things. Culture. I didn't want to be a father yet, and I refused to let my son or daughter grow up without me." Greg's shape shifts and the chair wheezes. "So I moved out. I told myself it was to protect you, but really it was to protect myself from seeing you hurt."

I was hurt anyway, I think, but I don't say it. I don't want to stop this voice, because it's going to apologize and then it's going to tell me that Greg wants me back, wants someone whose bare shoulders he held in the South China Sea and marveled, "God, they fit my palms exactly."

"And then when I saw you at the Gala, it hit me," says Greg. "You're the only person—"

The voice breaks off.

I've ever really loved, I hear him say.

"—in Los Angeles that I trust completely," Greg says. "My mother even said it, that I would always be able to trust you."

His mother. That specter of strength and bitterness and pain.

Greg is still talking. "But how could I ask you for help now?"

"Help?" I wobble back to the present.

Of all the apologies and reconciliations that I fantasized about, I never imagined this one.

"I'm the police's lead suspect. I have no alibi for Wednesday evening. I was out walking that night, too." There's a catch in Greg's voice.

I glance over at him, but it's too dark to see his face.

"I told them about Kim seeing Bas with some man she thought was stalking her. But I can tell they don't believe me," he says. "Frankly, I didn't believe Kim."

"She saw Bas with her *stalker*?" My stomach suddenly roils, and I sip the bubbly water.

"On Monday. On the West Side somewhere."

"But what kind of stalker was he? Was he following her, sending her messages? Was he threatening her?"

"She wouldn't tell me." Greg sounds hurt and defensive. "She said it was complicated."

"But she knew who he was?"

"She thought she did, but she wouldn't say."

"What would Bas be doing with him?"

"I don't know. She thought he wanted to get at her through her art. I don't know. The show was making her hysterical," Greg says. "She was barely sleeping, and she wasn't . . . taking care of herself."

It's dawning on me: why he hasn't seen her since Tuesday. "And you fought about that and she left. And you don't know where she went."

"Yes."

"Must have been a serious fight." I drink another slug of my water.

"It was. But I never thought—"

I hear the same dread in Greg's voice as earlier, when Babe reared beneath me, pitching us backward. I don't want to hear any more.

"You're absolutely sure it was Monday?" I interrupt.

Greg says he's certain. I tell him about Bas's bizarre behavior in the elevator, and the board vote on his directorship, and the press release that Jayme had me copyedit.

"That's impossible." Greg bolts up in his chair. "Kim needs that money as much as anyone. So does Nelson."

"As much as Bas needs his job? The gift would make him look really good. Especially if it was announced to the public. It might make it hard to fire him."

As I say it, I still can't see how the gift would be a motivation for Bas to make Kim Lord disappear.

"Giving away millions of dollars makes no sense for her," says Greg. He tugs a hand through his hair as if trying pull free an explanation for Kim's alleged donation.

He refers to her in the present tense. I notice this with a slow lurch inside.

"You need some more water? I'll get you some more," Greg says, and disappears into the house, the steel back door slamming behind him.

I hunch in my chair, trying to process the information Greg has told me. Their fight. Kim's departure. Her connecting Bas to her stalker. The pieces feel jagged, like they don't fit together. My sense of time has been mugged by the tequila, and I don't know if minutes pass or just a moment before I look up and see Greg in the window watching me, his face twisted with rage. I flinch, our eyes catch, and the expression vanishes. He waves and holds up a water glass.

"Here. You need to drink about ten of these," he says in his usual amiable tone when he returns.

I decide my vision must have been a warp of the old bungalow window, an odd reflection. I can't see any trace of anger or fear.

"I'll try to find out where Bas went on Monday," I say.

"Christ, if you could—" says Greg.

"But your new lawyer, what's she doing?"

"She says the police are getting a warrant to search my properties. There's nothing to find." He sits back down in his chair and sighs. "Except this." From his pocket he fishes something that looks like a thin, black finger. "I do have another favor to ask."

I'm shaking my head, but when he slides the object toward me, I take it in my palm. It's a flash drive.

"These are Kim's photos. The studies for *Still Lives*. She deleted them off her computer and camera, and she was going to destroy this after the opening."

I recall copyediting the pages in the *Still Lives* catalog devoted to Kim Lord's idiosyncratic process, the same one I first puzzled over so long ago in Thailand: first her study of her subjects, then her photographs of herself costumed as those subjects, then her paintings of her photos, and, finally, the obliteration of the photos. Smashing the flash drive is her last ritual. I would have thought she'd done it by now. She delivered her last painting to the Rocque on Tuesday.

"Why don't you just take a hammer to it yourself?"

"I can't," Greg says. "I just can't. Please hold on to it for me?"

"We might be obstructing an investigation."

"It's not like that, I swear. There's nothing on here that will help the police."

He closes my fist around the flash drive. I wince at his touch. *You shouldn't trust me,* I say in my mind, and Greg asks *Why?* And I say, *You shouldn't trust me because I still stupidly wrongly hopelessly love you.* But I say nothing aloud; instead, my fingers stay closed.

Greg stands up. I feel a squeeze on my shoulder and a tiny peck on the top of my head. "I hope you and the squirrels of NIMH get some good sleep," he says.

Still speechless, I stand and turn on the patio light for Greg to find his way out. The glow illuminates a low branch in a nearby bush and what looks like a white hose wrapped around it. As I lean close, the hose shifts, and inside its hollows, an elongated face gazes into mine. It has a sharp funnel for a nose and deep-set eyes. It looks like a distorted heart. I leap back, yelping, and there's an immense, heavy scrambling as the creature disappears deeper into the bush.

"Possum," Greg says in a wondering voice. "They've evolved into possums."

Kim is missing and Greg doesn't know why. He doesn't know *her.* He loves her, but he doesn't know her. After he leaves the patio, I go up to my bedroom, lie down, and brood with a spinning and bitter mind about this paradox. Greg doesn't know Kim or love Kim, but he thinks he does. He thinks he knows Kim because she is his mother. Not his mother, who is dead, but the mother of his childhood. The beautiful Theresa Ferguson, who was also an heiress and a runaway. And a genius. Theresa was the opposite of me, which was why Greg loved me until the moment his mother died.

Theresa Ferguson was born in 1932 to a wealthy New York family and ran away to Paris at eighteen. She enrolled at the Sorbonne, and drifted from lover to lover, all over postwar Europe. She learned five languages and never married. A "protofeminist," Greg called her. Her sculptures are in the collections of eight minor museums.

When Theresa gave birth to Greg, she was forty and living in a Swiss town filled with artists. Greg's father was just one of many who came through, an Irishman who never knew of his son. Greg didn't seem to mind much. Instead, he channeled all his filial devotion toward his mother, who alternately adored and ignored him. He grew up at the fringes of her all-night parties—waking in the mornings to find strangers filling the other bedrooms, and once an entire French circus troupe sleeping off hangovers, the acrobats still wearing their dusty tights.

Theresa relocated to a New York suburb in Greg's teens. He and I stayed in her gorgeous, art-strewn house one night before leaving for Los Angeles. I don't think Theresa disapproved of our big move, but she'd always disapproved of Greg's interest in me, a young woman with a country upbringing and no distinct ambitions.

That night, Theresa cooked a full French meal for the three of us. She chopped, she sliced, she stirred, pacing about the kitchen, her dark hair piled messily on her head. The one time she looked directly at me, her gray eyes carved holes. "Are you thirsty, Maggie?" she asked.

I realized I was.

"Oh no, I'm fine," I said.

She poured me a glass of water anyway, her bony fingers extending it. "You look thirsty," she said.

I offered several times to help Theresa. She finally handed me a chef's knife and asked me to cut some red bell peppers. I made a pile of chopped pieces before she came over and stared at them.

"Greg, can you show her how to julienne," she said coolly.

Wordlessly, Greg stood behind me, wrapped his arms past my waist and murmured in my ear, directing me, as we cut the rest of the peppers together. Theresa faded outside the fortress of our intimacy and the smooth movements of the knife. That night he also sneaked into my bed, and we had the best sex of our relationship, better even than the first months in Thailand, Theresa's old clocks wheezing in the hall while we touched in silence with the fever of teenagers.

When I opened my suitcase in a hotel in Ohio, I found the chef's knife, carefully wrapped in butcher paper. No note.

I showed it to Greg. He raised one eyebrow. "She's just funny that way," he said. "She gave my last girlfriend her extra blow-dryer. She likes to get rid of stuff."

Theresa's knife was an expensive one. After Greg moved out I kept it. I still use it, ignoring the pang it gives me every time: that I might never learn the right way to slice things.

Kim Lord knew who her stalker was. She knew, but she chose not to tell anyone who could protect her. Not Greg, not the police. Why? Did she believe nothing could happen to her, she who had spent years immersed in the accounts of killers who lurked in alleys and parks, in innocuous apartments, and in the very homes and beds of the women they murdered? Did she think she was safe, she who posed as, and then expressively painted, the Black Dahlia in her final position: arms raised, legs spread, gutted, with her intestines tucked beneath her? Did she think she could escape, when Gwen and Chandra and Nicole could not?

Or did Kim Lord have a reason not to name him? What could she be hiding? Outside my bedroom window, the branches of my avocado tree rustle and toss. The creature must be climbing higher. I push my aching head deeper into my cool pillow to block out the sound. The pressure makes me want to throw up again. I squeeze my eyes shut, longing for sleep, though I know it will come over me like a heavy sack, and I will wake feeling worse.

SUNDAY

12

My morning is a blur of sick and head split. A series of decisions followed by stunned immobility. Pulling on jeans. Lurching to the toilet. Back to bed. Glass of water. Kim Lord's flash drive tumbling from my night table. Retrieved. Its flat bullet shape in my hand. Why did Greg have it? More sleep, troubled by nausea and worry. Shoving off damp sheets and stumbling downstairs. The chairs still pulled away from the patio table, where Greg and I sat. My purse open. Phone on, messages blinking. More water. Slipping on sandals, sunglasses. A yearning for milky Thai tea. Coconut curry. I know a place deep in the Hollywood and Highland mall. I know artists destroy their work all the time. Claude Monet, Francis Bacon. Painting slashers. John Baldessari burned everything he made in a thirteen-year span: 123 paintings went into the crematorium; ten boxes of ashes emerged. He baked some of the ashes into cookies and ate them. What did Kim Lord do with the smashed pieces of her flash drives? Chuck them in the trash? Scatter them in the sea? I'm at the Thai restaurant now, slouching in a fish-sauce fog. Metal spatula clangs the wok. I order spring rolls, too. A huge Thai tea. Stagger home over the pink marble stars, sucking sweet orange toothache through a straw.

By the time I pass Grauman's Chinese Theatre, my head is finally clearing. The sharp pagoda roof and red columns draw my eyes, dizzy, upward into a massive relief of a dragon, while below my feet the hand-prints and shoe prints of Hollywood stars look absurdly small. Their signatures and well wishes loop in the concrete, made childish by the thickness of their lines. Joan Crawford, Clark Gable, Nicholas Cage, Myrna Loy. These are the names of those who made it in L.A., and they made it by falling in love and shooting one another and dancing and dy-ing on giant screens for everyone to see. They made it by being someone else entirely, and being their own selves writ large, by the same power-ful transference I saw in the galleries: Kim as Nicole Brown Simpson as Kim. Kim as Roseann Quinn as Kim.

Beside me, a flash of red and blue. A conspicuously unmuscular Superman flexes for a photo with a family wearing pasty midwestern complexions and jean shorts. Batman lurks behind him, tall, gangly in the thighs, another aspiring actor waiting to be discovered by no one, be-cause no one comes to Hollywood by day but the tourists. I don't know if a temp agency hires the superheroes or if they arrive of their own accord, but seeing their fixed fake grins ends my brief sugar high and plunges me into my hangover again. My hip aches from last night's useless leap from the horse.

On the far west side of the theater's maze of celebrity prints stands Skanky Spider-Man, with his ripped costume and duct-taped mask. Skanky Spider-Man is a frequent feature of this edge of the edge of fame. His ersatz getup and jumpy gestures tend to scare the tourists, so the other superheroes always pose a safe distance from him, with their backs turned, as if he belongs to his own cruddy parallel universe. He can't possibly make any money, but he shows up anyway. I don't like to think about what peculiar obsession drives him to shove his legs and arms through his stained blue nylon suit day after day.

Once Greg offered to buy the guy lunch. Greg loves buying lunch for panhandlers and transients—"A real lunch," he always says.

"No offense, man, but I'm done with that," said Skanky Spider-Man.

"I'm done with that. I'm *done* with that. What does that mean?" Greg kept asking me later, shaking his head.

It means what it says. *I'm done.* As I pass Skanky Spider-Man, I remember how he said it to Greg, brash and unapologetic, as if Greg were the one who didn't get it. Greg never gets it. He asks his ex-girlfriend to believe him when he says he knows nothing about his current lover's sudden disappearance. And then he gives that ex a key piece of evidence—a flash drive he shouldn't have in the first place—and asks her to hide it. He's either stupid or too trusting or cunning or insane. I don't want to find out which.

I'm done, too.

I'm going to send the flash drive back to him. I'm not going to spy on Bas. I'm not going to answer Greg if he calls. I can't help him, and I don't want to suspect him either. Let the professionals step in and handle this. I've got five more blocks in this dusty lemon light, five more blocks of loud traffic and gawkers and shoppers, and then I'll turn off Hollywood Boulevard to my palm-lined street and stroll the last block to my quiet bungalow to enter alone. I'll eat my salty takeout and jump in the shower. I'll curl up on my yellow couch and read until I fall asleep. And Kim Lord will soon be found by the police. And Kim Lord will be alive, unscathed, and she'll be the biggest story of the year in the art world: the artist who vanished and then returned to give all her paintings away.

My phone rings as I'm waiting to cross La Brea. I don't recognize the number, but the traffic light is taking forever, so I answer it.

"Is this Maggie?" says an alto female voice, and then without waiting for my answer, "This is Cherie Rhys, Greg Shaw Ferguson's attorney."

The hello is barely out of my mouth before Cherie relates that Kim Lord's phone has been discovered, and that a search warrant for Greg's properties has turned up a bloody cloth in the basement of one of his studios.

A bloody cloth. The phrase snags and doesn't process.

"At the moment, Shaw has just been placed under arrest, but it is likely that he'll be arraigned and held in custody without bail. I'm working on the bail part." She pauses. "On my advice, he isn't speaking to anyone, but he wanted you to know."

"He wanted me to know . . . ," I repeat, faltering over where to begin. He wanted *me* to know? Did something happen in his basement? Who found her phone?

"If you wish to communicate with him about anything," Cherie adds, "you'll need to do it through me."

My curiosity boils over. "Did *he* find her phone? Did he know about the . . . the blood?"

"I'm afraid I can't divulge many details right now," says Cherie. "But no, detectives found the phone in Echo Park."

"You don't believe Greg—Shaw—did anything to hurt her, though."

"Of course not." Cherie's answer is smooth and quick. I realize she must say this for every client. "Do you have anything you wish to communicate to Shaw?"

I cross La Brea, my mouth growing drier by the second. Does he want me to say something about the flash drive? About Bas and the stalker?

"Um, do you have any questions for me?" I say.

"Not at this time," she says. "I'll be in touch."

"Is he okay?" I ask, but she has already hung up.

"Call the rock critic," Yegina says in a muffled voice. It's past noon now, but she is the queen of sleeping in. "He's got to know something."

I am back in my tranquil kitchen, exhuming my takeout and nibbling tiny bites of the spring rolls. "I did. He didn't answer," I say. "Should I call Cherie back? I feel like I blew my chance to ask her any real details."

Yegina makes a soft sliding noise, like someone burying herself deeper in her pillows. She's one of those people who always has a fluffy, soft, floral-smelling bed, while mine invariably resembles gym mats.

"She won't tell you anything," she says. "Call Kevin again."

"I don't want him to feel forced."

"He has the hots for you."

I set down my spring roll. "What?"

"In our interview, I asked him if he liked you—"

I start to interrupt, but she cuts me off.

"And he said he thinks you look like a young Marlene Dietrich. But it doesn't matter because he's been engaged for five years to a rich girl he met in Tanzania when he was studying abroad and she was in the Peace Corps. Mindy's older than he is. She kept him a secret from her family until he graduated college, and now he needs a big career leap or he'll shame her."

"And then I suppose you told him about me and Greg," I say.

"Why are you so afraid of what people think?" Yegina asks.

Her exasperation hurts. I open the rice container and pour the curry on it. I eat a spoonful. The warm coconut flavor clogs my mouth.

"Just call him," says Yegina.

"All right." I swallow. "But—"

"Good." Yegina gives an enormous yawn and makes that burrowing noise again. "I'm really tired."

"Did Rick the ranch hand stay over?" As soon as the question slips out, I regret it.

There is a silence, and then Yegina says slowly, "If you hadn't gotten so bombed last night, you might know."

My phone feels hard against my cheek.

"Rick the ranch hand has a wife and a daughter," says Yegina. "And I am pursuing Hiro, the new grant writer. Hiro is very courtly and hasn't proposed a date yet, but I can sense his interest from the delicate increase in his stammering." She pauses. "What happened with you and Greg anyway? Did he stay over?"

"No."

"Something happened."

"Nothing happened," I lie. I can't tell her about Greg giving me the flash drive. I don't want to entwine her in anything dangerous, and since Cherie's call, Kim's disappearance feels more dangerous than ever. But I never lie to Yegina, and it makes my weak stomach quiver.

"And how was it?" she murmurs. "The nothing?"

"Greg told me that he's the police's main suspect. That's all. He was pretty upset." In my mind's eye I see my kitchen window last night and, in it, Greg's rage-distorted face, watching me. What was he seeing?

Yegina yawns again.

"He isn't guilty," I say, my voice shaking because I don't know what to believe.

She snorts. "Not of murder," she says. "He isn't innocent either. Now please go eat your crinkly lunch alone and let me sleep."

13

Of all the startling news I've received in the past twenty-four hours, Greg's comments and behavior nag me most—what he and Kim fought about, why he possessed the flash drive, and what or who spilled blood in his studio basement. I should be thinking about what to do next—send Cherie the flash drive? Use her to get a message to Greg? How does he need me now? Why does he need me? Deep down, do I still believe he's innocent?

Yet instead, as I drift on my yellow couch, listening to a helicopter ratchet the southern sky, my brain keeps routing me to a different question: why Kim would suddenly want to donate her entire show to the Rocque's permanent collection. Also, why hadn't she told Greg? The loss of millions would weigh on her mind, wouldn't it? She didn't strike me as rich. Neither is Greg, and it's quite possible that she owed him for living expenses. It's also quite possible he's leveraged to the hilt right now. Was that what they really fought about—money?

Yet Greg genuinely didn't seem to know about Kim's plan until I told him, and his reaction would be typical of any gallerist. The donation makes terrible business sense, short term and long term. Even if Kim can swallow the financial blow, she will sacrifice a pivotal reputation-building moment with collectors eager to purchase her work. It took years for her to complete this show. The Kim Lord I know is deeply ambitious. And her gift to the museum flies in the face of a main objective of artist and gallerist: to develop a wealthy and steadily more glamorous provenance.

Provenance is the chronology of ownership of a work of art. Who owns what. Who bought what from whom. The record of exclusive possession. Ownership is listed on every wall label, and it's written in a history that accompanies every object when it's sold. If a famous collector buys a sculpture, that sculpture will sell for a higher price the next time it goes on the market, sometimes hundreds of thousands more. Dealers know this. They keep long waiting lists of purchasers so that they can control who gets what, and which sales are known to the press. In Britain, collector Charles Saatchi practically made the career of Damien Hirst when he bought the artist's first major animal installation, a glass case with maggots feeding on a rotting cow's head. Saatchi later paid for Hirst to create his famous formaldehyde shark. Public display of the works catapulted them both to fame. And some could say that Hirst made Saatchi, because if Saatchi ever sells the shark, he'll probably get millions. The artist-dealer-collector triad is a symbiotic relationship, soaked in cash. Most of the time, the transactions happen behind closed doors.

Who owns Kim Lord's work? Who wants to own it? Could a collector have frightened her with his demands, with his obsession, enough to make her decide not to sell any of *Still Lives*? It's not easy to find the right information to illuminate the situation. Kim's gallerist, Nelson de Wilde, might know, but he would never share anything about his clients, and sometimes, especially when an artist's value is declining, different gallerists and consultants can sell a piece several times in quick succession, and it's hard to keep track of who owns it.

My cell starts buzzing. It's still lying on the floor, where I dropped it after I hung up on Yegina, and I have to strain to reach. The number on the screen has a New York area code. Kevin. Reluctantly I answer.

"Can't tell you anything. I mean nada. Cherie doesn't breach her clients' privacy," he says. "But can we meet somewhere cool? I'm flying out tonight and I want to give you something."

•

For a repository of dreams, the Chinatown wishing well is a surprisingly dumpy sculpture: a hunk of lumpy grottoes, smiling gold Buddhas, and blue-lettered luck signs. The well resembles an altar instead of a hole, and although it's supposed to replicate some famous cave in China, it seems more like a shrine to a bygone era when Chinatown bustled with actual Chinese residents. Pennies and pigeon droppings scatter the tin cups placed in front of WEALTH, LOVE, and VACATION. Nearby, shops sell bamboo plants, brass tins of tea, and hoary brown roots in big barrels. In the distance, the freeways carry constant streams of cars downtown. Yet here, by the well, it is perpetually hushed and still. Whenever Yegina and I walk past it on the way to our favorite dumpling shop, I feel like we are walking sideways through time, that we are connected to neither past nor future.

I'm staring at the sign for LOTTO, wondering about my choice of meeting place, when a penny sails over my head and plinks a metal cup.

"I got it in SUERTE," a voice says from behind me. "What's *suerte*?"

Kevin's wearing his tweed again, but it works tonight because there's a chill, and because he's going home to New York.

"Luck, I think."

"Why is everything else in English and SUERTE's in Spanish?" he says.

"*Suerte* sounds luckier, I guess." I pull out my pennies and aim for MONEY's metal cup, missing wildly.

"You in shock?" Kevin says.

"Yeah. I mean, I just saw Greg last night. Now he's in jail." I explain about the ranch, the ride, the fall, but not my drunken outbursts. "He's not guilty. He didn't even care that they were searching his gallery and studios."

We chew over the known details of Kim Lord's disappearance, though I still don't tell Kevin about the press release and Kim's intended donation to the Rocque. I secretly think Kevin knows something about Greg that he's not telling me. "Did your sister tell you if there's going to be an arraignment tomorrow?"

I understand a bit about police procedure from Jay Eastman, who was tracking the arrests and prosecutions of the drug dealers in Vermont.

The fact that it's Sunday today changes the usual timetable and gives the cops extra hours with Greg, but not many. They could hold him overnight, but if they're not going to charge him by Monday afternoon, they have to let him go.

"No idea. My sister is a vault," Kevin says, but his voice rises.

He's lying. I wait, hoping.

"You've given up on your Aimee Semple McPherson theory," I say.

"Entirely." He looks grim. "I think the head box in 'Disappearances' is Colleen Stan's," he says. "Homemade torture instrument made by the guy who abducted her."

The head box? Homemade torture instrument? Just two days ago, Kevin was deep into his theory of Kim Lord cunningly staging her own vanishing. Now he's decided on a different story in the same painting—the giant still life I have yet to view. It makes me skeptical that there's anything to find.

I ask what changed his mind.

"You'll see when you look at that painting," he says. "The more you study it, the more it looks like a prediction of something very, very bad."

He fishes inside his coat and holds out a packet of papers. "I've got to catch my flight. I'm giving you my notes on 'Disappearances,' though," he says. "I wish I could have made something from them myself, but"—he scratches his beard—"I can't."

I take the papers. "This is what you wanted to give me?" I try not to sound disappointed.

"You seem like you have a head for this," he says. "Don't you?"

Kevin's notes are a few loose sheets wrapped in rubber bands that make them heavier than they are. Inside I can see the shape of his handwriting: a jaunty, hasty print. I shrug.

"You know you do," Kevin says.

"Why are you going home so soon?" I say. "I thought this was a big assignment for you."

Kevin runs a hand down his tweed lapel and looks off to the freeway. "I can still focus on the Gala," he says. "That first evening."

"Doesn't sound like a cover story," I say.

His gaze remains on the distance. "I've encountered unforeseen complications," he mutters. "My sister doesn't want me writing about her client." He pauses. "She doesn't like what I'm seeing."

Kevin must mean that Greg looks guilty. He has to mean this, or why would it bother Cherie, Greg's defender? My stomach drops, but I don't say anything, studying Kevin's bearded face, his broad, honest brow. The edges of his notes prick my palms. Faded red lanterns sway behind us, tossed in a gritty breeze from the east.

When the silence gets too long, Kevin tells me that he's also soon to be "embedded" with something that sounds like "secret rows" and he needs to prepare.

I recover my voice. "You're going to Iraq?"

He chuckles and repeats the name. "Icelandic band on a big American tour. They're blowing up and I'm going to be riding the bus with them." He nods at the notes. "But this story is huge. And you know you're in the perfect position to tell it."

Now it's my turn to look away, to the wishing well, now collecting late-afternoon shadows.

Kevin aims for WEALTH, and the penny pings the rim. "Never going to get in that one," he mutters.

I offer him a penny. "Try WISDOM," I say.

"Never going to get that one, either," Kevin says. "Anyway, I've got to go." He gives me a long glance, one that feels heavy on my face. "I wish you well, Maggie Richter."

To my surprise, he grabs my hand and kisses it.

"Please be safe," he says, and walks away.

When I get home, I toss Kevin's papers in my work bag with the flash drive, call my parents, and tell them about Greg's arrest. Then I call my two brothers, John and Mark, and have the conversation all over again. As I repeat the same horrifying facts, my disbelief and worry pile up with their disbelief and worry, and the news begins to fall more heavily through me. By the end of Mark's call, it's a hard rain, soaking everything.

Then Yegina beeps in.

"Want to go on a double date with me and Hiro to a Jon Byron show at Bootleg? It's Tuesday night." There's something cagey in her voice.

"Who's the fourth person?"

"Well, he's not really a prospect for you. He's more of a fan of Jon Byron." She sighs. "Actually I just invited us both along on a man-date—"

"With who?"

"—in which we now both have to pretend we both like Jon Byron even though I think he's meh and you're clueless. With Brent."

"I know who Jon Byron is. He does all the soundtracks for the movies I fall asleep to," I say. "What am I going to talk about with a surly married man?"

"It's usually too loud to talk, remember?"

The last time we went to Bootleg, the loudspeakers were turned up so high that they caused a minor earthquake in Altadena, and the pasta dinner looked like it had been poured straight from a can, spat on, and gently stirred. I remember suggesting that we stuff it in our ears instead of eating it.

That night, Yegina and Chad were still together, and Greg was still with me, and Kim Lord was a famous stranger who blessed us now and then with her sharp conversation. I held Greg's hand all the way to the car afterward, and it felt ordinary, the night in the bar, our laughter and happiness, but now it seems unbearably precious.

"My brother got his last med school rejection yesterday," says Yegina. "I found out an hour ago. My mom is in pieces."

"Oh no. I'm so sorry." Much as Yegina makes light of her parents' pressure on their children to succeed, her half-white mother grew up hungry and outcast in Vietnam, then ignored by her American father's relatives. She wants to show them all. "What's Don going to do?"

"Maybe a nursing degree," Yegina says skeptically. "Maybe osteopathy. But he's stopped leaving the house. Just sits at his computer in his room."

"Count me in for any Don support you need," I say. "And for Bootleg. But can I ask something? Do you think we should look into what happened to Kim ourselves? I mean, we know the Rocque. We might find something the police missed."

"Absolutely not," she says. "We're not qualified, and besides, if she has been murdered, and if Greg is the killer, your judgment is too clouded to see it—"

"*If* Greg is the killer!"

"And if the killer is someone else, he's still out there and you're putting yourself in danger by snooping around. So no. Don't get involved."

"You'd rather let an innocent man get framed?"

She makes a frustrated noise.

"You don't care what the truth is?" I ask.

"Maggie, you don't come from a haunted people." Yegina's voice deepens. "I do. You can't just step into this pit and step out again."

She's right. I'm already in it. I've been in it since Nikki Bolio was murdered, and I thought I'd left for a while, but *Still Lives* brought it all back: the fear that any path is a bad one, that any surface beneath my feet can break and plunge me into a bottomless dark.

Yegina is still talking. Her tone has smoothed to a warm hum. It says, *I know you're hurt and confused, but time will heal you.*

"We're just laypeople. Rubes," she finishes.

"Fine. I have to go," I say.

She doesn't protest, and we hang up.

Maybe I am a rube. Maybe I always will be. I regard my living room and its possessions: Bare walls except for one print of fishing boats that I brought home from the Mekong Delta. The faded gold couch, the cheap glass coffee table, bookshelves in maple veneer. The only items of value are my books. Their titles gently pull my eye: *In Cold Blood. Slouching Towards Bethlehem. Kaputt. The Love of the Last Tycoon.* Only the books are arranged, cherished. Without them, the room would have no personality but neglect. Without them, a visitor might guess the occupant had just moved in, or was moving soon, or didn't believe in having taste. Or maybe that she didn't even notice what was missing.

Three days before the press preview of *Executed*, the Jason Rains exhibition about capital punishment, Lynne Feldman invited the staff to test it out. Twenty of us showed up, a little crowd, chatty and nervous. Although Lynne welcomed us, it was Brent Patrick, the exhibition designer, who told us what to do. As Brent stood in the darkened doorway to the show, the possessive pride in his face startled me. This show had Jason Rains's name on it. But it was Brent's vision, Brent's staging that would alter us.

"Turn off your phones," he said. "Don't touch anything unless we direct you to."

We filed into the dark theater and each took a number from a machine. Then we sat down on creaky wooden benches and stared through a one-way mirror into the room beyond, where Brent and Dee stood by the brown leather injection chair.

The red number 1 flashed above the doorway between the chambers, and Jayme, holding her number, went through the door in a pale-blue blazer and skirt. We watched in silence as Brent and Dee strapped her in. It took a long time, and Jayme's ordinarily elegant form flattened and bunched in the chair; her hands groped at air as Brent tightened the buckles. Then we waited again as Dee pulled over the syringes on a small cart. They were filled with lethal chemicals, their caps sealed but the needles aimed straight at Jayme. It was like watching a dentist's visit crossed with some kind of sick torture. Jayme wiggled in her restraints.

Brent pulled a lever and the chair tilted back. Jayme's brown knees and chin aimed at the ceiling. Her legs were pressed together, but if she let them open we would see her underpants. Her ankles looked helpless, bare. Brent and Dee could do anything to her now and she wouldn't be able to escape it. Then I saw Dee frown and touch Jayme's shoulder. She must have moaned aloud.

I shifted on the bench. I would have to endure ten more of these slow humiliations before I would take the chair myself.

A television screen in the corner glowed with a message:

CAPITAL PUNISHMENT IS OUR SOCIETY'S RECOGNITION OF
THE SANCTITY OF HUMAN LIFE.
—Orrin Hatch

Both rooms went completely black, except for the TV. Someone shrieked. We sat in the dark, reading Hatch's shining words. We whispered and joked about how creeped out we were, and then, as the dark persisted, we fell into silent and individual reveries. I sensed the bareness of the room, the warmth of my own body, my sleeve barely brushing Yegina's. I was glad not to be Jayme, but I felt like a prisoner anyway. I would have to become her soon.

When the lights came on, the injection chair was empty again. The red number 2 flashed above the door.

Executed. It was destined to be a blockbuster, and it bothered me that Jason Rains would get credit for Brent's genius. Jason Rains had come to the Rocque with his sketch for the chair and the assistants to make it. He had come with adorably mussed red hair and known relationship woes with a hot British sculptor. But he hadn't thought about the lag time between visitors trying out his chair, or about whether visitors would want to test it at all. He watched, dazed, at our exhibition-planning meeting as Brent took the sketch and the pen and began to fill in the viewing theater, describing the numbers that people would draw to wait their turn, the lighting. Harsh brightness and darkness would alternate throughout the experience, the way they did in criminal interrogations, to make people feel isolated and afraid.

"You can't just kill people in your chair," he said. "That part is pretend anyway. You need to make them part of the system that kills. That's real."

When the red 12 flashed above the door, I was almost grateful to enter the execution chamber. Being told where to sit and where to place my hands was a relief. The belts didn't hurt. I waved at the darkened mirror. Dee rolled the syringes over, and then my chair lurched back. The tipping changed everything. My head sank like an anchor, dragging on my body. The white ceiling had a slick, sickly sheen. I knew people were watching beyond the mirror. *Everyone is watching me,* I thought. I felt their eyes. I heard their silence. They were already inured to pity. I strained against the belts. Then blackout.

A second TV flashed the names of the hundreds of people who have been executed in California since 1778.

"That was really eerie," I said to Brent moments later as he helped me out of the chair. I wanted to compliment him, but my voice sounded false, chirpy. "It must have been something to see your stage sets."

He inclined his brown head.

"We should do a show of your shows," I added.

Brent finally met my gaze. Inside his eyes something glowed briefly, like an ember blown by breath. It burned into you, that look, and I could see why everyone worshiped and feared him. He seemed capable of reducing a person to ash. And now that his wife was worse, he acted like he was seeking a target—picking more fights with the curators, talking to his female staff in such an abrasive, flirtatious way it made one of them quit.

"Next person's up," he said, dismissing me.

Unsettled by the experience, I couldn't go back to my office, so I walked down to Grand Central Market in the hot sun and bought a fountain cola with lots of ice. The cold sweetness tasted good. The bustling *pupusa* stall, with its white counter and round slabs of dough, almost comforted me. The ice-cream place made me pause wistfully, staring down at the pink, green, brown, and speckled mounds. I watched two women bend to bowls of *caldo de camarones*, their fingers delicately peeling shrimp shells, piling the translucence beside them. Neon signs led me farther. For the first time, I lingered at a jewelry stall, touching rings couched in velvet and name necklaces of cheap, diamond-studded gold dangling from a display. *Isabella. Tracy. Samuel.* I listened to Spanish radio and rapid spoken Vietnamese. Light spilled into the building from both ends, and the concrete floor wore stars of sawdust. My straw made squeaks on the cup's Styrofoam bottom.

On the way back, I stopped at a water fountain, refilled the cup, and drank the slightly warm, slightly sugary sluice. I popped the lid and chewed the thin bits of ice until everything was gone. Then I returned to my desk. I did my job fine, but I was pursued all day by the dull sense that I had lost something valuable and could not find it.

After I hang up on Yegina, I go upstairs and try to nap but end up staring. I scrounge in my cupboards for a can of minestrone, heat it, set a neat table with a folded napkin and a full water glass. But I cannot eat. I flip open my phone and contemplate the keypad, but never dial.

Yegina's right, I tell myself again and again. *You can't step into this stuff and step out again.* But I just don't believe Greg is guilty of murder.

It's well past dark outside my bungalow when I unroll Kevin's notes on my little dining table and pore over them, shaking my head.

I still haven't seen "Disappearances" up close, but I know it resembles a real still life more than any of the others. It is packed with objects, and the objects are arranged, so why wouldn't the objects hold a meaning? The real question is: What meaning, and how do you know? *She doesn't like what I'm seeing,* Kevin told me. I don't either. Reading his translations of the symbols in "Disappearances" makes my skin crawl. According to him, Kim Lord's depictions of objects like a bottle, a notebook, and a bloodstained screwdriver each reference horrible crimes against women.

As I fold up the notes and raise my head, I can hear my own breath, feel its dampness. My body is cramped and prickly from sitting so long, but I have the feeling that if I rise from this chair, if I make any big movements, a dark, lurking presence outside will know I'm here alone and enter. I switch off the overhead light. Better. I switch off all the lights in the bungalow, until the only illumination is the orange glow of the rest of Los Angeles extending to the desert and the sea. The glow's dull persistence is comforting. It will go on until dawn.

I dig in my purse for the flash drive, pull it free.

There's no path for someone ordinary like me to find one missing woman in this whole city. To rescue her if she needs rescuing. To clear the name of an innocent man. It takes teams of police officers, laboratories, experts, courts. The impossibilities rise around me, steep and sheer. But I think of the hero of Fitzgerald's last novel, Monroe Stahr, flying over the highest mountains and talking to his pilot about the old railroad men and how they had to lay a track through anyway. *You can't test the best way—except by doing it. So you just do it . . . You choose some way for no reason at all.*

I stick the drive into the computer and open the files, scrolling through them fast. Ten. Twenty. Fifty. One hundred. Kim's in every frame, bending, collapsed, grinning, stripped and bound.

My phone rings. Yegina. She knows. She always knows.

I keep scrolling, wincing at what I see but not surprised by it. These are all studies for the paintings in *Still Lives*.

Four rings. Yegina doesn't leave a message. She calls again, hangs up again when I don't pick up.

At the very end of the string of pictures are five photos I don't recognize. They don't connect with the exhibition at all.

Yegina calls a third time. The rings are like shrieks to me. I take my hand off the mouse and answer.

"You awake?" Yegina says. She tells me that she was phoning to apologize, to say she understands how difficult this is, her kindness like a warm blanket she throws over me.

I close my eyes, close my ears.

"I'm not mad." I speak low to keep my voice steady through the lie that comes next. "And you're right. It's ridiculous to play detective."

"Phew," Yegina says. "It's hard to just sit on things, but that's what spin class is for. You in tomorrow?"

"I'm in," I say, surprised at how calm I sound.

MONDAY

14

Of the 231 pictures on Kim Lord's flash drive, 226 are studies for the *Still Lives* exhibition. This morning I scan through them a third time before I leave for work. Last night, in the dark, the whole experience felt like trespassing, my heart in my throat as I witnessed each thumbnail, but I am getting used to it now, and with that relief comes the sinking sense that Greg was right, there is nothing to find on here.

Blown up large, and viewed in L.A.'s cheerful morning light, the photos have none of the haunting quality of the exhibition. Instead, the whole slide show seems campy and overdone. Kim Lord donning her wigs, hanging from her arms, lying prone. Girl playing dress-up. Girl playing with mud. Girl playing with roses and blood. The studies for "Kitty Genovese" and "The Black Dahlia" look especially goofy. All that glistening splatter and gore. Finally, I come to Kim Lord sprawled on a table piled with objects—a study for "Disappearances"—her head in some kind of wooden crate. It looks like she tripped and fell into someone's garage sale.

After these are the last five photographs, the ones that don't fit. Four pictures show a random dog yawning and wagging for the camera. Whose dog? I don't recognize it.

The final photo shines on my screen. Last night, I thought it was Kim, disguised in heavy makeup, but this morning I decide it is someone else. Another woman who resembles Kim, only slumped, haggard, and glum-looking. A potential suspect? She doesn't look capable of standing up, much less hurting anyone.

I force myself through all the *Still Lives* studies one last time, finding nothing but the inexplicable gap between crude sketches and a finished masterpiece.

Still, anything could be a piece to this story. Today I'm going to find another piece: where Bas went on Monday. I leave early to beat rush hour, but by the time I make it to the Rocque, a throng of journalists is standing outside, white TV trucks behind them. Their frank, curious gazes follow me like guards at a checkpoint. I can feel their hunger for a new angle, something no one else knows. I duck my chin and hurry past, clutching my bag containing the flash drive and Kevin's notes.

"Miss . . . miss . . . ," one of the reporters calls to me. "Do you work here? Any comment on the Greg Shaw Ferguson arrest?" All the newspeople call him Greg Shaw Ferguson, in that three-beat crescendo that echoes other famous killers.

I shake my head.

"When was the last time you saw Kim Lord?"

I feel a hand on my shoulder, and Jayme's voice rings out.

"The director is preparing a press conference for ten o'clock," she says. "Until then, please let our employees get to work." She muscles in beside me. "Don't even glance their way," she mutters.

"Hey, Jayme," yells another one. "I hear that Kim Lord had a stalker following her to and from the museum. Any comment?"

There's a sudden silence, in which I can feel the Santa Anas breathing warm desert air on us all. Clearly, this is new and confusing information to everyone. Jayme goes rigid and stops. I keep walking.

"Press conference at ten," she repeats behind me. Across the glass front of the Rocque I see two pale, bare legs flashing and realize they're my own. Those are my own hunched shoulders, my fierce, hunted expression.

"You look like you slept about five seconds last night," Jayme says as we ride the elevator to our floor. She's ironed her usually springy hair smooth again today, the way she wore it to the Gala. It looks a bit like a helmet. "You talk to Shaw?"

"His attorney. I bet she's the one who planted the stalker idea with the media," I say.

Jayme eyes me questioningly.

"If it casts enough doubt on Shaw's case, then the police may postpone the arraignment until they have more evidence," I tell her. "She's trying to get him out."

The elevator slows and toggles. Jayme looks like she's about to say something, but instead she punches the button to our floor again.

"Do you need me to help with the press conference?" I ask.

She shakes her head, and I see the tremble in her shoulders.

"You sure?" I say.

There's a beat of silence, and then Jayme swings on me.

"I want you to stay away from them," she says with such force that I back up into the elevator wall. Jayme blinks, but she keeps talking. "They'll eat you alive if they connect you to Shaw. They're desperate for anything now, because the cops have clammed up. The detectives are not even coming today. It's just Bas talking for ten minutes, and me taking questions." She straightens to her fullest height. "You are not allowed, okay?"

"Okay," I say, cowed.

Ordinarily I might show up to help Jayme anyway, but now I'm thinking, *Ten o'clock might be the only time Bas's assistant leaves her cube all day.* I hug my bag closer to my body, gathering courage from Jayme's courage. Whatever happened to her, she doesn't let it rule her. The elevator shudders and the doors slide open.

"This is a terrible time for you," Jayme says gently. "You want to take a sick day, I'll sign off."

"I want to be here," I say, and stride out with her staring after me.

Press conference at ten. I've got an hour and forty minutes before Bas and his assistant, Juanita, vacate their offices. My stomach is a sack of acid, I'm so nervous, but I tell myself that this snooping is just another kind of copyediting—looking for things that should not be there. I'm watching what happened last week the way I watch the page.

Monday
Bas and stalker seen together by Kim Lord.

Monday or Tuesday?
Kim Lord offers massive gift to museum, negotiating herself out of millions of dollars.

Tuesday
Greg last sees Kim Lord.

Wednesday
My last sighting of Kim Lord, leaving the Rocque.

Thursday
Texts continue to come from Kim Lord's phone (could be someone else, pretending to be her). She goes missing on her opening night.

The police are so busy trying to nail the angry boyfriend, maybe they've overlooked Monday's meeting and Kim's gift. Maybe they can't see the possibility of a cold, calculating intelligence who covers his tracks. A collector who has become obsessed with her. Who panics when she threatens to expose him.

I plug in the flash drive and click through the files again, slowing down at the last five photographs.

The dog is standing on grass and sidewalk. He could be anywhere.

The woman in the last photo sits against a white wall. Her shirt is blue, collared, nondescript. Her gray-threaded hair is brushed, and lipstick darkens her mouth, but there's something violating about these improvements; they only serve to highlight the woman's pallor and exhaustion. The photo is dated a week before the opening-night Gala.

A friend? A new subject? The images are not labeled. The woman is looking not at the camera, but at something or someone beyond the photographer.

Should I call Cherie? If I call Cherie, she will requisition the flash drive. If Greg wanted his lawyer to requisition the flash drive, he would have told her to ask me for it. I am supposed to hold on to these images as art, not evidence.

For now.

I remove the flash drive and chuck it deep in my drawer.

When I reach the entrance of *Still Lives*, I don't look at the walls. The museum has not yet opened for the day; the galleries are as dim as crypts, and the paintings hard to see. I hurry toward the third room, but I can feel the gazes of the dead following me.

Unlike Kevin, I don't believe Kim was painting secret messages, but her monumental still life, "Disappearances," is one of the last things she touched before vanishing. She delivered it on Tuesday with the paint still drying, hours after Brent went over to her studio himself and demanded it on behalf of the nerve-racked exhibitions crew.

According to crew gossip, when Lynne saw "Disappearances" go up on the wall, she stared at it for ten minutes—in disgust? in awe?—and then stomped out of the room.

Still Lives has never been Lynne's pet show. Its origins on the Rocque exhibition schedule are unclear; Yegina thinks Janis Rocque was behind it, because it was not something our curators proposed. Most of our exhibitions originate from the scholarly agendas of their department—they like to be the ones who decide which artists matter.

Regarding *Still Lives*, Lynne made her own position clear. In her catalog essay, she professed a faint admiration for Kim Lord's much-heralded career and her initial concerns about the show's content and the artist's self-declared turn away from portraiture. "Still lifes have long been considered a lesser form of art, a decorative or feminine form," Lynne wrote. "Instead of looking outward to epic characters and scenes, the still life looks inward, to the possessions of a family." Tables of peaches and flowers. Tables of dead birds. A glass of half-drunk wine. "In *Still Lives*, Kim Lord has inverted the form, to examine today's commodification and consumption of the images of female homicide victims." Lynne steadfastly refused to praise the move, however; I think she felt that no matter what artistic process Kim used, the blood and gore were beyond the realm of good taste.

The text was finished months before the images; Lynne asked Yegina to approve all the copyedits, which, for a control freak like Lynne, was the equivalent of washing her hands of the whole thing.

Now the faces of dead women follow my progress through the gallery. When I reach the threshold of the third room, I realize I am holding my breath. I don't see these pictures as treasure maps, but, reluctantly, I find them haunting. And like Lynne, I don't yet know why.

Why here? Why subject us to these scenes in an art museum, when we've seen them practically everywhere else? For decades, the spectacle of female homicide has spattered the news. A couple of weeks ago a former actress was found dead in a record executive's house. Her beautiful face glowed from every crevice of the media. Another blond smiler. Another bloody mess on someone's floor. We've seen her and seen her and seen her. We've witnessed victims in every feminine shape, young to old. The child pageant winner with her sexy lipstick, duct-taped and garroted. The teenager abducted from her suburban bedroom. The elderly woman raped and strangled by a stranger she allowed in the door. What we haven't seen, we've read or overheard. How could Kim Lord's depictions move us beyond disgust and visceral fear, into an emotion that is deeper and richer, freighted with pain for humanity? It's just paint around me now. Shape, texture. It's also more.

Until now, I've avoided Kim's portrait of Judy Ann Dull, victim of the Glamour Girl Slayer. It's the main feature of the third room: Kim-as-Judy is wearing only underpants, gloves, and thigh-high stockings and is bound to an X of wood, her blond head slumped, bare breasts exposed. The life-size painting hangs low on the wall, so you can stare right into the victim's shuttered and drained face, her eyes closed, her skin glowing against a black background. "I can't tell if she's dead or still alive," Evie said to me about this image when she handed the catalog pages back, and

I wondered the same thing, then and now, looking into Kim's depiction. It's impossible to tell if Kim-as-Judy has perished already or simply lost the will to respond to another torture. She just sags there, strung by her wrists.

I hate this artwork. I hate the abject powerlessness it projects. I hate it because it reminds me there is an end for women worse than death. I will not look at it again.

I exhale and turn my gaze to the monumental canvas hanging on the back wall.

In the weak sun from the skylights, the painting looks like someone's overloaded buffet table, strewn and heaped with objects and fruits. The colors glow with a lushness absent from the rest of the exhibition, but here, too, red appears more than any other hue. I am halfway across the room when I finally discern a woman's shape underneath the chaos. As with the photo on the flash drive, she is lying facedown, as if someone has flung her to the table. She is all contour, her body covered in a rough gray robe, her head thrust in a dark wooden box. The only spot of bare skin is her white, exposed neck. The neck pulls my eyes back, again and again, even as I try to catalog the rest of the things Kim Lord is showing me:

A gold blanket.

A book marked 5¢.

A bloodstained screwdriver.

An empty bottle of absinthe tipped on its side.

A cloth hanging behind the figure, a cream-colored curtain, alternately patterned with jugs and fruit.

A heap of apples, one of them split and lying open, showing its pale meat and seeds.

The old-timey radio microphone with a cross on it.

A toy bicycle with an oddly numbered license plate leaning in one corner.

That white neck.

A clock.

That neck.

I open Kevin's notes and read about the five-cent notebook that eleven-year-old Florence Sally Horner stole from a store in Camden, New Jersey, prompting a pervert who witnessed the theft to tell her he was an FBI agent. If she didn't follow him, he'd have her arrested. He then proceeded to make Horner his sex slave as he traveled across states, masquerading as her father. *May have inspired Nabokov's* Lolita, wrote Kevin.

The bottle of absinthe and the robe: *Favorite libation of Elizabeth Smart's captor, who dressed her in a burka when he took her in public.*

The clock: *The passing of time. Significance of no hands? You're out of time when you're dead?*

The apple: *Symbol of female sexuality. Cleft apple = woman's reproductive parts. Also, implied violence.*

The screwdriver: *Could be the weapon used to kill Carol Jenkins, a young black woman stabbed in the chest while selling encyclopedias in a white Indiana neighborhood (1968).*

I fold the notes and just look at the painting: at once artifacts of opulence and of pain and debasement.

I don't see what Kevin's decoding can possibly add up to. I step closer for one last study, when I notice something odd.

There was no drape behind the figure in the flash-drive photographs. Kim had set up no curtain, no backdrop at all. Instead, the space behind her body was a blank wall. This section of the painting doesn't have the classic Kim Lord exactitude. The curtain behind the figure is smudgy, the brushstrokes less precise than in the rest of the canvas. Oranges, apples, and jugs decorate the fabric, but they, too, seem hastily applied. Oranges, apples, and jugs? What can those mean? And why do they seem painted in a hurry?

Evie is alone in the registrar's office, stroking her nails with her thumb while staring at her computer screen. In the artificial basement light, she has a pale, stoic appearance, like someone guarding a bunker. She's changed a lot since our first day at the Rocque. We met at orientation. We made the quintessential provincial pair: me in a floral cotton sundress and chunky sandals, and Evie in the cheap gray pantsuit and white blouse of a supermarket manager. Neither of us looked like we belonged at the museum, where half the staff slinks around in svelte black, the other half in steampunk or couture.

As we waited outside the HR office that day, I smoothed my wrinkled dress and made awkward small talk with Evie about summer movies and their infinite depictions of the apocalypse by stray meteor, aliens, and global epidemic.

"You're so calm!" Evie said to me after a while, and I couldn't tell if she was talking about the end of the world or our new jobs.

"Not inside, I'm not," I said. I asked her where she was from.

She shrugged. "All over small-town California. My mom moved us around a lot, depending on the guy." Then she gave a hard little laugh that I didn't understand until later, when she explained about Al, her stepdad, whose more-than-fatherly interest in her spurred her to run away.

Evie liked dropping hints about herself and her tragic past, and I liked alluding to my own secret reasons for leaving the East, but there was a game to it, where neither of us would ever fully explain the truth. Sometimes, in our early days at the Rocque, we would take coffee breaks outside by one of the many corporate fountains and smoke her cigarettes, staring pityingly at the bankers around us while we made cutting remarks about their predictable lives. But we never said much about what had been different in our own. It was as if we were living in a Raymond Chandler novel, and confessing anything sincere would make us less interesting, too gushy, too feminine. We both needed to pose as savants of cool to feel like we belonged in L.A. I'd never had a friendship like this, and it fascinated me, especially because Evie dressed like she wanted to belong, body and soul, to an insurance agency. And then Yegina entered the picture, and I found myself with a real friend, someone who needed me and, later, who lifted me from my own misery.

Evie's clothing tastes have remained plain, but her appearance now exudes upkeep and expense. The material of her navy jacket has a silken luster. Her chin-length blond hair never gets a millimeter longer; her plucked brows are straight as a line of ink. Last year Evie got a loan to buy a loft near Boyle Heights, in a block of deserted warehouses on the other side of the L.A. River. It's as austere and pretty as the rest of her:

sun spills down onto the spare geometries of her modernist furniture. I didn't like how empty the place must feel at night, but Yegina cooed over it and approved of the investment. "In five years, you could quit on what you'll make from this."

I hope Evie doesn't quit. She's good at her job of caring for our art collection and our loans to other institutions.

As I knock on the threshold, she startles and looks up, her eyes unfocused.

"Sorry," I say, nervous. "I just wanted to see if you wanted to go to spin class with me and Yegina."

A friendly expression slides over her face. "Thanks. I'll try," she says. "I have so much work. It's ridiculous."

I nod, casting about for a segue. On Evie's desk, I spot a magazine, open to an interview with Janis Rocque. "What's J. Ro got to say?" I say, stepping in, picking up the issue.

"She's talking about her sculpture garden," Evie says. "Dee's been doing some installing there. She says she can get me in for a tour."

"Wow. Lucky you." The cover photo shows a steel ellipse by Richard Serra, big as a barn and flowing like a wave. Janis Rocque's Bel Air estate has more art than most museums, ours included, and her sculpture garden is the stuff of legend.

"You want to go?" Evie glances at me. "You should ask Dee." She turns back to her keyboard and resumes typing.

I page through the photos of Goldsworthy and di Suvero sculptures, oohing and aahing to a silent Evie. There's a pull quote from Janis Rocque: "I like my art to cast a big shadow, but don't get me wrong, I don't buy something because it's famous. I buy it because it's a masterpiece." J. Ro sounds as bossy and all-knowing as ever, but she gives the camera a shy, harassed look, as if she wished she weren't being photographed.

I can't keep it in any longer. "Did you hear that Shaw Ferguson was arrested?"

"He was?" says Evie, without turning around. "Are you relieved?"

"What?"

"I mean, he could have hurt you, too, right?" she says, her head framed by the gray glow.

The odds are stacked against Greg. His arrest makes sense to people. He is the victim's boyfriend. He has no alibi. He rose so fast, from being an unknown personal assistant to opening his own gallery to dating a famous artist. From receiving no invitation to the Rocque's annual Gala to sitting at its head table. Maybe he rose too fast.

I perch on the edge of Evie's desk. "Look," I say quietly. "I think they've got the wrong guy. We know Kim had a stalker, and I think we could find him. If you had time to help me."

"You know who her stalker is?" For the first time in our conversation, Evie sounds interested. She swings around to me, searching my face.

"Not yet. But I have a good idea," I lie. Then I hesitate again, reluctant to ask the favor.

Evie continues to study me. "You're really scared for him," she says softly. "For Shaw."

Yes, I try to say, but the word gets stuck in my throat, so I just nod.

Evie's brow wrinkles. "Of course I'll help you."

"Great," I say, swallowing the lump. "I need someone to find out the provenance of Kim Lord's paintings. All of them. Every one she has ever made."

On the way out of the registrarial den, full of warm feelings toward Evie, who swore herself to secrecy, I pass a small, handwritten sign taped to the wall. The word *Batcave* is crossed out and replaced with *Lascaux*, with an arrow to the vaulting cavern that holds the permanent collection storage, the carpentry room, and the loading dock. I'm glad I'm not the only one who feels like this dim subterranean space is the real temple of the museum, precious and distant from the hubbub of the surface. Because we can't possibly put on view even a fraction of the thousands of artworks the Rocque owns, there's more art and history in our storage room than in most of Los Angeles: Pollock lined up beside Krasner, Krasner beside Kline, a Chamberlain wreck beside a Ruscha ribbon drawing. When our old director resigned, the space overflowed with gifts to the collection. Evie is now seeking a second, off-site storage facility. "You have no idea what it's costing the Rocque just to own stuff," she once told me, and then went into a copious explanation of the superb climate-control capacities of a new place in Van Nuys.

A shrill noise blasts from the carpentry room. I pop my head through the doorway to wave at Dee, who is slicing up boards with a table saw, goggles on.

"Spin today?" I shout.

She nods and gives me a froggy grin, then goes back to the saw. I envy Dee her underpaid job sometimes. I envy this sawdusty room. The stacks of plywood, the painting tarps. The pegboards hung with tools: mallet, chisel, hammer—worn handles, oiled blades, all neatly arranged. Here Dee makes tangible things—frames, pedestals, crates, scaffolding—that smell of trees and glue and metal. At the end of the day, she can touch them with her hands.

I also envy Dee because everyone loves Dee. With her biceps, her smooth British accent, and her boyish look, she epitomizes white cool, like the guys on punk album covers from the seventies. She navigates both the office and the crew world with equal ease. When Brent learned of the onset of Dee's diabetes last year, he bargained for her to get full-time status and health insurance so she could stay on at the Rocque.

"Because you're so talented," I told her.

She snorted. "Because I keep my mouth shut."

"About what?" I asked.

"Ha-ha. I told you. I keep my mouth shut."

An addiction? An affair? I thought booze or drugs. Yegina thought affair, maybe the woman on the crew who quit.

Why was Dee missing last Wednesday and Thursday? Sickness seems like a feeble excuse. And she seems fine today.

There's a grinding sound as her saw sticks, and I see something stir in a chamber at the far end of the carpentry tables. Brent's office. It's the only office down here with a door, and while the crew was hanging the exhibition, he'd offered it to Kim Lord as her changing room so that she could doff her disguises for jeans and a T-shirt. She must not have changed on Wednesday, because she was wearing her trench coat and wig when I saw her hurrying toward Pershing Square. She must have been waylaid almost immediately after she arrived at the Rocque.

A phone call on her cell? An encounter here? Perhaps she saw her stalker outside the museum?

Through the open crack, I spot Brent, frowning over a pile of papers. I wonder how long he'll stay at the Rocque, if he'll leave on his own or be ousted for his hostility, maybe even for harassment. He doesn't belong among us almost-somethings and has-beens anyway. Brent's heyday on Broadway—the 1990s—brought the world *Rent*, *Chicago*, *Angels in America*, *Hedwig and the Angry Inch*. He specialized in epic urban decay, Gotham crossed with Rome. His office has the air of a shrine, hung with black-and-white pictures of industrial sites—steel girders, half-finished roofs, crumbling bridge pilings. Track lights cast a moonglow over the man himself, now scribbling furiously, his dark head bent. He looks like a child caught in a feverish make-believe. When he glances up, directly at me, I swear I am completely invisible to him. His expression is still inward, transfixed.

Dee switches off the saw and yanks the board free.

"Need something else?" Dee asks, holding up the board. I catch sight of the clock above her head. It's 9:31. Almost time for the press conference.

I tell her no, and hurry away.

Out in the loading dock, the massive door to the permanent collection is up, revealing the museum's hidden trove, packed with leaning frames, canvases mounted on rollers, and plastic-covered sculptures crouching on shelves and standing free. It looks half like a labyrinth and half like a really expensive rummage sale. I spot our chief curator inside talking to someone obscured by a tall, bubble-wrapped Giacometti. Would Lynne know anything about the cloth behind the figure in "Disappearances"?

As I hesitate beyond the threshold, hidden from view, I hear Lynne say, in a voice raspy with emotion, "I want you to understand something: I didn't want this exhibition any more than Janis did. Sure, Kim was Nelson de Wilde's shiny penny back in the early nineties, but I thought she was highly overrated. Until I saw these paintings. And then—"

The saw from the carpentry room drowns out Lynne's next words, giving my confusion a chance to register. Janis Rocque didn't want Kim Lord on the exhibition schedule either? Then who did? Bas, obviously. A director can throw his weight around to make a show happen. But why this one?

I creep closer to the collection, keeping concealed behind a shrouded sculpture the size of a horse. A male voice is saying, ". . . In search of the miraculous. I'll have to look it up." The voice sounds familiar, the way it softens and lengthens the *I*, but I can't place it. An artist, probably. Lynne hates being interrupted when she's with artists—it's like bursting in on a high mass for a nun—so I'm turning to retreat when from behind the bubble-wrapped Giacometti steps J. Ro's private investigator. He's in jeans and a hoodie today, making him look younger. He doesn't say anything, just chews his lip a little, as if he is equally startled to see me.

"I was just walking by," I say.

"Who's that?" says Lynne, appearing behind him. She glances at me without interest, but I'm surprised by the change in her appearance. Her hair and suit are black and sleek as ever, but her collar bunches; she looks damp and unwell.

"Do you know Detective Hendricks?" Lynne asks, and then turns to him again. "Someone made a documentary about Ader in the nineties, but it glosses over some things. You really need to read the catalog."

I regard them blankly, trying to slow my speeding pulse. I don't like the way this Hendricks person has been watching me since the night of the Gala. He's studying me now, so I study him back, but it's as if he has one of those nictitating eyelids that hawks have—an almost imperceptible veil slides over his blue eyes, and I can't see past it.

They've both fallen silent.

"Ader?" I say.

"Bas Jan Ader," Lynne tells me impatiently, and then I remember: Dutch conceptual artist, used to film himself falling off things. In his last project, he set sail from Cape Cod, intending to cross the Atlantic. His empty boat washed ashore a year later.

"He disappeared, too," I say.

"Exactly." Lynne's face tightens as if she has just stepped close to a fire. "After he vanished, everyone thought he meant to die. But he didn't. He was making new work, he was devoted to it—" She cuts herself off and turns away, almost stumbling into a large Mondrian canvas. "Excuse me," she mutters, and moves down a row of canvases hanging one after another on a large rack, the way they hang rugs in department stores.

I've only once witnessed Lynne at a loss to articulate her feelings, and it was at an opening for a photographer documenting white supremacist gatherings. Lynne's mother was a Bergen-Belsen survivor. Now Lynne wanders farther off, into rows of shelves holding smaller sculptures—she is a vanishing silk jacket and trousers, bound black hair. A waver in her walk, as if it hurts to step. She must have changed her mind about Kim Lord. What's more, she seems terrified for her.

"Journalists won't leave her alone," Detective Hendricks says. The drop in his voice suggests he dislikes the breed.

"Are you helping the police?" I ask. "Because Greg wouldn't have hurt Kim Lord."

The detective says nothing, but I feel his eyes on me.

"And I wouldn't have either," I say, "so you can stop wasting your time spying on us and start looking for someone else."

"You have a someone else in mind?" he says.

"No," I say quickly.

"I'm still free to talk," he adds as Lynne rejoins us, folding her arms. She is paler than usual, but her eyes are hard and clear again.

"How about tomorrow morning?" I say, realizing the time. "We have a press conference—"

"Surely you can spare a few minutes," hisses Lynne, but Detective Hendricks holds up his hand.

"Tomorrow morning is fine." The long *i* again. Southern? "But let me give you my phone number, in case that changes." The detective hands me a card that is blank except for his name, RAY HENDRICKS, and the digits, in a glossy typeface.

I tuck it in my pocket and then blurt my question to Lynne. "Do you know anything about the cloth behind the figure in 'Disappearances'?"

Lynne frowns. "The cloth? What about it?" Her question drips with distrust.

Predictable heat floods my cheeks. "It looks like it was painted in a rush."

"It probably was," says Lynne. "She told me she wasn't finished." She turns to Hendricks. "She wanted to finish it." Her voice cracks. "She was not suicidal."

"No," says Hendricks. "I don't think so either." He looks at me again, with sober eyes. "At least not in the conventional sense."

"Excuse me?" says Lynne.

He turns to her.

"Maybe she didn't run away," he says, "even though she knew someone wanted her dead." He shrugs and reaches out with his palm open, toward a massive all-black canvas propped beside Lynne, as if he sees something hidden inside it. "Or maybe she did."

"I'm sorry, but you can't touch that," snaps Lynne. "It's a Stella."

Hendricks takes a step back, still absorbed in the painting.

"No, I wouldn't," he says in a gentle, respectful tone. "It looks ugly enough as it is."

I leave them before I can fully hide the smirk on my face.

15

Within the next hour, I lie three times.

First I lie to Jayme, who wants to know what behind-the-scenes stories I've gathered for the museum's annual report.

"I've done a few interviews," I fib. "I already finished the write-up of Evie's."

Then I lie to Kaye, who calls with a twang of payback in her voice for my drunken behavior at her post-cancer party. She can't believe they've arrested Shaw and wants to know how I'm holding up, it's so crazy, is there really a killer on the loose, and oh my God, she can't even get tickets to the exhibition for three whole weeks, do I think there's a way I can just sneak her and a couple of her survivor friends in today?

"I wish," I say, and fumble through an excuse about the fire marshal counting the people in the galleries. "Next week?"

Then I lie to the *ArtNoise* fact checker who calls about Kevin's article. "I'm in a meeting right now, but fax me the article and I'll look at it." I hang up on her protests.

Then I tell the truth to Phil and Spike, because it is impossible to fib to two grown men wearing fisherman sweaters and Andy Warhol wigs, and carrying sitars. "We did some busking outside today," says Phil. "How much do you think we made?"

"Honestly?" I say. "Nothing."

"We had our fifteen cents of fame," says Phil. "Hey, you could wear a blond wig and be part of our revue. Then we could be Edie Sedgwick and the Andies."

"Maggie *is* blond," Spike points out.

"Yeah, but not the right kind," says Phil.

I tell them I don't know how to play the sitar anyway.

"Neither do we. Chad traded us three lessons in exchange for designing his flyers," says Spike. "He's an awful instructor, though."

Chad, as in Yegina's ex-husband.

"Wretched," says Phil, sliding the Warhol flop back to expose his broad brow. "Does not bode well for the new business."

"Business?" I say.

"Teaching music to spoiled Silver Lake kids. Like us," Spike says. He raises his hand and whack-strums the instrument, Pete Townshend style.

"He's started a music blog, too," says Phil. "It's wildly popular with his mother."

I don't have time to listen to more twin patter, because it's almost ten o'clock. So I feign extreme frowning over my copyediting until they trundle away, instruments banging their sides. Moments later, here's my chance: Juanita T. Filippa, senior assistant to the director, is following Bas to the elevator. Juanita is wearing her usual conservative navy suit and alert but expressionless gaze, and I wonder what she thinks of the recent events. She is one of the Rocque's oldest employees, and her manner seems to belong to another era, when cultural legitimacy was dispensed by a ruling class rather than earned from the masses. A thin gold bracelet slides along her arm as she presses the down button.

I wait until the elevator doors close, then another two minutes to make sure Juanita and Bas have reached the ground floor. In the dozen steps it takes me to round the maroon wall of cubes to Juanita's, my heart starts beating so fast it feels like a flash mob is assembling in my chest.

Juanita T. Filippa has served as assistant to every director the Rocque has ever had. She is a broad woman, but not fat, with brown hair that she puffs into a smooth bob above small gold hoops always glowing in her ears. She sits twenty feet from my door, but I've never heard her on the phone. She doesn't go out for lunch, and whatever she eats, she must consume with catlike neatness, because her desk gleams, crumb-free, under tidy stacks and files. She signs every e-mail with her full name and her full title. If Juanita has any unkind feelings toward the office's congregation of raging egos, she keeps them inside. If she has a sense of humor, it must be buried somewhere deeper than the tar pits on La Brea.

I know Juanita keeps two calendars, one in a blue leather cover that she brings to meetings, and one on her computer. I figure it will be easier to check the handwritten calendar because I don't need a password. I stand in the threshold to her cube's neat expanse, scanning for blue: Upright file marked TO DO. Horizontal file stacked with bills and invoices. Headpiece for phone calls. Virgin Mary candle, the kind you'd buy at a botanica. Framed photograph of a grinning boy, the print faded in such a way that I know the boy is much older now, possibly grown. No blue calendar. The computer screen is dark. I take a breath and step into the cube.

"May I help you?"

Juanita is standing behind me. She's so short I can see her pale scalp through her parted hair, but somehow it still feels like she's looking down on me.

"Is that your son?" I say, wishing she would move so I could, so I don't have to continue standing inside her private space. "He looks just like you."

"Nephew," she says, her eyes sweeping over my body as if she suspects I have something stashed under my clothes. "What is it you need?"

"Development said you might have a folder on Bas with his bio and background and stuff," I say. "They want me to write a 'meet the director' type thing for a fund-raising campaign."

She repeats my last sentence, sounding particularly doubtful. "Who in Development?" she says.

"Hiro Isami," I say. How easily the lies are coming to me, Maggie of the butterfly earrings, who always stutters through the slightest falsehoods. "He's new."

There's a pause as Juanita digests this, and then she finally steps aside. I stagger out of the cubicle.

"I'll put something together for you today," she says, pulling back her chair, sitting down.

I gasp my thanks and don't dare look back as I leave her threshold. Out of the corner of my eye, though, I see she is waiting, unmoving, hands on her keyboard, screen dark, until I am out of sight. Only then do I hear the beep and sighs of her computer turning on.

16

Two hours later, I'm still wincing about Juanita's suspicious eyes as I walk to the gym with Yegina, Evie, and Dee. Fortunately Yegina is holding forth on the latest board efforts to jettison our boss. Prominent local artists have begun to voice their concerns about the schlockification of the exhibition schedule. How can a museum founded to predict the future of art defend a glorified car show? "The road to mediocrity is paved with product placement," said one. "When's the *Art of Cola* show, next year?"

"I'm starting to feel sorry for Bas," Yegina admits. "He came into my office this morning and asked how hard it would be to strike *Art of the Race Car.*"

Dee and I cheer the news, while Evie looks dazed at the work she'd have to undo. We wind our way between skyscrapers and reach a short down-flight of brick steps. The descent lifts me in my ribs.

"But do you know why?" I ask. "This sudden change of heart?"

"Because it's a bad idea," says Yegina, a new note of pride in her voice.

"He won't last against you," I say.

She gives me a sideways look. "Art of Yegina," she says appreciatively.

Our shoes clack, thud, and slap the bricks: me in Mary Janes, Yegina in platforms, Dee in construction boots, and Evie in pumps. We toss our long hair, tuck our short hair, blink in full makeup or lipstick only. We're so different, I sometimes don't know what holds us together—is it just this moment of extended youth? Is it that we don't know how to grow older? Or why we should? None of us are married or mothers, none high enough in our career ladder, none younger than almost thirty. At this age, our own mothers were already raising their children, and their friends who never wed mostly chose from a short list of occupations: teacher, nurse, secretary, or nun. Our generation knows—we've known since childhood—that we could be anyone. We are pioneers in the brave new land that feminism and birth control have opened: sexually free, unencumbered by kids, able to pay our own way. We don't exactly need men, and they get this and maybe bank on it, in a way that their fathers couldn't. We support each other through their departures, and watch our age tick higher. Some of us marry our jobs. Some of us date women instead. Some say we'll just wait until thirty-eight, find a sperm donor, and raise a kid ourselves. We read about extraordinary women, women our age leading companies and curing malaria, and remind ourselves we should work harder, be smarter, don't waste time. We plan for a second master's degree, in something practical. We try capoeira and knitting. We take care of our slim bodies. We can be fascinating in conversation, and fearless in bed. We can do anything. So why do I feel like we are frozen, too, set on display until someone rearranges us? Still lives.

I ask Yegina if she knows about her ex-husband's sitar school. To my surprise, she doesn't seem especially interested.

"Good for him," she says. "Los Angeles was *really* lacking in businesses started by washed-up musicians."

"Speaking of exes, heard anything new about Shaw?" Dee says to me.

I shake my head, willing Evie to stay silent. She looks blankly at a man in a dirt-smeared plaid shirt picking in a trash can, and says nothing.

"Kim's parents were on the news earlier," says Dee. "Seemed like a normal Canadian couple, if you ask me. Distraught, of course, but they didn't place any blame on Shaw." She rubs her tattooed right arm, a sleeve of roses. "I'm just shocked that no one mentioned her sister."

"Whose sister?" Yegina and I say in unison.

As we cluster closer, bumping elbows, Dee tells us that Kim Lord spent a whole afternoon at the crew office a couple of weeks ago because she was concerned about the lighting in one of the galleries. And then she got to talking to Dee about light sources—because, apparently, this is what artists talk about—and Kim said she'd grown up with long, dark winters in Toronto and so was acutely sensitive to L.A.'s brightness. Also, that she associated white light with fear, because her older sister used to wake her up every night by shining a flashlight in her eyes.

"She literally said to me, 'Voices were telling her I was dead,'" Dee says. Kim also told Dee that her sister had vanished from her rehab facility in Toronto a month ago.

"Do the police know?" says Evie.

"They must," says Dee.

Kim Lord has a troubled sister. Was she the older woman in the flash drive photo? Is she dangerous? Dee's news is like a minor chord, altering the tone of the scene around us: the flow of the marble fountains deepens to a harsh rush; the stark sun and shadows of midday seem locked in battle. It's odd information to come from Dee now. She could have mentioned it during Craft Club, but instead she brought up Greg then, too. She's always so interested in Greg. Or so eager to cast blame on him? We're almost to the gym now. We halt together at a busy intersection near the crest of Bunker Hill and the steps down to the public library, and wait for the light.

"How come you never told us this before?" demands Yegina. "Here Maggie's been on a quest to prove her stalker theory."

"I love stalker theories," Dee says. "But come on." She spins on me. "Don't you suspect Shaw just a teeny-weeny bit?"

"No," I say flatly. "He was out walking on the night she disappeared."

"Walking," Dee repeats. "In Los Angeles. All night long?"

I hate the conclusions in Dee's pale eyes, in this whole sensationalizing city.

"Why didn't you mention her sister before?" I say.

Dee watches a flurry of pigeons ascending from some scattered bread. "Kim didn't sound afraid of her sister," she says slowly. "But I did hear her complain about Shaw."

"When did she complain?"

"Down in the crew office. Her phone kept dinging. She said he wouldn't leave her alone."

"But when?" I ask again.

"I don't know. Tuesday?" Now she gives me a pitying gaze. "I'm sorry, mate. This must be wretched to hear."

"Look. Greg told me he was innocent. He . . . he only talks about her in the present tense," I say. "I know him. He's heartbroken." My voice catches on the last word.

My friends' heads all swivel.

"Oh, sweetie," Yegina says. She's wearing black today. It heightens the contrast in her complexion, her darkness and her paleness, and turns her into a woodcut of disapproval. She doesn't believe me either.

None of them do.

I really need to get off this subject.

I nudge Dee. "Hey, I heard you're taking Evie on a tour of Janis Rocque's famous sculpture garden. Can we all go?"

Thankfully Yegina practically explodes into rainbows at the idea, and this topic takes us all the way into the gym, through the locker room, and up the stairs to the spin studio.

Our spin instructor is a Frenchman with a lavishly hunky sense of himself; he stares at his own gyrating body with infectious longing as he rides up nonexistent hills. Denis has a huge following and people mob every class. My friends and I each have to hurry inside for a bike and slam down onto it. The lights dim. Denis's techno track layers beats over our buzzing wheels. We sit on our hard seats, trying to keep pace. A wall of mirrors reflects us, pumping and frowning, but Denis is faster. His legs blur at measureless speeds. His sweat pours like a libation to the floor.

"Find a friend and catch up! Make a team!" shouts Denis as we log our thirtieth minute. This is one of his tricks: first we compete, then we compete again and pretend it's collaboration.

I look back toward Evie, who always spins so fast her wheels are humming clouds. Her face is a slick of sweat. Her thighs and upper arms bulge with flexed muscle. No one works harder in this class, or at any other workout. I never catch her, but that's why she's good for me.

"Someone very scahhhh-ry is chasing you both! He's gaining. He's gaining. Go faster!"

I look for Yegina's glowing face in the reflection. We don't like when Denis does his boogeyman tactic in class, but we put up with it because the workout is so tough. And because Denis is so delighted with his dumb idea and his sexy accent that it comes across as a joke.

"He's gaining! Go faster!"

Today the threat feels different to me, and I wish Yegina would meet my eyes in the mirror and silently agree. We don't need this. We need fake mountains to climb, and fake wind in our faces, and fake victories over fake finish lines, but we don't need fake perpetrators. *Look here*, I will Yegina, staring her down in her reflection. *Let's stop pedaling. Let's stop together.* But she's staring off into space, her lips parted, unreachable.

"He's gaining! Faster!" Denis shrieks.

He's gaining. I picture Kim Lord's stalker: a balding man with shiny skin. No. A guy who's almost handsome except for the weak chin that he tries to hide with a scraggly beard. No. A businessman, gray suit, coppery hue, chilly and elegant. His image doesn't stay fixed in my mind except for the stare, its calculation, its possessiveness. For years, he's been patient. For years, he's bought up everything she's ever made, but he can't wait any longer. He wants to own all of her work; he wants to own her. She will be the ultimate treasure in his collection.

"Don't stop now!" Denis shouts, pointing to my wheels. I look down at my slowing feet and pump them until they're blurs again. Another face slips into my mind: the woman from the flash drive, with her pretty, haggard eyes, her downturned mouth, a blue collar. Who is she? Then another face: Kim Lord as Roseann Quinn, casting her vague, doomed smile over Grand Avenue, Fairfax Avenue, Western, and Sunset, this entire enormous city. Where is she?

I ride so hard I am gasping.

On my desk when I return: a green folder, a sticky note that says *Per your request* in Juanita's nunnish cursive. Inside, yellowed and new clippings, Bas's name highlighted in each article. Most are from 2001, when the

Rocque hired him, and they recap the same biography: Yates graduate, a long stint at Catesby's auction house, then a slew of development and administrative jobs at East Coast museums.

The oldest clipping, from the Yates alumni magazine, transcribes an interview with Bas when he still worked at Catesby's as an auction specialist. In the accompanying photo, Bas smirks with smug boyishness. He stands between two Yates friends, clearly the handsome one, the budding star, arms looped over their shoulders.

I skim the text, about to turn it over, when something Bas says catches my eye:

> *Auction houses are changing the playing field for*
> *contemporary artists. Some artists—like Chris*
> *Branson and Kim Lord—have proved that they don't*
> *need intermediaries to determine their value. They're*
> *skipping the gallerists and selling straight to collectors.*
> *Big collectors. I know this will sound sacrilegious*
> *to some, but houses like Catesby's could become as*
> *important as museums in determining the Old Masters*
> *for future generations.*

The article is dated 1996. Kim Lord had just had her first show, *The Flesh*. Bas must have watched the paintings sell at Catesby's for high prices, riding the artist's wave of talent and daring. How strange he must feel now to watch his career come full circle, to work at a museum and be offered a priceless but monetarily useless gift from the same artist. And then to have her vanish. My eyes snap on another statement:

> *It's all evolving because of international money. First*
> *the Japanese got in on it, and now the Russians.*
> *And they can be different about provenance. Some*
> *view ownership as a private investment, not a public*
> *statement like most American collectors. I have a friend*
> *who makes a great living buying contemporary art*
> *for collectors in Asia who don't want their names and*

ownership public. Everything is under an alias. And
he's having to buy twentieth-century work because the
Rembrandts and Monets—they're just gone. Snapped
up. It's making the contemporary art market even
crazier. Just wait ten, fifteen years and see how the
prices have skyrocketed.

I flip through the rest of the folder. Nothing there exactly, except an unsettling feeling that Bas hasn't changed since that interview. Not underneath. He's always been dazzled by money, especially by how money shapes the art world. That might have blinded him, or tied his hands, when it came to an obsessive collector who wanted to buy everything an artist had ever made.

I dial Cherie.

"The arraignment is scheduled for late this afternoon." Her voice has lost none of its clip, but deep down I hear a note of defeat. "There's enough evidence."

I tell her Dee's story about Kim's sister leaving rehab.

"Rachel Lord, missing since March," says Cherie. "I've been following that lead, but—" She stops herself. "Is that why you called me, or did you want to get a message to Shaw?"

"How's he doing?"

"He's surprisingly stoic," she says. "Nights there can be hard."

And grief is hard. Greg in a jail cell is an image that refuses to materialize in my mind. Instead, I see him in the weeks after his mother died, his face hawkish, badly shaven, his clothes hanging like wilted leaves. Truth be told, I didn't know what to feel about Greg then: he was so far gone into himself that he was a stranger to me. He sat at the kitchen table and stared into space, or went on walks alone. Sometimes he held books but didn't read them. I roamed his periphery, making useless soups and toast, wondering if I should turn on the radio or let the silences cloak us. That was the beginning of the ending: I couldn't be Theresa for Greg, and I couldn't be myself either, because I reminded him too much of how he'd resisted her influence all his life. How he'd settled on an ordinary, pretty girl from the country, when he was the son of a queen.

"Do you have a message for Shaw?" Cherie repeats.

I can't ask her to ask him about the flash drive. "Not really," I say. "Tell him I'm thinking of him."

"Can I ask you something?" says Cherie. "Shaw said he tried to talk with you at the Gala, but you avoided him. Why?"

For a stunned moment I wonder: *Is Greg trying to implicate me?*

"I was embarrassed," I say. "Humiliated might be a better term. We hadn't seen each other much since our breakup."

"You were humiliated by Shaw Ferguson," she repeats.

I know where she's going. Where Detective Ruiz was going. Angry ex. Prime motive, right?

"Yes, humiliated. In an ordinary, dumped kind of way," I say coldly.

"I see." She waits. "Why did you call Shaw on the night of the Gala?"

I remember my phone in Yegina's hands that night. "My coworker asked me to call him, to find out where Kim was."

"But you hung up before he answered. Were you upset with him?"

And so we go on for several minutes of useless prying, until I've had enough, and tell her I have to go.

I click end on my phone, but I waste the next thirty minutes googling Cherie Rhys to see how many cases she's actually won (turns out, quite a few). I scroll through page after page of her pretty, intelligent face, a thinner and sharper version of Kevin's. It bothers me to think of them discussing me. Did he give her the idea that I might be a suspect? Then I remember Kevin's article, the call from *ArtNoise*, the faxed copy of it I was supposed to review.

Downstairs, the fluorescent mailroom is neatly stuffed to the brim with boxes of museum letterhead, shipping materials, and one sluggish photocopy machine. A wall label beside the copy machine says:

Copier, 1998
5 x 3 x 4 feet
Metal, lights, toner, infuriating paper jams

I check my mailbox. Empty. I check the boxes around it. Also empty. I check the fax machine. Nothing. I can't believe Cherie Rhys—anyone—would think I could hurt Kim Lord. But who did? I wonder if Evie has had any luck with the provenance question. Although I only asked her this morning, it feels like years ago.

When I return upstairs, Yegina is marching out from Jayme's office with a big binder, her cheeks still pink from our exercise class.

"*Art of the Race Car* is almost off the schedule," she says. "I just have to win over Development. They're going to hit the roof, though."

"The Art of Yegina."

She rolls her eyes. "Art of J. Ro, more like it," she says, but the flush deepens. "You want to go out for happy hour tonight?" She follows me into my office. "Sliders and fries half off at Luster's."

Luster's is our default after-work place, a dark steakhouse right across the street and dirt cheap if you hit it before seven.

"I'm saving my energy for tomorrow and Bootleg," I say, sitting down and grabbing my folder from Juanita. After she leaves tonight, I intend to sneak over to her cube again and check her calendar.

"Yeah, Bootleg. But that's with *them*," Yegina says, sounding as if she's slightly dreading our plans with Hiro and Brent. "Come on. We should catch up, just us."

"We've talked sixteen times a day since 2002," I joke, opening the folder.

Yegina stands there, the binder perched against her waist, tucking her black hair behind one ear.

She never begs like this. I want to say yes. But if I say yes, it ruins my plan to search Juanita's cube.

"Early drinks tomorrow night. Just you and me. I promise," I say, rooting through the clippings. I hold up the Yates picture. "Check this out."

Yegina stares at the twentysomething Bas in the photo.

"Before the facelift," I joke, and put the clipping down.

Yegina winces. "I'm worried about my brother," she says. "He's not answering my calls."

"Maybe you should invite him out for drinks tomorrow, too." I turn to my keyboard. "It's high time Don started anesthetizing himself to failure like the rest of us."

"Yeah, right," Yegina mutters. The light in my office brightens as my friend walks away and I rise to shut the door after her, knowing she'll hear it click.

I've met Yegina's brother a few times. A more categorical opposite to Yegina could not be invented: Don is tall and skinny, and he blinks a lot. His music tastes halted somewhere after Barney; obscure pop culture references sail over his head; and he favors khakis, Hondas, sincerity, and holidays at Disneyland. In college, Yegina backpacked alone through Europe and rode the Moscow-Beijing train all the way to China. Don has never left California. Yegina learned to spray-paint graffiti; Don dutifully colored the entire illustrated *Grey's Anatomy*, page by page, never going over the lines. They spent their childhood caged together, Yegina always disappointing her parents, Don always winning their approval, and sometimes I think their resistance to each other was the only thing they had in common.

But when Yegina's parents were flipping out about her divorce, Don supported her. He told her without a trace of sarcasm that she was the best person he knew in the world, and she shouldn't settle for someone who didn't believe that, too. She was profoundly touched, and it has ushered in a new era of perplexing closeness between them. "I actually like Don now," she told me once after they went bowling together. "What a funny feeling."

I think of my brother John, who has offered to fly out. Siblings need to rescue each other. I go to my inbox, open a message, and write to Yegina:

> *Sorry for sounding glib earlier. Just keep telling Don you care about him. And if he doesn't respond, say you're going to come kidnap him tomorrow. I'll make sure he has fun.*

I hit send. A few minutes later:

> *You don't know my brother, but okay, I'll try.*

•

The parking garage is dim as usual, but somehow tonight all the vehicles I pass are sheer and shining, lined up like bottles in a vending machine. There's Phil's little coupe, Spike's Vespa, Evie's spotless beige sedan. The rows of glimmering chrome hoods and bumpers stretch half a football field, looking as new and untouched as if they just drove off the lot. I could go blind from all the reflections. My skirt swishes on my bare knees. My sandals skim the concrete. Even the walls' dirt streaks look premeditated, gestural. I am tingling with my sleuthing success.

I found Juanita's calendar and read it without getting caught. Bas did indeed meet someone on Monday. I have a name for him.

"You look happier," says a voice. I turn to see Jayme, standing by her white car. She has sorrowful lines around her mouth. The hairs above her ears have started to kink into tiny scribbles. Although I know Jayme is older than I am, I don't know by how much. Too old to want to marry anyone? Too old to have children? I don't usually worry about her vitality—she's so lovely, so competent at life—but something has unmasked her age tonight.

"Just glad to go home," I say. "I heard the press conference went well." Another lie, but what does it matter? I found a piece of evidence. I can feel it. Even my clothes fit differently, looser, like I just dropped five pounds—my dress barely touches the skin of my waist.

"It went. That's about all I can say for it," says Jayme. "You ready for tomorrow?"

I try not to look blank.

"The big meeting about the annual report," she says, studying my face. "We talked about it this morning? You said you were putting together some stories."

"I am," I say brightly. "I just found some good info for Bas."

"All right, then." She puts her hand in her big red purse and beeps off her car alarm.

It was all so easy, I can't believe it happened. I waited for Juanita to leave and then I slipped over to her cube. I found her blue calendar, right there on her desk. It practically opened on its own to last week.

I read the entries. No meetings on Monday for Bas except one, with a Steve Curtain. Funny name. Distinct name. How many Steve Curtains can there be? I'll figure it out tonight, safe from prying eyes, in my own apartment.

"Although, you know, Bas might get the ax," Jayme says without turning around. "The board votes on Wednesday."

I wonder if I should act surprised, and don't respond for a moment.

"He gets fired, and the reporters will be all over this place, looking to connect it to Kim's disappearance," Jayme says, fury in her voice. "TV, too. Tabloids. I'll quit before I have to deal with that."

She opens her door: the car's interior is as dark as a safe.

"If they don't think I'll quit, they're nuts," she mutters.

I've never heard Jayme angry like this.

"Don't quit," I say. "The Rocque couldn't run without you."

"Yeah." She doesn't turn. Down the row, a minivan squeals as it wheels up the spiral ramp to the street.

My throat constricts as I say, "I hate Kim's show, too."

Instead of answering, Jayme slowly sinks into her car seat and stares over her steeling wheel, through her windshield, to the concrete wall beyond. But she doesn't shut the door.

I hover over her, trying to articulate what I felt when I looked at the Judy Ann Dull portrait earlier. It comes out clumsy and broken, but I say it anyway. "I mean, I don't hate what it is. I hate what it says."

Jayme continues to gaze at the wall, her face in profile, frozen in an expression of sadness and exhaustion. Then she looks down at her hands on the wheel, her graceful, tan fingers, and they tighten until the knuckles flex.

"It wouldn't bother me so much, but he's out," she says finally, in a calm voice, as if we're discussing some tedious office matter. "He served twenty-two years for abducting another thirteen-year-old. But he got out in November."

I don't know what man she's talking about. I'm afraid to interrupt, though.

"I always thought I was one of the lucky ones," she says, still gripping the motionless wheel. "The police did nothing about him following me, but my mother moved us here and let me change my name. She knew she had to save me, and she did."

Jayme abruptly twists away and rummages in her purse and I think she's searching for something to show me. She searches and searches, her hand grabbing in the bag, coming up empty, grabbing again. All this time she doesn't meet my eyes. Finally she pulls out her key and slides it into the ignition.

"He's out now?" I say softly. "Here? In California?"

She makes a noise of derision. "Who knows. Maybe. Guess I think I'm safe now, though, old lady like me."

"Jayme, I'm so sorry . . ."

Her hazel eyes finally meet mine. They are full of an ancient bitterness, her loveliness like a halo around it. "Be careful," she says. "Don't take any chances for Shaw. It's not your job."

Then she slams the door and turns the car on. The air between us fills first with the roar, then the taste of oil and fumes.

17

Steve Curtain does not exist in Los Angeles. There are dozens of Stephen Curtins—a spelling variation—in the United States, but mostly in Massachusetts. A doctor named Stephen Curtin in Pleasanton, California, and a doctor named Stephen Curtin in Arizona appear to be the same person. A Stephen Curtin is a district judge in Idaho. Another is an online consumer watchdog with an expression of such fake, shiny pleasure that he reminds me of the plastic sushi in the windows of Little Tokyo.

Juanita could have heard the name and written it down like the noun is spelled. Or she could have written the notation as shorthand for a name and a place, but I can't find anything for Curtain—no restaurants, no cafés, no galleries. Nothing except a factory outlet for drapes in El Monte.

My screen glows with cold light. The Internet streams beneath the glass, shifting with the clicks of my mouse.

Greg Shaw Ferguson was arraigned late yesterday in connection with the disappearance of Kim Lord. He had no comment for the press. Photos taken outside the courthouse show him gaunt, with lank hair that hangs in his eyes. Most articles detail the same four things about him: he was Kim Lord's boyfriend; he is a "young entrepreneur" whose gallery and studios were "hot" or "edgy" or "up-and-coming"; a cloth with blood matching Kim Lord's AB blood type was found in the basement of his gallery; and he allegedly made more than seventy phone calls or texts to Lord on the day before she disappeared, demanding to see her.

Seventy. Every time I see the number, I get a fresh shock.

A statement by Detective Ruiz crops up frequently: "Greg Shaw Ferguson is currently our only suspect." Kim Lord's phone was found in the bushes in Echo Park, less than a mile from Greg's gallery. Her texts beg him to leave her alone.

A few articles probe deeper: Greg Shaw Ferguson graduated from Williams College and worked as an office assistant for a New York art festival before moving to Thailand to teach English. The years skip ahead to Los Angeles, to Greg's job for the Beans, the famous movie star and his art collector wife. The Beans said, "We can't imagine that this is the same Greg Ferguson who worked for us. He was exemplary in every way. A real gentleman." A photo shows seventy-year-old, white-haired Sandahlia Bean with Greg at an art fair, her frail, crepe-sleeved arm around him, smiling. These articles also mention Greg's fondness for papaya salad; his warm, scratchy voice; the death of his mother; the make of his car; his admiration for Jack White's guitar; the philosopher he's never read (Nietzsche); and his recent sunset horseback ride over the Hollywood hills.

No one in the media should have access to the texts Greg sent Kim Lord, but nonetheless two texts are often quoted: *You have to see me. If you don't meet me, I will come find you.* And *You have no right to do this.*

I think about what Jayme told me in the parking garage, and what she didn't tell. It sounded like someone stalked her, maybe some man she knew. She escaped, but also she didn't. Jayme's alive, she's even highly successful by all external indicators, and yet I can't imagine her without her rigid self-control, her isolating sense of privacy. I don't know who she would be.

I look up statistics on stalking: One in six women have been stalked, and more than half of those before the age of twenty-five. The average duration of stalking is almost two years. Stalkers of domestic or intimate partners are more likely to use violence than are stalkers of strangers.

Homicide occurs in only two percent of stalking cases, but when it does, the stalker is usually an intimate partner: a husband, a boyfriend.

As I read this, my head grows dizzy and dizzier, as if the oxygen in the room is draining away.

I scan the e-mails from my parents and brothers, asking me to return their calls. My mother writes three times: first casually, about wrapping chicken wire around the apple tree that she and I once planted so that the deer won't eat the buds; then worried that I am letting the news overburden me; then forcefully reminding me that she is my *mother* and she has a *right* to know if I'm *safe*.

In my mind's eye, I can see her furrowed brow, her blond hair wound up in rollers, her trimmed but unmanicured fingers clattering the keys. I picture her on the day I learned of Nikki Bolio's death. I am hiding in my bed in my cramped Burlington apartment when my mother storms in, her mud-season boots thudding the floor. "Are you in danger, too?" she demands. "Because if you are, I'm picking you up in my arms and taking you home." And then she did, without waiting for a reply.

I'm safe, I type now. *I'm doing okay. Really.*

John also sends me a sample itinerary. *I can fly out on Friday if you need me.* I tell him no. I love John, but I can't translate my life for my family right now. I just need to press deeper into it.

I read about why med school applicants get rejected: no clinical experience, lackluster academics, badly written documents. I'll offer to edit Don's application if he tries again next year.

I look up Rachel Lord, Toronto. There's a record of a Rachel Lord arrested for being a public nuisance. Nothing else.

I look up Bas Jan Ader, and there's a photo of a young man holding his head and weeping. *I'm too sad to tell you* is written across the frame in a delicate hand.

I get an e-mail from Ray Hendricks, who wants to interview me at nine tomorrow morning. A Ray Hendricks was an almost-famous musician in 1930s and '40s Los Angeles. He played with the Benny Goodman Orchestra. A Ray Hendricks once pitched a no-hitter for a minor league baseball team. A Ray Hendricks is mentioned in an obituary in an Asheville, North Carolina, newspaper as the surviving half brother of a

Calvin Teicher, a young art history lecturer, who was found dead in a Los Angeles hotel; it appears he fell in his bathroom and struck his head. Teicher also left behind his mother, Willow Teicher, sixty-two; his son, Nathaniel, four; and an ex-wife who lives in Florida. I search "Ray Hendricks North Carolina" and find another mention, in an article about state police busting up meth labs in the Smoky Mountains. Special Agent Ray Hendricks, a Boone native now working for the North Carolina Bureau of Investigation, calls meth "a scourge in our rural counties." No picture accompanies either article, but I can't help feeling it's the same Ray Hendricks who is working as Janis Rocque's private investigator.

Special Agent sounds impressive. A big career for a guy from a small mountain town like Boone. Is he out here for his job or for his half brother? Either way, I don't buy his sleepy, laconic mask; underneath it, there's something else playing on a loop, some huge grief or desperation. *I'm too sad to tell you.*

It's getting colder and I want to go to bed, but my mind is not tired and I won't sleep. I sit in the dark, staring into a box of illuminated fog, and hope for the miracle of Kim Lord's life—hiding out or locked away, waiting to be found—instead of the commonplace fact of her death.

One last peek at my inbox.

A note from Yegina: *Don said he'll come. (!)*

A note from Evie, who says she has unearthed a perplexing pattern in the provenance of Kim's work: *I've never seen anything like this. I'll show you the list tomorrow.*

TUESDAY

18

M ind if I shut this?" Ray Hendricks says, and waits for me to nod before closing my office door. I have a small office. Shutting the door makes it shrink to a pay-phone booth, tight and muffled. In this space, Hendricks is bigger than I thought he would be—he barely fits on the other side of my desk, but he doesn't look uncomfortable as he sits. He has an easy looseness in his limbs. His eyes scan my shelves, roving over the spines of catalogs and copyediting books, then flickering to my window, my wilting ficus. They touch anything and everything but me.

Hendricks's watchfulness is something that has perturbed me since the first night I saw him, at the Gala, wearing that horrendous mustard-colored jacket. Most people look at the world, but they don't watch it. They don't try to see what's coming at them. Hendricks couldn't have known the fallen earring was mine unless it was somehow loose in my ear that night. He wouldn't have brought it the next day if he hadn't guessed I was an employee at the Rocque. He was curious about me. And knowing that he might be from the same eastern mountain chain as I am, that he's a detective, that his half brother died here in L.A., makes me curious about him. And unnerved. For all the time I spent with Jay Eastman learning how to interview sources, for all that Hendricks and I must be close in age, I feel amateurish in his presence, almost precarious. It's as if inside me there's a plate teetering on the edge of a table, and one false move could make it fall.

"Nice place," he says in an unreadable tone.

"I'm lucky to have an office." I fumble for things to say. "They almost put me in a cube."

Hendricks's roving eyes finally stop on a little Zen garden that's gathering dust on my sill. The square wood frame holds sand and pebbles; a black rake perches on the corner.

"Yours?" he says.

I nod. My brother John gave the Zen garden to me as a joke when I told him I was moving to California. "If you rake the sand, it's supposed to make you feel peaceful," I say. "I keep it because the rocks are the only things in L.A. that remind me of my childhood creek." I hesitate, then add, "I grew up in the mountains." *Too,* I add mentally. *I grew up in the mountains, too.*

Hendricks listens to all this with his head angled, as if he can't quite understand my English, and then nods.

"Try it if you want," I say.

To my surprise, he lifts the Zen garden down to my desk and starts combing.

"I told everything I knew to Detective Ruiz," I say.

The rake makes gentle scratching sounds. "I don't work for the police. I work for Janis Rocque," he says. He piles all the rocks but one in a corner. Then he combs the sand so that it radiates out from the pile, like ripples in a pond. Finally, he puts the lone stone across the garden and presses it deeply down; the flowing sand almost drowns it. "She's an inquisitive woman," he adds.

I peer at his work, surprised at how he made the crude materials so expressive. "I like the splash."

Hendricks sets the rake down on the frame's corner.

"What does Janis Rocque want to know about me?" I ask.

"She doesn't want to know anything about you." Hendricks raises his head, and for the first time his sleepy guardedness is gone and I see a different man, blinking at me, the way people look when they emerge from water. It's so shocking to see his direct gaze that it momentarily steals my breath.

"Cases like this . . ." He pauses as if steeling himself for what he has to utter next. "There's often collateral damage. Sometimes, people get hurt who shouldn't. People like you." His blue eyes lock on mine. "I just want you to understand that you can call me anytime, day or night. If you need help."

"Okay," I say with a little unintentional laugh. "I have your card."

He almost looks bashful. "Good," he says.

A shadow passes my door: Yegina. She's carrying that *Art of the Race Car* binder around again. She waves and gives me a grin just as Hendricks turns to look. I wave halfheartedly back.

Hendricks sets my Zen garden on the sill. "I'll see you around," he says.

"That's it?" I say. "That's all you wanted to say?"

He pauses with his hand on the door handle.

"There is one question I had," he says. "Did you know that Kim Lord was pregnant?"

19

The loading dock door inches up. Morning light floods the cave where the crates are stacked. Fritz, our security guard, stands in the glare, his head craned toward the underpass. A large truck is backing up outside, beeping its way, and the noise ricochets against the walls and floor. Red lights flare above the truck's giant bumper. Their glow looks garish, menacing, but my senses are hardly reliable now. Everything shimmers as if someone has punched me between the eyes.

Evie emerges from the registrar's office, a clipboard in her hands. The light from the underpass throws her features into sharp relief. She told me once that she came to L.A. to become an actress, but I can see why she didn't succeed. She's undeniably pretty, but in an impenetrable way. Even as she waves at me, her face looks as carved and immobile as a mask.

"Just let me handle this first," she says. "Can you wait a minute?"

I could wait all day. It's not like I can work with my mind like this, playing the end of my conversation with Hendricks over and over. How did he know Kim was pregnant? "Shaw told me," said Hendricks, and then his voice changed, interrogating me.

I hadn't known? No.

Had anyone known? No one here. Not Rocque gossip. Not common knowledge at all. I was so stuck on refusing the idea—of Kim Lord's ripening belly, of a mother-to-be painting herself locked in some pervert's torturing head box—that I couldn't ask Hendricks why it mattered if I knew. All I could think about was Kim in a few months' time, strolling slowly, full of Greg's child, running her hands absently over her curving stomach while he hovered protectively, watching her step. I put my head in my hands, and probably—no, definitely—moaned, whereupon Hendricks fled my office like there was a dog inside threatening to bite him.

I try to focus on the moment at hand. "What's coming in?" I ask Evie.

"Going out." Evie points at two large crates. "Two Rothkos."

The truck stops, and the driver hops down and opens the back door. Empty truck. Pickup. He spreads the base with packing quilts.

"Major loan," I say.

"Abstract expressionist show at the Hirshhorn. I should be going with them instead of using a shipper," Evie says. "They're fragile."

The way she says *fragile*, it sounds so protective, almost maternal. I wish I loved objects the way Evie does, investing them with a precious presence, because I want to feel more about things. Or feel less about myself.

"Why can't you go?" I ask Evie.

A shadow crosses her face. "A conflict," she mutters. "I'm supposed to accompany four Judd sculptures to Amsterdam on Saturday. Can't do both." She leaves me to meet the driver.

Small talk concluded, my haze returns. I clench and unclench my fists, feeling like I want to get in my car and drive north, until the gas runs out, and then keep going.

Brent Patrick bolts from the carpentry room, frowning. He doesn't look mad. He just looks, once again, like his mind is boiling something down to a concentrate. I wave.

"I hear we're going to Bootleg tonight," I call out. Brent glances toward the open door before giving me a puzzled nod. "The Jon Byron show?" He doesn't move any closer, so I walk over to him, blinking as I enter his steaming, hypermasculine presence, and prattle on about the venue's horrendous food, outrageous volume. I've never had a nonwork conversation with Brent, and it's hard to launch one. "I heard the owner turns up the speakers if you complain," I add with a little laugh.

Brent regards me for a moment, but he doesn't seem to focus. "Excuse me, Marie," he mutters, and charges off, past the truck, out the loading dock.

"Excuse you, Brando," I mutter. I hope to God that Don takes my place at Bootleg. I am not in the mood to third-wheel with a caveman tonight. If I started driving right now, I could be in San Francisco by dark. Or Vegas. Or Baja. Or Death Valley. Wouldn't there be a maudlin irony in that? Wouldn't it be pleasing to see the starkness and bloom of a spring desert? Except that I actually hate driving by myself. I wonder if my brother John would fly out and man the wheel while I stare into the passing miles.

"What did you want with Brent?" Evie is back at my elbow, her voice barely audible above the rumble of the truck driving away.

"Oh, we're supposed to go to some show tonight. With Yegina and Hiro and Yegina's little brother." I register the look on her face. "Want to come? It's at Bootleg."

"Bootleg," she repeats, like it's a foreign name. "No, thank you."

"Good choice."

She squints at me.

"The food's so bad," I tell her. Why I am having such a hard time communicating? Maybe because my insides are melting into the saddest lake in the world.

Evie shakes her head. "Would you care to see what I found?" she says.

"Sure." I follow her into her office, noting that she manages to blow-dry the back of her hair with the same meticulous care as the front. Blond strands curve toward her neck, touching the raised tendons. She sets her clipboard down carefully, releases three forms, and sticks them in a binder.

"I'm sorry you couldn't go with the Rothkos," I say. "But Amsterdam sounds like more fun."

She makes a small noise of assent.

There's a movement behind me: Brent storming back to his office with some papers in his hand, slamming the door. Evie watches him rigidly. The table saw shrieks from the carpentry room.

"What's in the air down here today?" I say.

Evie opens her binder again, fingers the forms to count them. One, two, three. Then she shuts it a second time. There's a deliberateness to the gesture that reminds me of my days as a grocery cashier, when I watched overwhelmed mothers excavate their carts with slow, exact movements, ignoring the shrieks of their children.

How cold I sound. "I'm sorry. Everyone down here must be so freaked out about Kim Lord. Where do you guys think she is?"

Evie picks up a yellow legal pad, holds it loosely, as if testing its weight. "Most people think Shaw did something. But I believe you," she says, then hands the legal pad to me. "Here is the provenance on every work I could find."

I see the names of Kim's artworks first, about fifty of them from her first two shows, all oil paintings, varying dimensions. All but a few are titled by the names of women: the prostitutes Candi, Tonya, and CiCi, and the film stars Barbara, Rita, Jane. Mentally I add the *Still Lives* list: Nicole, Elizabeth, Roseann.

And then I notice the collectors, not one of them with American or Anglo names except Janis Rocque, who owns one painting from Kim's first show, and Nelson de Wilde, who owns three. The rest sound Japanese or Russian: Akira Naoki . . . Sanjugo Ishibashi . . . Vladimir Daniloff . . . Tanaka Ikuta . . .

I read the names twice, hoping to find a *Steve* or a *Curtain*.

"Notice anything?"

I feel Evie's eyes on me and look up. She's resurrected her usual cool expression again, but there's a hint of pride in it.

"Who are they?" I say.

"I don't know." Evie sounds triumphant. "They're not recognized collectors. An artist like Kim Lord, you'd figure she'd be in the collection of a Peter Benedek or Eli Broad, but she's not."

"So she has a big international following," I say. "And no collectors in the United States but Nelson and Janis?"

Evie hesitates.

"Or you think these names are fake," I say.

"I think they're fake," she says. "I think someone or, maybe, a few people are using aliases to buy up everything she's ever made."

The statement hangs in the air. Evie and I are standing together in a small, dingy underground room, but it feels suddenly like we've risen high above the earth. Maybe I didn't fully believe my own theory either. Maybe I never thought I'd find actual proof, but this seems like a kind of proof, especially after Evie shows me the buyers who are publicly recorded for purchasing work from Kim Lord's first show, *The Flesh*, the one that sold out at auction. It's not the same as the list on the yellow pad, not by a long shot. The only one I recognize is Janis Rocque, but Evie says that all the other collectors must have resold the work privately later on.

"And this isn't normal?" I ask.

"Not at all! You look at the provenance of a Chris Ofili or a Mike Kelley, and there might be an avid collector or two, but it's pretty spread out over a dozen people and institutions." She taps Nelson de Wilde's name and says that the gallerist would have to be in collusion with the one mega-collector, or such a monopoly on one artist's work would never be possible.

"But wouldn't Kim Lord know?"

"Not necessarily. If the work got resold through someone other than Nelson," she says.

"I can't believe we'd be the first to figure it out," I say.

Evie raises an eyebrow. "Maybe we're not." She tells me about a collector who is suing a Harlem gallery because it did not offer him first dibs on buying a painting by Julie Mehretu, despite the fact that he supported the same gallery with a $75,000 loan in return for the chance to snap up hot artists. "He got so steamed about it, he went to court."

I'm not seeing the connection. "So?"

"So what if Janis Rocque wants another Kim Lord and she can't get one? Why else would she hire that sleazy guy to snoop around?"

He's not that sleazy, I think. But what Evie says makes sense. Janis Rocque invites her private investigator to the Gala to find the person who is hoarding the Lords. Then Kim doesn't show up and J. Ro keeps him on, suspecting something darker. Janis Rocque has been way ahead of me since the beginning; she worried someone was trying to manipulate Kim Lord's work in the marketplace. I am struck again with the uneasy pleasure of having my convictions confirmed.

"God, how did you find all this so fast?" I ask her. "You're amazing at your work. I'm so grateful."

Evie smirks, as if she feels sorry for me for finally noticing. She points to the yellow pad in my hands. "What are you going to do? Could this help Shaw?"

The hurt floods me again. "I hope so," I say, averting my eyes.

Outside there's a loud, rolling sound as the loading-dock door comes down. The light behind me darkens. Evie is saying something about Thursday. Visiting J. Ro's sculpture garden on Thursday.

"I'll be there," I manage to say, and wave my thanks, although Thursday feels as far away as the Atlantic Ocean to me. I can feel Evie's eyes on my back as I cross the cavern to the elevator. Fritz the security guard enters my field of vision, his tinted glasses still darkened from the recent flood of light. He's waving something thin and brown.

"For you," he says cheerfully. "UPS came by. Save you a trip to the mailroom."

I grab it, thank him, and keep walking.

Once, in Thailand, I was sure I was pregnant. My period was late, and I didn't know where to buy a test. As I sweltered in front of my chalky classroom blackboard, rode on the long bench of the covered taxi, strolled the fly-infested market where pig heads rested on ice, I felt myself expanding, becoming more than me. I wrote a letter to Greg, who was teaching two provinces away from me, but I did not send it. If I sent the letter, it could be true. If I waited, it was merely a secret, a threat. Also, a wish.

The blood came the week before I visited Greg at his house. As we lay on hammocks under his covered front patio, I told him about my scare. He sounded relieved. His relief made me angry.

"Is this a trial?" Greg flared back, and then added more gently, "Do you really want to have a baby? Because we should talk if you do."

I denied the desire, but I sulked because I couldn't express what I did want. Not a baby. Certainly not the diapers and co-sleepers that clogged my brother Mark's life. But the feeling of our future inside me, mine and Greg's? I liked that. It anchored me.

I punch the elevator button and the doors open immediately, the interior thankfully unoccupied. After the doors slip shut, I rip open the envelope, addressed to me in plain caps.

Inside: a torn notebook page, and a smaller white paper, folded. I read the notebook page first. The handwriting is Greg's, hasty and scrawled:

> *M—I only have a couple of minutes to write this because the police are here, and it seems like they've found something incriminating downstairs, but one of my assistants said she'd mail this for me. (1) I am NOT guilty. I know you believe this. (2) Please don't try to help, like I asked you last night. Let the police do their work. I got this under my studio door this morning and it's freaking me out. Stay safe. Stay out of this. I love you, my friend.*
> *—GSF*

I unfold the second, smaller paper. Six words in black marker:

YOU'D BETTER WATCH OUT FOR MAGGIE.

20

Donor wall," Hiro says. He is standing outside my office door, wearing a pine-green T-shirt for a bonsai society. He holds up two sheets of paper. "Can you look at these really fast?" he says, recoiling at my grimace. "We're ninety-nine percent sure they're correct, but you need to sign off on everything, right? For typos?"

YOU'D BETTER WATCH OUT FOR MAGGIE. The words on the note blaze through my mind. Now I understand Cherie's suspicions. Greg thought someone was warning him to protect me; Cherie interpreted the opposite. Better watch out for Maggie, as in *Maggie's dangerous.*

Who in the world would think I'm dangerous? Maybe Nikki Bolio once thought I was, when I asked her to expose the people she knew. Yet in a ruthless city like Los Angeles, I'm as harmless as a lamb. I make homemade cards for people's birthdays. I exclusively wear practical shoes. I bring maple-bran muffins to cocktail parties.

Then again, if Greg's interpretation is right, who is out to hurt me?

Wordlessly, I yank open my office door and throw Greg's envelope on my desk.

Hiro follows me in, spreading the list of names that will each receive their own shiny chrome plaque on our outside wall. He sets the paper down as if it is delicate, and backs away. "Are you okay?" he asks.

YOU'D BETTER WATCH OUT FOR MAGGIE. There's something provocative about the message. It's deliberately unclear. Like a work of art, it invites you to interpret it.

"Maggie?" says Hiro.

"I'm fine." I try to focus. The black and blue pens of the Development department have slashed through a few names, corrected others. They're vigilant about this stuff because rich people go ballistic if they are not acknowledged properly.

"I won't hover," Hiro says. "But can I come back in an hour?"

I see that Thalia Thalberg's name has been edited to Thalia Thalberg-Talbert.

"You can't be serious," I mutter.

"Two hours?" Hiro says politely.

"Thalia Thalberg married someone named Talbert and they're hyphenating?"

"She's *getting* married," says Hiro. "In July, I think. Cheapest time to pay the city of Paris to evacuate so she can fill it with her wedding guests."

I gape at him.

Hiro holds up his palms. "Kidding. She wants to have the wedding in France before her surrogate gets too pregnant to travel."

"You're still kidding."

Hiro gives me a huge, wondering grin. "Actually, no."

For the first time today, I find myself smiling, too, and not in a snarky way, but an astounded one, at the marvel of Thalia Thalberg-Talbert and her superior ability to hypermanage every life moment. It feels unbelievably good to grin. I pull the list across my desk. "Just come back in fifteen minutes," I say.

Hiro nods and leaves, pausing at the top of the stairwell to gaze out on my favorite view of the city. Most people just clop on down the steps, focused on their daily tasks. Hiro really soaks it in, his brown eyes blinking. Yegina told me his apartment is full of bonsai trees, that he hopes to make a living from them one day. In his longest conversation with her, he held forth on branches: how the tree always wants to grow, and it grows by trunk and branch, so the bonsai artist's art is also the line, but his material is a living thing. "Very slow and very unpredictable," he told Yegina. She repeated this to me with a wry smile.

With a radiant surge of hope, I wish for the two of them to fall in love. Real love. Yegina's brother is right. She needs someone who is worthy of her, someone who is sincere and kind and who won't let her down. Maybe it can all begin tonight. Maybe I should just tell Brent and Don so we can quietly slip away.

My eyes fall on the envelope from Greg. Do I tell Yegina about this? She'll put me under twenty-four-hour surveillance.

Hiro begins to descend the stairs. Juanita crosses my line of vision. She glances from Hiro to me, and I duck my head. *Please don't ask him about the Bas article,* I will her, and she doesn't say a thing, just drifts on, but I think she knows I am a liar.

I stare at the donor lists, gripping my pen, until I am sure Juanita is gone. The Founding Donors—Victor, Hilda, and Janis Rocque—get their own donor category at the top. Then there is a slew of Charter Donors, who've given between half a million and a million dollars. Among them are the Beans, Greg's employers, who gave a public interview this morning in which they defended Greg's character but said they were "puzzled" by the evidence the police had discovered. Their voices sounded hurt and old.

James and Marie Terrant, Bas's parents, are also among the Charter Donors. Supposedly they sold their Palm Springs house and gave the proceeds to the Rocque as a welcome gift. They're joined by collectors and politicos whose names I've read so many times I know they're correct without checking. But when I get to the lower categories of funders, I have to look up and double-check every person and company because last year someone slipped the name Sparkle Jollypants into the list and no one caught it until six months after the plaque had been hung. Among the Gold Donors, a longer name is inked out and replaced with *CJ Gallery.* I look it up and find nothing, and make a note to double-check it with Hiro.

"Knock, knock," says a low voice. It's Jayme, resplendent in a teak-colored tunic and white jeans, her hair bound back in a scarf. Her face betrays no sign of the anguish she displayed last night. In fact, it looks defiant. Whatever she told me, she won't voice it again. "What are you up to?" she says. It comes out like a challenge.

"Just looking for Sparkle Jollypants," I say, and show her the donor list.

Out of the corner of my eye, I see the top of my inbox darken with a new message from Yegina, the subject heading: *Don.* Jayme asks me if I'm ready for the annual report meeting, and I assure her I am, because I'm going to blow my lunch break on developing a few more story ideas from my files. Jayme steps inside my office to say sotto voce that *Art of the Race Car* is completely off the schedule and, as of this morning, we're replacing it with a tribute to some board member's personal collection.

"Well played," I say, wondering if the new exhibition is Yegina's idea. "What a relief."

Jayme doesn't respond. She is looking at my Cy Twombly drawing, her head tilted back, as if she hasn't seen it before.

"What if it is just a scribble?" I say. "Don't you ever wonder that?"

"Did you see that report on Kim Lord's family?" Jayme says. "Her sister's been found. She never left Toronto. She contacted the parents, and she's back in rehab."

Kim's sister never left Toronto. That means she can't be the woman on the flash drive.

"Thank God she's safe," I say. "I can't imagine how their parents are feeling right now."

Jayme gives a convulsive little shrug.

"I'm sorry, I—" I begin.

"I always thought it was a scribble," she interrupts dryly, gesturing at the Twombly. "Excuse me." She pulls out her phone, dialing a number.

Hiro appears behind Jayme. "Just two more minutes," I call to him.

Jayme departs, hand to her ear, already deep in conversation. I'm amazed at how she can compartmentalize so fast. I ought to try it. I gesture at Hiro to sit while I scan through the last few names. He lowers himself into a chair and folds his hands. I mention Bootleg, and we joke about their awful food, about filling up at a happy hour before. Even to my own ears, I sound cheerful. Maybe compartmentalizing is the only way to cope this week. Kim's sister is safe. That should be good news. But, then, who is the woman in the photos on the flash drive?

"So . . . CJ Gallery—is that what this says?" I ask, tapping the list.

He looks at the list, frowns. "No, CJF. MeiMei wrote that. I think it used to be Curtain, Jug, and Fruit, but they changed their name before they opened."

"Curtain, Jug, *and* Fruit?" I repeat. "I can see why they shortened it. Let me check the punctuation, though."

I open a search engine, make sure the initials have no periods, and hand the whole list off to Hiro, who thanks me profusely and splits. I am about to click on Yegina's message when the back of my neck prickles. I look again at the search results.

CJF is a brand-new Santa Monica gallery, run by proprietor Steve Goetz. I've seen that last name before, but can't remember where—another donor list?

Curtain, Jug, and Fruit is a painting by Paul Cézanne that sold for $60 million in 1999, making it one of the most expensive still lifes in the world.

Steve Curtain was the notation in Juanita's planner. Steve *at* Curtain?

Kim Lord's hastily painted backdrop in "Disappearances" features a hanging cloth depicting oranges, apples, and jugs. Curtain, jugs, and fruit.

Kim Lord was warning him. Or the rest of us. But warning us of what?

Steve Goetz—proprietor of CJF Gallery, art collector, former Catesby's consultant, master's degree from Yates—is burly and dish-faced, with thick brown hair and a flush in his cheeks like he just swallowed a hot toddy. In the photo accompanying one news article, he stands erect, legs spread, in front of the Guggenheim Bilbao, hands in the pockets of his indigo suit. The article is about art philanthropy. Steve Goetz has started an organization called the Patron Foundation to pair wealthy international collectors with individual up-and-coming artists. "Like the micro-loan movement, but for New Masters," he says.

A call to my contact at the Yates library turns up his thesis from

1993 called "The Supercollector and the Artificial Artist," keywords: art market, economy, Damien Hirst, Tracey Emin, Charles Saatchi, YBAs.

The librarian says she has the abstract. Do I want her to fax it?

"Can you read it to me now?" I beg her.

> *In our new international contemporary art market, the artist's value is no longer principally attached to the artist's work; rather, it is attached to other factors such as wealthy collectors, media hype, and the increasing trend to collect "wet paint" artists. This thesis proposes that key individual non-artists (i.e., collectors, critics, curators) may have a greater influence on artistic movements than the artists themselves, and that the future is ready for a new figure, the "supercollector," to shape a new canon of "artificial artists."*

"Say that again—a 'supercollector' . . ."

"Shapes a new canon of 'artificial artists.' Geez. I'll be an artificial artist if someone wants to hype me," she says. "Too bad I can't even draw."

"It's disgustingly cynical," I say, thinking of all the artists I know who would be mortified to be called *artificial*. "Like the process and the appreciation of art don't exist, just its market value, which can be influenced at will."

The librarian makes a noise of assent. "Yeah. It'll never happen, though. What's the payoff for being the so-called supercollector? That everyone knows you really are a douchebag?"

"It could happen," I say. "It could have happened."

There's an expectant silence.

"That's all I'm saying," I say.

"Really," she says thoughtfully. "You know, you're the second person to request that thesis this month."

"Who's the first?"

"Can't tell you," she says reluctantly. She'll copy the thesis itself and fax it to me by tomorrow morning.

I gaze out the window, and then down at the splashing sand of my

Zen garden, formulating a plan. It's hard to concentrate when bile keeps rising in my throat at the thought of someone manipulating an art career this way. The preening superiority of Steve Goetz's thesis dismisses dozens—no, hundreds—of generations of artists who have dedicated their whole lives to making pictures and sculptures that move us, that make us think, that shape our understanding of the world. To turn that effort into some rich person's economic operation, to turn Kim Lord into a commodity that only the rich could trade—no wonder she wanted to donate all her paintings. And yet. She was also giving up millions of dollars. It was a courageous choice. Or a desperate one.

I send a quick note to Jayme saying I don't feel well, and close my inbox without opening Yegina's message for fear that some fresh worry about her brother will slow me down. I have never left the Rocque in such a rush, flinging the flash drive into my purse, flinging my purse over my shoulder, digging for my car keys and holding them out in front of me blocks before I reach the parking garage. I slam the door, start the car, and roar up through the ramps to street level, hoping not to be seen by anyone from the museum.

I am not seen. Now the lights go red and I take my place in line on Beverly, leaving the sheer, mirrored corridors of downtown for the two-story sprawl of the rest of the city. I love driving L.A.'s east-west boulevards. It always dazzles me: each broad avenue has its own flavor, shaped by pockets of immigrants—Thai Town, Koreatown, Little Tehran—and each one aims toward the sea. Whenever a song from Beck's *Sea Change* is playing on the radio, I think I could spend the rest of my life flowing over these passageways to the Pacific.

A calm has descended through me since I got in the car. Or maybe it's detachment—I'm traveling through space, but I don't feel entirely connected to it, like I'm entering an ocean mist, everything glittery and indistinct. That's Fairfax I'm passing, and if I glanced right, I'd see the dusky red-and-brown walls of Bootleg, where we're supposed to meet tonight to hear music. It seems so far away.

I reach into my purse and close my fingers around the flash drive. I may not need it, but having it with me feels like I have Kim along, and all the hours and heartache she must have poured into making her paintings—ambitious Kim, and then pregnant Kim, Kim the mother-to-be, frightened and angry, knowing in those last days before *Still Lives* the stakes of her sacrifice: to give up everything she'd made. Vanished Kim. Who must have badly underestimated what could happen to her. I have to be very careful. I have to look eager but guileless. I have to ask the right questions. I don't need to know everything—just enough to make a case for others to follow up on. Just a piece of the picture. Before it's too late.

Santa Monica is what I once naïvely pictured all of Los Angeles would be: the palm trees, indoor-outdoor restaurants, views of the ocean, trim green parks. Temperatures sway gently between warm and cool; the air is either muzzy or sparkly. Attractive people lead their Weimaraners on leather leashes. *If you deserve the good life, why choose anywhere else?* the city seems to ask the moment you pass under its big, blue, invitingly readable street signs.

Instead of this paradise, Greg and I moved into the bustle and grit of Hollywood, on a small street halfway between the old movie theaters reviving themselves and the giant billboards of the Sunset Strip. Every day, going east, we drove past the glamorous edifices of another era decaying over bright, cheesy bric-a-brac shops; going west, we hit the great mirages of commercialization and beauty, slender-legged models fifty feet high, smiling in white sweaters and jeans. Both directions seemed like routes away, and never routes home. Nowhere in L.A. seems like home to me.

I wasn't raised to deserve anything but my own struggling existence. I grew up down a dirt road next to a family of rednecks whose favorite sport was drinking Budweiser and Ski-Dooing doughnuts in their backyard. When I was twelve, I babysat for them, wiping their kids' noses and bums for five dollars an hour and a daily assault of dumb-blonde jokes from their Uncle Larry. He called me Faggie Maggie, as in "Hey, Faggie Maggie, how does a blonde like her eggs in the morning? Fertilized!" When I was fourteen I bagged groceries at the A&P; at fifteen I cleaned the cafeteria at the local ski resort. I know the cramps of overworked hands. I know the bored, haggard faces of my supervisors, who were overseeing the same dismal landscape of cash registers and dirty tables at forty because there were no other jobs for them. I know I am lucky to have escaped.

My rust-freckled station wagon rumbles into a parking spot. CJF Gallery gleams straight ahead, a full bank of windows, a gallerina sitting at a desk, a staircase leading up to a loft. The gallerina looks like most gallerinas: young, dark-haired, groomed to flawlessness, her eyes glued to some papers on her desk. The room beyond her looks like most galleries, blank and chilly as an empty refrigerator except for a few paintings hung here and there. And yet. The light is so bright and white inside, it sets the whole scene off, makes it look sinister and fake.

I grab my cassette recorder from my glove compartment. It's a ridiculous apparatus: black, bulky, clacky, and prone to chewing up tape. Jay Eastman mocked me for it ("Did you get that from the town dump?"), and he made me carry his own little digital machine when I interviewed Nikki. I keep this big one because my father bought it for me one Christmas when I worked on my high school newspaper. Back then, it was a top-of-the-line device. My parents, with three kids and a lackluster income from their elementary school teaching, tended to gift the cheap and homemade. Dad believed I could be a great journalist one day. I don't know what he imagines for me now.

I set up the machine to record and slide it in my purse, but I can't muster the nerve to leave the car. I shouldn't be doing this alone.

As if she senses my presence, the gallerina glances out the window. Her eyes travel over me, assessing and dismissing my car, then the person inside. The coldness in her gaze demoralizes me. I flutter in my purse for my drugstore lipstick. My lips redden in the mirror as if someone has just pumped blood into them. I look childish and middle-aged at the same time.

Did Kim want to keep her baby? She was thirty-eight, almost on the brink of too-late.

Did Steve Goetz make her afraid? Say he did spend fifteen years coldly collecting and planning, building to his great statement about Kim's career as his own artwork—what would he do if she found out and tried to unravel it all? Would he stop her any way possible? Would he benefit even more if she died?

I won't go into the gallery without knowing there's someone waiting for me on the other side. I try Yegina, but her phone's turned off. I try Evie, but I only get her voice mail. "I think I've found something else. Call me," I say, and hang up.

I need to reach a real voice, to set a time when I should be arriving somewhere. Reluctantly I pull out Ray Hendricks's card, stare at it for a while, heart pounding. Finally I dial.

"Yes," he says in almost a whisper.

"Uh, sorry, did I wake you?"

"Maggie. Hold on. I'm in a movie." I hear the creak of a chair, the blare of a soundtrack, then a hush. "Did something happen?" Then traffic. "Are you all right?" He sounds genuinely concerned.

"I just—you said—if I was ever—" I can't tell him where I am yet. "There's someone at the Rocque I'm worried about."

"Yes," he says.

His seriousness alarms me. "What were you watching anyway?"

Hendricks mumbles something.

"Did you just say *Piglet*?" I say.

"*Piglet's Big Movie*," he says in a resigned voice. "I'm screening it for someone."

So you have a kid, too, I think. Apparently everyone has a kid these days.

"My nephew," he adds.

His nephew. The son of his deceased half brother?

How was it? I intend to ask about the movie, but it comes out, "How is he?" I cough. "I mean, do you think he'll like it?"

"Even at the tender age of five, he might find it beneath him."

"I always liked Piglet," I say, stalling.

Hendricks makes a noise. "Your point?"

"What?"

"Your point in calling me?"

"Can you meet me at Luster's Steakhouse at five? It's a few blocks from the museum. I can't talk here."

Hendricks doesn't answer immediately.

"I'll be there," he says, his voice retreating from the phone as if he's writing something down. We say awkward good-byes, and then I jump out of my car and charge toward the gallery before I have time to change my mind.

The air is so cool and sharp inside that it hurts my nose to breathe. Everything has a hard shine in here, the glass frames on the wall, a sculpture made of broken test tubes, the red nails of the gallerina, now clicking away at a keyboard. I stroll to a couple of paintings, pretending to look at their bold, simplistic lines, working up my courage. Then I reach in my purse and click the record button on my machine before approaching the desk.

"I'm here to see Steve Goetz," I say to the gallerina, who is ignoring me with a deep intensity.

She types a few more sentences before turning. "Your name?"

"Sheilah Graham," I say.

She starts typing again.

"I'm here from the Rocque."

The gallerina smooths a single brown hair back into place, stands up, mutters "Excuse me," and slowly climbs the stairs to the loft. Her dark suit ascending through the white space reminds me of an insect mounting a wall. When the gallerina disappears through a door upstairs, the silence thickens. I am recording it through the muffling leather of my purse, and I know that if I listen to it later, it will sound like nothing, a blank interval of time. But the sensation of it now is heavy and textured, like sand.

A quick exchange of voices. The door opens again, and he is standing there, looking down on me, tanner than in his photographs. He has broad, high brows, the shadow of stubble, puzzled eyes.

"Yes?"

"I'm here for the profile," I say brightly. "For the Rocque's members' magazine?"

He frowns. "Is that on my calendar?" he says to his assistant.

She peers at her computer. "I don't have any record of it," she says in a brittle voice, darting a nervous look at him.

"Juanita told me she set it up for three o'clock today," I say, doing my best to look very young and very crestfallen. "I'm sorry. Is there any way? I have a deadline—"

He gives an exasperated, wouldn't-you-know-it sigh and gestures for me to climb the steep steps, no railing, each one lifting me farther away from the safety of the door to the outside. I feel like I am ascending into a hive.

When I reach the top, Goetz calls down to his assistant. "Do get us some coffee, will you."

She looks up. From this angle, her once flawless face looks mousy and frightened.

"Oh, that's okay—" I say.

"No, no. Fresh coffee, please," he says, and I suppress a flinch as the gallerina grabs her purse and stands up to leave.

Goetz opens the door to his office. I enter first. He shuts it behind me and stands against it a moment, regarding my face, before circling to his desk. The room is filled with shelves of art catalogs. I recognize their bulky, oversize shapes, and the smaller bound paperbacks that are auction catalogs. Ordinarily such a collection would reassure me. Thinking people read. I like thinking people. I like people who like art. But the air in here is musty and oppressive, and there are several boxes on the floor, also full of books, and no place to put them.

"So, Sheilah," he says genially. "Tell me about this profile."

He takes a seat behind his desk, and instead of waiting for my answer, he begins clacking at his computer. I can't see the screen.

"Well, I'm awfully sorry it's a surprise," I say earnestly. "Development wanted us to do a profile in each issue on our biggest donors, and we're really grateful for your support. It's helped enormously with shows like *Still Lives*."

His typing pauses. He sits back in his chair, making it creak. He is heavier than he looks in his photographs. He has large hands. But the scariest thing about him is the overbearing friendliness in his features, as if he wants to drive me into the ground with his pleasantness, as if he wants to smear it all over me.

"How nice," he says, smiling.

"So I got a lot of good information about you online," I say, and tell him what I know about his philanthropy and his schooling at Yates.

Goetz's shoulders relax as it becomes clear how much research I've already done, and he corrects only the date of his degree. All the while, I'm trying to glean what I can from scanning the titles around me. They're all contemporary art. I don't see any book pertaining to Kim Lord. What else is here? A long modern desk, a computer, a leather chair. An empty vase with a broad base and narrow flute—could it be Japanese? Back in a corner, a white birdcage hangs from its own stand, its door ajar. In the other corner sit stacks of embroidered textiles, their colors too bright to be American. The souvenirs of a world traveler.

As Goetz tells me about the latest beneficiaries of his Patron Foundation, my eyes return to the birdcage, the thin, straight bars banded once in the middle, and what looks like a winged carving inside, also white. The stand is white. Even the links of the short chain it hangs from: white. A lustered white, almost cream, and smooth as bone.

The cage, its captive bird—the entire piece is made of ivory.

So maybe he bought something illegal, or maybe he collects antiquities. It's an odd piece, but not unusual for a rich man to own something so ornate and rare.

Yet as I stare at the cage's open door, all the book titles I skimmed moments ago start playing like credits: Marlene Dumas, Barbara Kruger, Cindy Sherman, Kiki Smith. Every catalog, every artist lined up neatly on his shelves: they are all women.

"Promise you won't put my messy office in your profile," Goetz says, catching my gaze. "I haven't finished unpacking."

"Of course not." We both laugh.

He leans toward his screen and clicks the mouse a few times. "Anything else?"

I need more. I make my next move.

"There's one last thing," I say. "I'd like to get a quote or two to spice this up. Are you okay with playing a little word game?"

"A little game," he says, with another mouse click. "What does that mean?"

"It sounds silly, but it's a fun way to get to know people," I say. "Our members love reading the answers, too. It goes like this. I say a word, and you say whatever comes to your mind. So if I said *sunset*, you might say *boulevard*. Or you might say *beautiful* or *beach*."

"Why not," he says. "I like games."

"Okay," I say. "The first word is *museum*."

"Treasure."

"*Art*."

"Necessary," he says.

"*Artist*."

"Maker."

"*Collector*," I say.

"Creator."

I almost falter. "*Andy Warhol*."

"Factory."

"*Agnes Martin*."

"Faded."

"*Kim Lord*."

"Missing," he says in an unreadable tone. The fake smile is on his face, but he is watching me.

"I'm sorry," I say, coughing, because I can't think of another word. I can't think of anything. I just want to bolt from here.

"You're not on the Rocque staff contact list, Sheilah," he says.

"I'm new there," I say.

There's a pause. His plastic smile warps into a pained leer. "Did Kim send you?" he says, a thickness in his voice.

"No," I say, astonished.

"Where is she?" His eyes bore into me, and he doesn't move, but his words are clogged with emotion. "Why don't you tell me before I call the police?"

I reach the door before him. I take the stairs just as the gallerina is coming up, bearing her cardboard tray with two coffees, and push past her, knocking her off-balance so that she cries out and the coffee splatters on the stairs. "Sorry," I shout, and make it to my car before I can breathe again.

He could have caught me easily. He could have even locked me in. But he didn't. I look back at the gallery. Steve Goetz is standing in his bank of glass windows, a silhouette, staring after my escape. He didn't stop me. He's not afraid of me. Or, rather, he's not afraid of being caught in his game. *I like games*, he said. I'd hate to find out what other games he is playing, but I don't think he knows where Kim Lord is. I think he was genuinely hoping I would tell him.

21

Piano music trickles over the sound of clinking glasses at Luster's Steakhouse. I hunch alone with a Manhattan at the dark and velvety bar, staring into the bovine carcasses in a huge glass cooler just beyond the dining area. Red meat, marbled with white fat, dangles from hooks. The torsos are motionless, but their skin-stripped shapes look so bare it almost appears as if they are slowly revolving, showing every side. Occasional fog patches cover the glass, blurring the carnage to a crimson haze.

My whole body is caked in sweat, and I have to keep pulling my blouse loose so it doesn't stick to my damp chest. Every time I do, the air-conditioned breeze touches my breasts and I shudder at the memory of CJF Gallery and how empty it was as I bolted away from Steve Goetz.

I've called Yegina three times already. No answer.

I leave her a message. "Hi, I left the office in a rush. I thought I was getting stomach flu, but I guess it was just a little food poisoning. Are we meeting at Luster's? That's where I'm heading now. Hope everything's okay."

It surprises me that she didn't answer. I have a bad feeling about her brother, but I can't check my e-mail without a computer.

Someone passes behind me, and Hendricks sits down, two stools away. He is wearing a faded black T-shirt with a spiky skull-propeller thing and the words CORROSION OF CONFORMITY on it. There's a new cast to his face now: it has gone from sleepy to sharp. He also seems inexplicably longer and taller, like an animal extending from its hole.

"You look surprised to see me," he says.

"I'm not sure this is where we're supposed to be."

I meant about meeting Yegina later, but Hendricks nods and glances into the meat cooler. "Me neither."

An awkward silence falls. Where do I begin?

"You called me because you were worried about someone," he says. "Who?"

"It's gotten more complicated than I thought," I say.

"Try me," he says.

I take a breath. I can't look at him. "Did Janis Rocque ever try to buy one of Kim Lord's paintings? I mean, a more recent one?"

Hendricks doesn't answer right away. I sneak a peek at him. His expression is a cross between curiosity and regret.

"Is that what you were investigating?" I say.

He jerks his head at the giant carcasses.

"Can we continue this somewhere outside?" he says.

We rise and leave the dim, dark air-conditioned interior for the cooling night, the surge of skyscrapers around us. Above each table, the heat lamps are on, their dull fires glowing. Beyond them, I catch sight of the line of red street-pole banners with Kim-as-Roseann-Quinn smiling down on us. Hendricks knew what I was going to ask. I feel triumphant but fearful. If I'm right about Steve Goetz, if Ray Hendricks knows, too, then why isn't the collector a suspect in Kim Lord's disappearance?

We sit down at a patio table, suddenly close and alone. Hendricks is older than I am, but not much older; he has the faint facial lines that you start to get in your thirties.

"Okay," he says. "Tell me again why you called me."

"I know about Steve Goetz," I say plainly. "I think you do, too."

He threads his fingers slowly together until his hands knot into a single fist.

"They exhumed Kim Lord's body this afternoon," he says slowly.

"Her corpse was discovered a few hours ago in the Angeles National Forest. Sniffed out by someone's dog."

I must be gaping, because it feels like my whole face is spilling open. My palm slides over my mouth.

"There was a significant blow to the skull," he says.

In my mind's eye, I see an anonymous female head, hair streaked with blood, and then my imagination fails and my shoulders start shaking.

Kim Lord is dead. Her unborn child as well.

I put my fingers over my eyes and try to press the image from them.

"Maggie," Hendricks says.

I feel him move nearer to me, and then pull back.

I breathe in hard to keep from crying. I don't want to cry in front of him.

"I wasn't sure how you'd take it," he says, almost to himself.

"What caused the blow?" I say. "Do they know? How many days was she there?"

"I only have the details I told you," he says. "I'm sorry."

"Are you? Why are you wasting your time with me?" I say, blinking back tears. "Don't you cops have better things to do now that you have a body?"

"I'm not a cop. I'm a private investigator," he says. "But you're right. Janis Rocque wanted to buy a painting by Kim Lord and she couldn't," he says. "And when a woman of her power and wealth can't get what she wants, she gets ticked. Ticked enough to pay someone a ridiculous sum to find out why."

His composure isn't contagious, but it helps. I raise my head.

"So you found out about the supercollector," I say.

"Weeks ago," he says.

"And when Kim disappeared . . ." I pause, struggling to suppress another wave of shock. "You wondered if he had collected her, too."

He nods. "Very briefly."

"But you don't anymore."

"No," Hendricks says. "Steve Goetz did not kill Kim Lord."

I may be distraught right now, but something in his delivery is off.

The inflection landed on the wrong words. Instead of saying "Steve Goetz did *not* kill Kim Lord," he said "Steve Goetz did not kill *Kim Lord*." As in, Steve Goetz killed someone else? Who? He looked entirely calm when he said it. Maybe it was just the southern accent.

"Who did—" I say.

Hendricks cuts me off. "But you recognize his connections with Bas Terrant and Nelson de Wilde, and you want to know more," he says. "I was curious how you figured that out." He sounds almost impressed.

"At the eleventh hour Kim Lord wanted to donate all the paintings in *Still Lives* to the Rocque, with the stipulation that they never be sold," I say. "It made me suspicious."

Hendricks looks stunned by the news.

At that moment, the waitress materializes. I order another Manhattan. Hendricks asks for grapefruit juice.

"Tell me again about this gift," Hendricks says when the waitress leaves.

"I proofed the press release on the night of the Gala," I say. "I thought it was fishy, especially when Bas didn't announce it. And then I started thinking about provenance, and then I looked up all the people who had collected Kim Lord's work. With our registrar's help. All the names appear to be fake."

Hendricks folds his arms and studies me again. With some effort, I keep my chin up and study him back, noting the nicks in the collar of his T-shirt. The waitress brings our drinks. Hendricks lifts his and drains it. I gulp at mine, the bourbon burning my tongue.

"What did you find out?" I ask.

"Finish your whole story first." Hendricks begins smashing the ice in his glass with his cocktail straw as I tell him about Steve Goetz's super-collector and artificial artist thesis, and about Bas's history at the Catesby auction house, the article where he spoke admiringly of collectors influencing an artist's success. I stop before I get to my journey to the CJF Gallery. Hendricks doesn't need to know that I took such a stupid risk. Downtown darkens around us, erasing Kim-as-Roseann-Quinn's face on every street pole nearby, leaving only her white smile hanging there and the white letters:

KIM LORD
STILL LIVES

Hendricks smashes more ice, then shakes the glass and slurps the juice and water.

"That's it," I say. "Your turn."

Hendricks sets his glass down. He's about to speak when my phone rings. It's Jayme. I hit decline.

"You have cops in your family?" says Hendricks.

"No. Mostly teachers."

"Uh-huh," says Hendricks, as though settling an argument with himself. Then he slumps over the table. "What I would do for one humid night here," he mutters.

"Why did you move to L.A.?"

He gives me a wary blue look. "Career change. Why did you?"

"Mostly wanderlust, I guess," I say. "Moving to the big city was the next thing on our list."

I hate that I sound so directionless.

"Your brother . . . ," I say.

The tremor in Hendricks's face shuts me down.

"I'm so sorry," I add. If I lost John or Mark, I would feel severed for the rest of my life.

"Tell me something," he says, pushing away his glass. "Look at that couple over there and tell me what you notice about them."

He gestures to a man and woman seated by the railings over the street.

I scrutinize them, puzzled. They both have corporate suits; both their faces are tense and unhappy. Otherwise, they couldn't be more different. He is tall and dark-haired, his shoulders rounded and sloped, and she is slight and fair, with a big bust, pale eyes, hair that needs lightening. He drinks wine; she drinks water. He wears a wedding ring. She does not.

I tell Hendricks all this.

"What do you think they're fighting about?" says Hendricks.

I blow out my breath. "I don't know. They had an affair and he wants to break it off because he's married and won't leave his wife."

"Could be," said Hendricks. "You see her left shoulder from here?"

I peer harder. "There's some crud on it, I guess."

"Spit-up," says Hendricks. "My guess: There's a baby. His baby? Hard to know, but judging by her profile and her choice of beverage and her dark roots, the baby's new. Judging by her expression, he might owe her child support, or be the lawyer for someone who does. The point is, I actually don't know, and you don't either. We only know what we see, and then we intuit." He slows down for this word, *intuit*. "But the interesting thing about intuition is how little it tells us about the external world, and how much it tells us about ourselves. You think he's dumping her. I think he owes her money for her child. Our theories reveal us." He settles back in his chair, past the ring of candlelight, and the next statement emerges from the dark silhouette of his head. "Your problem with that murdered girl in Vermont—you trusted intuition, not facts and logic. You didn't believe she'd betray herself."

It takes me a frozen moment to understand that he is talking about Nikki Bolio. He has been spying on me. Digging deep.

"The police never found the killer because it could have been anyone in that ring," Hendricks says. "She bragged about talking to Jay Eastman, one night when she was drunk. Everyone in town knew what she had done. But she didn't talk to Eastman, did she? She talked to you."

Nikki, by the lakeside, turns to me, her long, dopey face flashing with fear and eagerness. "I could show you the Ski-Doo map they use in winter to take heroin over the border, but I know I'll get caught," she said. *I know I'll get caught.* Was there a thrill in her voice when she said that?

"Why are you so curious about what happened to me years ago?" I say to him coldly. "It's none of your business."

To my surprise, he looks sheepish and squirms in his chair.

"You're right," he admits. "But something about you didn't add up. So I asked Shaw, and then I looked into it."

I push back from the table. Hendricks makes an abrupt movement with his arm, as if to grab me, detain me, and then, just as fast, his hand lands back down.

"Listen," he says, and falters, rowing back in his seat, sighing, looking off toward the skyscrapers around us. "I'll tell you what I know about Steve Goetz, but then will you please drop this?"

"For how long?"

Now Hendricks's phone buzzes and he glances at it. "I may have to go," he mutters, rising. Now that he's the one leaving, and I'm still full of questions, my curiosity surges like a wave.

"Okay," I say. "I promise."

"You won't talk about this with Shaw, or any of your colleagues, at least until we find the killer."

"I said I promise."

Hendricks gives me an appraising glance and then lowers his voice. "Steve Goetz didn't just underwrite *Still Lives*. He gave two million dollars to the Rocque in order to guarantee Kim Lord a high-profile spot on the exhibition schedule."

I knew it. "Driving up her prices," I say.

"And fattening the budget for his pal Bas Terrant," says Hendricks. "Not illegal, but certainly not in the tradition of the historic Rocque."

My phone rings again. Jayme. I hit decline again.

"So Kim must have figured the whole thing out. She must have felt betrayed at such career manipulation, and decided to donate *Still Lives*. And they freaked," I say. "Is that reason enough to kill her?" But even as I'm saying it, I know Steve Goetz didn't do it.

"Both Goetz and Terrant have solid alibis for all day Wednesday and Thursday," says Hendricks.

Of course they do. *I like games*, Goetz said. I wish I hadn't gone to the gallery now. I wish he hadn't seen my face.

"Goetz can't be prosecuted for what he did, can he?" I say, thinking of the shelves in his office, all the catalogs of women artists. "What if there are more victims than Kim?"

Hendricks hesitates before shaking his head. "Nothing to prosecute. Some might even see it as a career boost."

"But Bas could still be fired by the board if they learned of this."

"For what?" Hendricks says. "He got a huge donation to put on an exhibition by a rising star." He tosses down his napkin and moves to rise.

He's right, and I am being naïve, but their maneuvers still infuriate me.

"Something I don't get," I say. "If the supercollector never sells an artist's work, how does he earn his money back?"

"Steve Goetz is a patient man," says Hendricks. "Art investments usually take a couple of decades to pay off. Kim Lord's first show was fifteen years ago. What if he starts slowly selling the work at auction and through the gallerist, all the while paying privately for more media hype? He could quadruple his early investment, and"—he takes one last slug from his glass—"the supercollector becomes a powerful and influential figure in contemporary art. More original than Kim Lord herself."

"And she goes down as a fake, created by hype and back-door dealings," I say. "But she's a genius." I hear Brent's agonized cry on the night of the Gala, *It was all her. It was all her.*

My phone rings again. Jesus, Jayme will not give up. I hit decline for the third time.

"A genius because of this last show," says Hendricks. "I suspect that Goetz thought she'd be a flash in the pan."

"She burned up the pan," I say.

"She burned down the whole kitchen," Hendricks agrees.

For one unshuttered instant, across the table, our eyes meet and I see longing in his. For what Kim stood for? For me?

Hendricks abruptly stands. "Now you have your answers. Do we have a deal?"

"No leaks," I promise. "But who killed her?" I ask. "You must have a theory."

Hendricks wavers for a moment above me, the night sky inking his shirt, his hair. "It won't do you any good to know my theories," he says quietly. "And I think your boss wants to speak with you."

I turn to see Jayme frowning behind me, her arms folded.

Jayme starts her lecture with the same lacerating poise she maintains in her media previews, her voice cool as a blade. But the deeper she gets into recounting my behavior in the past seventy-two hours—skipping the annual report meeting, giving Juanita the impression that I was trying to steal something from her office, and now sitting at a restaurant when I'm supposed to be home sick—the more a moan of betrayal creeps in. How could I, of all people, do this to her? Jayme trusted me with her past last night, with the anguish she keeps buried, and almost as soon as she did, I started behaving like I want to distance myself from her as fast as possible. Like I want to be fired. I stare down at my empty drink. How do I ask her to forgive me? How can I tell her about Kim's death?

"I insist you take a leave for the rest of the week," concludes Jayme. She has not sat down or unfolded her arms. "Starting tomorrow. Okay?"

"Okay," I say. Silently, I practice saying it to her: *They found Kim's body.* I see Jayme's eyes go dull and her shoulders slump. Then I see her once again hoisting herself straight and tall, marshaling her strength to tell me I need a break, I need time, when whatever pain she is carrying has rooted so deep she can't pull it out for fear of destroying herself. *They found Kim with her head bashed in.* The words don't come because I don't want to be the one to utter them. I don't want them to be real.

"You need me to call you a cab?" asks Jayme.

"No." I get up carefully from the table and grab my keys. "Thanks for tracking me down. I'll be at home if you need me."

When I get to my car, I call Yegina again and get a curt text in return. *I'm home. Everything's fine, thank you for finally checking. I'll call you in the morning.*

It doesn't seem like her, but I'm so overwhelmed that I can't think about it as I inch my car along the freeway, careful not to weave.

Ray Hendricks's revelations are pinging around in my head. Should it ease my mind to know that Nikki squealed on herself, and that she never named me? It doesn't. It doesn't restore Nikki to life; she won't be snickering at herself for tripping in her snow boots, or fingering her delicate ears when she's searching for a word.

It doesn't make her un-murdered, either. From her family and friends, the real Nikki was stolen forever. The living girl has been erased, and in her place marches a death's-head, a warning. A panel in my memory slides open, and here comes the whole gory parade again, images I've seen, stories I've read: the little girl strangled in the basement, the stabbed woman, the bludgeoned woman, the woman severed in half, the woman who put her mouth around a loaded pistol, the woman bound at the wrists and ankles, dragged through icy black water. Nikki. Nikki comes at the end, flopping behind a dark boat. No. Not at the end. There is one more pale figure, straggling along, and she wears Kim's face. Then my face.

The freeway exit finally opens to the dense, honking slow-and-go of Hollywood. The traffic becomes nasty enough to keep me alert to it, every Lexus and Range Rover fighting for its slot. I'm grateful, because I want to stop thinking and feeling. I'd like to be as simple as the car I'm driving, as plain as the alley I turn down, as empty as the dark, narrow garage I slide into, just a slot in a row, with a broken door and a history no one knows. The car coughs as the engine stops, and I have to slink and twist to get out of the garage without touching the dusty chrome or the cobwebs on the garage wall. I emerge to the smell of my neighbor's wilting roses.

My bungalow is part of a 1920s courtyard with a dozen apartments. Our walls are peeling; our pipes run slow, but the old clay rooftops look pretty and everyone's got the same high ceilings. My neighbors include a retired Ice Capades star, a Hollywood makeup artist, an old man with a carefully preserved British accent, and some bearded twentysomethings with band aspirations.

I know everyone well enough to feel a protectiveness descend as soon as I stride down our walkway, but they're not real friends. Everyone here liked Greg for his gregariousness, and I think they got the impression I'd run him off until his face started appearing all over TV with headlines like "Gallery of Death?" Once my neighbors avoided me out of loyalty to him; this week they avoid me out of pity.

My bungalow looks dark and cold, the windows black. I always forget to leave lights on to fake the appearance of someone inside. It takes a while to dredge out my keys, even though I just tossed them in there, because my purse is so stuffed with the recorder, the flash drive, my phone. The rest of the courtyard notices this, I'm sure. And my tired, aching swaying as I search. *Where'd she stumble home from?* There the keys are, wrapped in the handle of the recorder. My keys, museum keys, gym locker key, even the stupid key to Greg's gallery, all on a ring. It amazes me how quickly things get lost. Or maybe not lost. Enmeshed. Tangled up so badly that you can't separate one thing from another.

The branches beyond my patio fence toss and heave. I jump. Drop the keys. Pick them up again. Avoid looking at the bush. I don't want to see the possum again.

Gold key in the heavy screen door, silver key in the inner door, even these small rituals of entry seem sadder and clumsier when you're entering a house where you live alone. All these months, and still I am not used to it. I push inside, hear my phone buzz with a text: *I really hope you'll get some rest.* Jayme.

I drop the phone back into my purse. Then I click on the living room light, illuminating my blank walls, my Fitzgerald biography lying closed on the coffee table. I go to my computer and turn it on, hoping to read Yegina's original message about Don. As the machine wheezes and grinds, taking forever to boot up, I see dust streaks on my arm. Stupid too-tight garage. I go to the bathroom to wash.

The faucet warms up slowly, so I run the cold over my skin. Soap, rinse. Night air gusts through the open window, giving me goose bumps.

I don't remember leaving the window open.

I do, however, recall leaving the Fitzgerald biography whacked down on the table in that spine-ruining way that my mother always told me not to do. I do remember feeling a twinge of guilt about it.

Someone was here.

Or is here.

Steve Goetz isn't Kim's killer. This means there is someone else. There has always been someone else. And that someone knows who I am, and might even know what I've been doing.

YOU'D BETTER WATCH OUT FOR MAGGIE. What if Greg was framed by the same person who sent him the note about me? And what if that person intended to implicate me next?

Untangled backward, the logic would be simple, believable: jealous Maggie kills Kim, then frames Greg.

Meanwhile, the real murderer gets away.

It wouldn't be hard to construct my guilt: just find a way to break into my not-very-secure bungalow and hide more objects from the crime. Then an anonymous tip. The police would follow the clues and recalibrate their case: Greg framed by Maggie, who did the actual deed. Jealous ex-lover. Again, this theory doesn't point to a stranger. It points to someone who knows us, who knows where we both live. Someone from our circle of acquaintances. Maybe even someone from the Rocque.

The bathroom doesn't lock. I wash my arm and hands again, noting with sudden acuteness my nail-bitten fingers. My ugly and vulnerable palms.

This is crazy. I must have moved the book myself and forgotten.

But I didn't. I left it upended, bending the pages.

The house throbs with quiet. My purse is by the door, with my keys and phone. If I run, I could grab it and be outside in less than a minute.

But what if a killer is standing right outside my door?

I could climb out the bathroom window, but he would hear me doing it, burst in. Besides, I want my car keys and my purse so that I can drive far away.

I could yell. I could yell out the names of everyone in the courtyard. How long would it take for them to recognize the cries and come running? How many people heard Kitty Genovese screaming? He could kill me before they arrived.

I turn off the faucet and stand there with my dripping hands. Then I wipe them on a rough red towel. I could just stand here and listen until I hear a noise; if I don't hear anything, then maybe he's gone. A long time passes after this decision, but it's probably just a few minutes.

Something creaks upstairs.

I throw open the bathroom, looking left and right, sprint to the kitchen. The kitchen is empty, my breakfast dishes messily stacked in the drain. I grab Theresa's knife from the counter and stagger into the living room, ascertaining that, yes, the biography is in a different place, and, yes—worse—my desk is different, too. The drawer where I keep staples and scissors is slightly ajar. But this room is also empty. A broom stands in the corner. I hold the knife high.

Five steps. I'm at the door. The living room light pulses. The back of my neck feels sunburned; even the motionless air in here chafes against it. I fling the knife into my purse, grab my keys, and bolt outside into the courtyard, slamming my doors behind me.

If my neighbors glance out their windows now, I am a shadow fleeing across the grass, head down, not stopping to breathe until I get in my car and lock it. I drive eight blocks away, making sure I am not followed before I park, dig in my purse for my phone.

Out comes the recorder, then my wallet, the knife, the flash drive, wrappers and receipts, a lipstick, a cinema ticket, until there's nothing inside but a few stray pennies, jingling when I shake the leather. I know I dropped the phone in here, so I search again, hands fumbling through my possessions. Then I prop the purse open in my lap and swipe the silky interior, in case a hole has developed in a seam, in case things have fallen through.

When I finally look up, the street is also empty, the cars parked, the houses locked and glassy. Nothing moves but the jacaranda trees, waving their dark, bugle-shaped buds at the evening. The trembling comes from so deep inside me, it makes my teeth knock together. Someone was there, in that room. Someone took my phone, the way he took Kim Lord's phone and sent messages to convince people that she was still alive. Why? I don't know how long I sit there, but it doesn't help. Neither does driving away, east.

Yegina lives in an Evergreen Queen in Silver Lake. She rents from the crazy old hippie who paints all his hilly East Side houses the same shade of deep pine and undercharges his tenants in exchange for underfixing things. Yegina's place has hardwood floors, a built-in washer-dryer, views east toward Hollywood, and free parking for her canary-yellow Mazda.

But the Mazda is not in her driveway as I race up her winding steps, so shaky on my feet that I trip three times on nothing and almost fall flat on my face. Where is Yegina's car? It's clear she's home; I can see the wooden inner door open behind the screen door. The threshold beckons: a portal to safety. Beside me, Yegina's terraced gardens of cacti have silhouetted to menhirs in the fading light. I gasp for breath, reaching the top, when a man speaks inside the house.

I recognize the voice but can't place it, not with this tearing in my chest. I'm about to ring Yegina's bell when I hear softer sounds, little smacking, breathy noises. Yegina is kissing someone. He says, "Wow," and now I recognize the depth and treble, though the voice is stripped of its usual heartiness. I peer through the gray scrim: Bas Terrant is sitting on the leather couch, and Yegina is sitting on him, her dark hair falling in his face. They are both still fully clothed, but his hands are probing under her shirt, his knuckles pushing out the cotton. I stare, paralyzed, watching the way Yegina arches and presses into him.

A black car drives slowly, slowly down the street below, the windshield shining. Didn't I see that car behind me on Sunset? I can't make out the driver.

Fear is like an itch all over my body. I must emit some sound, because just then Yegina looks up from Bas's lap and sees me. Her eyes narrow.

I take the stairs two at a time.

22

Greg's key fits into the deadbolt in the back entrance of his gallery. It turns easily. I always wondered if it would still work, or if he'd change the lock on me. More likely, Greg forgot that he ever gave me a copy. *In case you need it for any reason*, he'd declared with a magnanimous air. On many lonely nights that casual offer loomed in my mind, and I would come up with a thousand reasons to arrive at Greg's place. They all dissolved by morning. In case *you* need it. Translation: *You may need me. I assume you will.*

I hated the key, but I kept it. And now I want to search his apartment before it's too late.

Yet as soon as I push Greg's door in and shut it behind me, all willpower deserts me. I slide to the floor, hug my knees, and sit there a long time, unable to do anything but catch my breath. I can't think about the killer, or Yegina and Bas; I can't think about anything but staying safe. I'm safe here. No one will guess I'm at Greg's. After a while, my breath slows, but not the trembling. It's as if a two-by-four is slamming around deep inside me, the vibrations reverberating out. Even the veins in my wrist throb and twitch.

Beyond my knees, the dimensions of the rooms materialize, the white-painted walls of two galleries, artworks, a metal desk with a laptop on it. I stagger to my feet. A series of black ropes hangs from corner to corner; a TV monitor sits on a pedestal. Postcards dot the walls at intervals, odd messages on them, part of some conceptual project in which the artist did not stop walking around Rome until he collapsed. I stroll the galleries for a long time, examining every object, until the shaking ebbs.

There is a lone door at one end of the room. I open it and see plywood stairs down to a dark basement that smells of mildew. Somewhere down there, the police found a cloth with Kim Lord's blood on it. The killer must have sneaked into this space—how? Through this entrance or a separate opening below? The blackness of the space reaches for me. I'm too tired to meet it. I shut the door.

Another staircase rises behind the metal desk. I know where it goes. I know Kim and Greg must have taken these steps many times, and that in the silent room upstairs, their love bloomed, and a child was conceived.

By the time I get to those stairs, there is another Maggie in the gallery, moving with dragging steps. Her purse swings from her shoulder. She looks like me, but she is outside me and inside me at the same time. I am inside and outside, too, but we aren't combined. I don't stop her as she takes off her shoes, as she climbs, her bare feet whispering on the slats. When she reaches the small apartment above, the photograph of Greg's mother is the first thing she sees, propped on the nightstand. Young Theresa Ferguson, dark head cocked, in a long sheath dress. Young Theresa Ferguson leaning against old Parisian stone, hiding her hands.

The other Maggie stares at the picture and slowly unzips her skirt, pulls her blouse over her head, bends to drop her bra and panties. Then she walks naked to Greg's king bed and climbs into it. The sheets are freezing, but her prickling skin feels distant. She lets her head sink on one plump pillow and pulls the other to her, hugging it. Her body feels heavy and quiet now, and fully alone. The rest of the world is far away.

She lies there, staring at a blank wall until it wavers and vanishes.

When I wake, the room is dark and I have to grope around the bedside to find a lamp. The shade, made out of an old detergent bottle, casts a mellow orange glow. Scanty furniture unfurls along the walls. The whole apartment is one room, with a sink, an oven, and a fridge in one corner; a wardrobe and a mirror in another; the bed in a third; and a lime-colored sofa and a coffee table in the last. Low walls part the spaces. Three paintings on the wall follow a ball bouncing. Skylights in the ceiling reveal a cloudy, reddish night sky.

The room feels staged. Despite the carefully chosen decor, or perhaps because of it, the space has the air of a display. No messiness, no dust bunnies or stray hairs. Didn't they strew things like Greg and I did? I was always picking up his damp towels, wiping his coffee stains from the counters.

I sit up and look down at my naked breasts and thighs. And blush. My cheeks and face are soaked. I was crying in my sleep. What did I dream of? I don't feel any better, and I don't feel any more like myself, but I know I'm running out of time to search this place before one of Greg's assistants finds me here.

I wind the sheet around me and patrol the room, finding no possessions that look like Kim's. Greg's checkbook. Greg's socks, paired in his drawer. A curled rubber glove in the trash can, which makes me curious. Probably left by the police, who've been here already. The oven looks unused. The fridge holds a few apples, a brick of cheese, and a can of expensive lemon soda, which I crack and drink.

Theresa Ferguson watches me as she always has. Her photograph sat by Greg's bedside in our bungalow, too. Theresa is eighteen and wearing curled hair and a hat, a tube of a dress, and an expression of guarded triumph. Her hands are hidden behind her. Greg told me this was because they were burned and scarred; she was learning to be a glassblower.

I toss the soda can, go to the wardrobe and open it. Finally, some evidence of Kim's life: his side, her side. Greg's shirts and pants hang straight and pressed, like uniforms; Kim Lord's billow and sag, so many different sizes and shapes. Her items are fewer, but they dominate the closet, these ludicrous-now-tragic costumes that didn't protect her. The pale-pink Ann-Margaret dress; the high-waisted straight skirt and suit jacket straight from *Vertigo*. A navy trench coat. Two wigs, one coarse and black, one brown and curly. A few paint-spattered shirts and jeans. I check the pockets, all empty. She didn't own much. Or she didn't intend to stay long.

For several minutes I stare at the clothes, puzzling. I let my hand drag down the waist of the dress, squeezing its cool threads. Then I shut the wardrobe.

Greg's mother continues to watch me from across the room. The day she died, Theresa told Greg that although I was "thoroughly nice," I wasn't "worthy" of him. But it doesn't hurt anymore, her rejection of me. What hurts now is that there's a clue to Kim's death here, and I can't find it.

I yank open the wardrobe again and start with the Ann-Margaret dress, pulling it over my head, yanking when it strains. The black wig next, and then jeans barely reaching my thighs. None of this fits me. All of it constricts, even the wig, which pins my ears. Kim Lord was almost two sizes smaller than I am, and the woman in the mirror looks like an ogre who stumbled into the closet of a princess. I put on gloves from the bottom of the closet, slip my toes into her tiny shoes, then throw my purse over my shoulder and pirouette back and forth.

Who killed you? I ask my reflection. *Why did you die?* I say, pursing my lips, cocking my dark head. I run my hand over my flat, empty stomach, and sicken myself by imagining it full.

Finally I turn away and look back to see my own shoulder blades poking from the unzipped spine of the pale-pink dress. It's too tight to close. My skin and bones look smooth and winglike, but mostly they look exposed.

A narrator inside me begins to murmur: *See now? Feast your eyes. You're alive. You get to live. Leave this place. Leave L.A.*

I take everything off, get dressed in my own clothes, and put Kim Lord's neatly back except for the black wig, which I keep on my head. Then I take Theresa's knife from my purse. The blade's still sharp, though duller than it once was. The silver reflects pieces of the room around me, faintly and without depth or proportion. In Theresa's last months, when she was dying, she sometimes called our landline. Her voice would gravel and grind so deep, it sounded like a man was speaking through her. A collector of debts. *Why,* she said to me once. *Why am I still here.*

I slide her knife in the rack with Greg's other blades, and I leave.

Outside, the deadbolt locked again, I throw the key into the dumpster behind the next building.

Then, wearing my dark, limp crown, I drive around Echo Park, Silver Lake, downtown, Mid-Wilshire, until I find a parking garage I have never seen before. The city night dissolves behind me as I take the ticket and ease the car through the rising gate. I'm not tired, but I need to be safe. Anonymous. Anyone. Dark hair frames my face. I find the ramp, find a random spot on a random floor, cut the lights, lean my seat back, and stare up at my ceiling for a long time, listening to others arrive and depart. Listening to their door slams, their engines, and the silence. And the silence.

WEDNESDAY

23

arly today!" Fritz beams. It's 6:00 a.m., but he's crisp and exuberant in his navy security suit, his hair still showing the furrows of a comb. His tinted lenses are clear for once, and I can see him studying me.

"Yeah," I say sheepishly, not breaking stride. "I'm probably the first one here." I clutch my purse, hoping he won't notice I'm wearing the same clothes as yesterday, that I look like I spent much of the night cramped up in my locked car, sleepless, afraid to get out.

"Nope," says Fritz, and counts off on his fingers. "Fourth."

I pause, hoping one of them is not Jayme. I want to make a call first, and I want to take my Rocque work with me, to get it done while I'm away.

"Lynne Feldman was first." For a security guard, Fritz is a bit of a gossip. He and his wife are empty nesters now, and he gets lonely. "Then Juanita Filippa. Then Brent Patrick. But Brent is gone again already. Vacation, he says." He shakes his head. "Took a heap of stuff with him. Left his puppy in there for Dee." He gestures to the carpentry room. "Wonder about his wife."

I wonder, too. I wonder what Brent was drawing in his office yesterday, if his inevitable resignation is coming. I wonder what happened at Bootleg last night. It sure didn't look like Yegina was preparing to go on a date with Hiro or to meet up with her brother. Every time I think of the expression on her face when she spotted me outside her door, my stomach turns. So I'm not. Thinking, I mean. I'm just grabbing my work and calling Hendricks and telling him I'm leaving the city, but could he please case my apartment for me.

"You need some gigantic coffee," Fritz says, and thumps my shoulder.

I thank him and scurry away, past the various crates arriving and departing. I wonder if Evie's Rothkos are in the air somewhere over America now.

I stop by the mailroom, grab the stack of paper in my box, and rush for the door. Kevin's name jumps out from a typed manuscript with a yellow sticky on top: *Sorry, Maggie! Snaked this from your box by accident. —Dee.* Since her last name is Rager she gets her mail right above me. Dee, whose behavior keeps sticking out like a thorn on a branch. Home "sick" last Wednesday and Thursday. And now this. What is she up to? I can't puzzle it out.

Instead, I start to read Kevin's article, and almost finish by the time I reach my office. It covers the night of the Gala, and the party's slow realization of Kim Lord's absence. The writing is precise and stark, the atmosphere noirish. Shadows flicker, men scowl, and women glitter. If someone pulled out a pearl-handled pistol, I would not be surprised. Kevin introduces me as his PR rep, "a languid, saucy blonde" named Richter. Good ole Richter seems to perceive the dark undercurrent of the evening before everyone else. "Richter won't even accompany me into the final gallery. She hovers on the threshold, a fairgoer reluctant to enter a haunted house. When I look back, she is shading her eyes."

I throw open my office door and skim through the rest of the story before tossing it down. As the Gala night continues, I fade out and Kim Lord and her career take over, and then Kevin is back on the roof with the last few crew members. They linger like "desperadoes after a show-down, their hands in their pockets, faces studiously cool." Most admired Kim Lord. A few thought she was yesterday's news. They'd laughed at her Hollywood getups, but now they feel guilty about it, in a deadpan sort of way.

Say you're Kim Lord. Where are you now? Kevin asks them each in turn.

Baja.

Oh, come on, let her get to Oaxaca at least.

Marfa.

Antarctica.

Torrance.

Up in that window there (pointing toward a skyscraper), looking down on us.

Stuck in traffic.

Eloping to escape her suck-up of a boyfriend.

She's at LACMA. She got confused.

And then, as if they rehearsed it, the crew falls silent as the first limos start pulling up to bring the guests home. Satin-clad and coiffed attendees disappear into dim interiors. One by one, the party is vanishing, a party ruined by the absence of its guest of honor, but from up here, "close to the starless orange ceiling of Los Angeles," it still seems like it was a grand celebration.

Serves them right, says one of the crew finally. They all wanted a piece of her.

I'm going to go climb into my crappy Corolla now. Anyone want a ride home?

I'm too depressed to go home. Cole's?

The last limo pulls away. Valets start plucking up the orange cones. They pull their tips from their pockets, counting the bills.

The crew members start to mumble again.

Those guys probably made more money tonight than I made all week.

Yeah, but we made art history. Didn't we?

Before I gather my books and folders, I get online to let Kevin know I've read his article when I see the headline: "Ferguson Released." It jolts me so hard that I bite the inside of my cheek, making it throb and bleed.

The medical examiner has divulged little, except that Kim Lord died at some point on Friday morning, the morning after the Gala. That, with some other unnamed evidence, exonerates Greg. Greg has an alibi for Friday morning: he was meeting clients. Greg is in several media photos with his face averted; it looks misshapen to me, as if someone broke his jawbone and stapled it back together.

"Clearly there's been a miscarriage of justice here, but who's responsible? We don't know yet," says Cherie Rhys, also pictured, her brown hair pulled back, sleek and composed. "But we hope the LAPD finds out."

Death on Friday. It's hard to believe. Friday means whoever killed Kim knew we all were looking for her, and murdered her anyway, in cold blood. At midday on Friday, I was with Kevin staring at the Angelus Temple, plotting Kim Lord's implausible self-abduction, wondering if it was just a ploy for more publicity. On Friday afternoon, I was at Craft Club with Yegina, gossiping and dreading Kaye's horseback party.

Yegina's message from yesterday, the one I never clicked: *Don tried (ineptly thank god) to hang himself. I am on the way home right now. Will update you when I can.*

I scan the rest of my inbox, the words not sinking in.

Your phone's not picking up. Tour is changed to tomorrow, Weds!; meet downstairs at 11am, writes Dee.

Wow! writes Evie. *What did you find? Tried calling you back but just got VM. Do you want to come over after work?*

My head lowers itself to my desk, my eyelids prickling as if someone scattered sand under them. In my mind's eye, I see Yegina's brother, Don, mounting a bicycle for the first time, home on break from college. He was nineteen. He wanted to learn before he turned twenty. So Yegina and I took him to the broad bike path at Venice Beach. Don's head looked huge in his helmet, and his legs so skinny in their dark jeans. Ignoring the passing Rollerbladers and moms with strollers, he wobbled and fell and rose again, dozens of times. When he had finally gone the length of a block, Yegina and I whooped and hugged each other. "I made it," Don shouted back, triumphant, righting his crooked helmet.

I don't want to cry right now. It feels ridiculous to cry. I need to leave. I hold my skull for a while and then pick up my office phone. I dial my parents' number. It's one of the few I know by heart anymore.

The sequence of digits draws me back to my teenage years, standing at pay phones in parking lots, waiting for my mother to glide up in her blue station wagon, with its flurries of dog hair, the scent of her lavender soap. Before the phone rings, I hang up and dial another number.

Hendricks takes a while to answer. "Yes?"

Suddenly the words will not come. I'm holding the phone so hard my fingers hurt. A fan starts inside my computer, making a mechanical hum. I reach with my other hand and touch the cool dust on my windowsill, wiping it away. The street below is beginning to choke with morning traffic. I have to get out of here before Jayme arrives.

"Hello?"

My philodendron is drooping, the leaves dark and wilted. I rub the silk of one leaf; it rips.

"I just have to ask you a question," I say. "You really grew up in the mountains?"

"I did."

"You know those cold shadow places?" I say. "The canyons where the light never touches because the hills are too high?"

"Where are you?" Hendricks says.

"They're so dim you start shivering the moment you enter them— you know those places?"

He doesn't answer, but he isn't hanging up either.

"Whoever killed her reminds me—I have reason to believe—" I swallow, trying to summon my inner Cherie, calm and lawyerly. "I have reason to believe there was an intruder in my apartment last night." Without waiting for Hendricks's response, I tell him about receiving the handwritten note to Greg, then coming home last night, hearing the footsteps, and exiting swiftly. I tell him about my missing phone. I use clinical, distant words: *enter, object, situation, egress.*

Hendricks is quiet on the other end. I wait for him to dismiss the whole thing, tell me I am crazy, I am raving about mountain canyons. I can almost picture him, sleepy-eyed, watching my unraveling.

"Linville Gorge," he says. "I found a patch of snow there once in mid-July." Then he clears his throat. "You should have told me about the note."

I don't answer.

"Did someone follow you? Where did you go? Where are you now?" And then he's hammering question after question at me before I have a chance to answer.

I tell him I slept in my car and I'm safe in my office with the door locked.

"Steve Goetz called me right after you and I met yesterday," says Hendricks. "He wanted to inform me about a young blond woman who came to his gallery under false pretenses."

"Strange," I say. "I wonder who that was."

I hear a skeptical silence. "Is there anything else I should know?" Hendricks says.

I tell him about the flash drive Greg gave me. I explain that the photos are all studies for *Still Lives* and, as such, they are also artistic property. "The artist wanted them destroyed."

"They should be examined first. I'll get them to the right person on the squad," he says, sounding more relieved than anything. "They've got a big team on this now." He pauses. "And that's it? No more hidden evidence?"

I say no. "Did they find out anything else? About how she died?"

"There were other complications." There's a noise like a car door slamming. "And I have no clue what they are yet, so don't ask." An engine rumbles to life.

He asks me if there's a spare key to my apartment, and I explain about the one under the flowerpot. "If you find anything there, I mean, something that connects to Kim's death—you have to believe it's not mine."

"Who else knew about your spare key?" he says.

I tell him Greg did. "But I think the intruder went through the bathroom window. It was open."

Hendricks asks if this is the best number to reach me.

I realize it's the only number I have. "For now," I say, embarrassed.

I should tell him I'm planning to escape L.A. after rush hour. I have an old college friend in Tucson. I could drive there today, just as soon as I see Yegina first.

"Be good and careful," I say instead, and immediately feel silly. "That's what my grandmother always said when we went out the door."

Hendricks hesitates for a moment and hangs up.

I'm about to call Yegina when I spot Juanita mounting the stairs, slowly, her hand on the railing as if she's afraid to lose her balance. Already? It's not even eight o'clock. I shove my chair back and sink beneath my desk. It has a front panel that I can hide behind, with a cube of space big enough for me if I sit with my knees curled into my chest. I climb in.

Please, be patient with me, I tell Yegina in my mind. *I love you and I'm sorry.* My heart hurts for Don, for the whole family. My body is tired.

I must drift off because when my phone rings, my heart pounds so hard I feel my pulse in my ears. I wait for a second, then dart up and grab the receiver, pulling it by the cord down into my hiding place. "That was fast."

"You're there." Greg's words are raspy, as if he hasn't spoken aloud in a long time. He also sounds congested, like he's holding the phone very close. But more than anything he sounds painfully glad to hear my voice.

For a moment, I see Greg years ago, shooting up both hands to wave at me, a victory salute, as my bus glided into the station of his small Thai city.

"Are you home?" I say, rubbing my sleep-glued eyes.

"I'm at the house. I mean, your house. I was freaking out. I rang the bell a hundred times. Why are you at work so early?"

"Long story." I sit up and bump my head.

Greg has started talking again, his voice like a faucet that won't stop running. He says he doesn't know what to do and he can't sleep and he can't eat and the press is following him everywhere and he can't go back to his gallery because they'll be lurking, so Cherie let him come to her apartment and take a shower but then she kept fussing over him, and all he wanted to do was see me, so he slipped out when she went to get breakfast and took a taxi to Hollywood but I wasn't there. "When I couldn't reach you, I really freaked out, Maggie."

I don't even know where to begin, what to ask, what to answer. How to tell Greg how sorry I am and how over him I am at the same time. How exhausted and filthy I feel, and how the word *shower* fills me with longing. A hot soapy shower, with steam so thick it's hard to breathe.

"Someone stole my phone," I say.

Greg's flood resumes, as if he didn't hear. "I can't come to the Rocque because there are probably reporters there, too—"

I should wait here for Hendricks to call.

"I'll meet you," I say.

By the old, closed funicular railroad, Angels Flight, there's a small stretch of park above a row of bougainvillea bushes. It's usually littered with trash and bodies in various states of hunger and drunkenness and brain rot. I've never wanted to sit on that grass, though it looks warm and thick and the city must water it, but no one notices anyone in that park. I tell Greg to find me there in forty minutes.

I'm awake now, and I can hear the muffled voices of other employees coming in, and I wonder if I should just emerge instead of hiding. Instead, I hug my knees and tuck my chin, closing my eyes. I don't want to talk to anyone at the Rocque except Yegina, and she must be on the drive to work now. She never answers the phone when she drives.

Meanwhile Hendricks must be entering my empty house. Why hasn't he called yet?

Minutes pass. I call my cell phone several times, awkwardly pressing redial from my crouch beneath the desk. No answer.

I slide the receiver into its cradle and feel in my purse for the flash drive. I can't help wondering what the police will do with it. The woman in the photos, she could still be someone important—maybe I should look one last time. I slip out from my hiding place.

Too late. Jayme and Juanita are rounding the corner, Juanita pointing toward my office. They see me. Their looks of disbelief and displeasure throw me into a blind panic. I grab my papers, sling my purse over my shoulder, and bolt from my office, saying, "Just getting some work! To take home with me! I'll see you Monday!" and make a dash for the stairway without waiting to hear their response.

I take the stairs, two at a time, all the way down to the first floor and then the elevator to the loading dock. If Jayme is following me, I've got a good lead on her, long enough to sprint to the carpentry room, where I see Dee petting a large black dog with a wide head. Hold on a minute. It exactly resembles the dog on the flash drive. I slip through the doorway. Jayme won't think to find me here.

"Hey up, Maggie." Dee's face splits into a grin when she sees me. "I'm glad you came in. The Janis Rocque tour got changed to today, and I wasn't sure you could make it. Can you meet here at eleven?"

Black dog. Brent's puppy. Dee's sick days. Brent's sudden departure.

"Is that Brent's dog?"

"Dickson. Yup," Dee says. The dog noses her face. "He's a good boy. He's such a good boy," she croons. She sits with her legs splayed, elbows on her knees, loose and unconcerned.

"Where did Brent go?"

Now she tenses. She looks back at his office, then shrugs.

"Fritz said something—" I begin.

"He went on vacation." Her London accent sounds especially clipped.

"Brent Patrick goes on vacation?" I drift to his door and peer in at his photographs of New York, the striated underside of a bridge looming over a brick building with arched windows, sprays of graffiti. Then my eyes fall on another picture—small, angled away on his desk—and I step around to look at it.

There she is: younger, prettier, with blond 1980s hair poufed away from her face, her eyes dark with liner. Mouth painted pink. Brent Patrick's wife. The woman in the flash-drive photograph.

"What are you doing?" says Dee.

"I just love Brent's photography," I say, emerging, trying to sound cheery and calm. "I never get a chance to study it when he's in there. He's too intimidating."

"Truer words," says Dee. "He does go on vacation, though. And he doesn't want people to know where, and I think that's perfectly fine," she adds. "Not everyone has to be in everyone's business."

No, but not everyone seems like they're fleeing a murder case, either. Wherever my eyes fall now, the room looks sharpened, the saw and hammers, the nails, the pointy corners of the art crates. Only the eyes of the black dog are soft as he gazes at me and yawns.

"Good boy," Dee says again, and runs her hand slowly over his head.

"So, eleven?" She turns to me, and there's sorrow and determination in her narrow face.

"I'll try," I say, distracted by her expression. "Are you . . . okay? You seem a bit off."

Dee stops petting the dog and holds him around the neck.

"Dee?"

To my surprise, she gives a forlorn sigh. "I'm sure I will be fine," she mutters. "Now that my new girlfriend is no longer publicly ignoring me."

"Oh," I say. "I didn't know you were seeing someone."

"It's a new thing. Not quite common knowledge." Dee pulls Dickson closer and he sniffs her ear. "Especially not here."

An actress? An artist? A board member?

"Oh," I say. "I had no idea."

"That's the way she wants it." Dee's voice is grim. "And she always gets what she wants."

I pat her bony shoulder, my thoughts derailing like trains. Dee is sad. She is also protecting Brent, and Brent is running away. Strong, burly Brent. He would have enough strength to bash a woman's head in. But what would be Brent's motive? To end an affair with Kim Lord? Was she pregnant with *his* child? He has been so off-kilter lately. What if he did kill her, and was protecting himself by framing Greg? Or what if someone else was protecting him?

"Do you think Brent and Kim Lord were ever . . . ?" I ask.

"He admired her. She admired him," says Dee. Her tone is noncommittal. "They wanted to collaborate on a show sometime. But sex? I don't think so." Her eyes narrow. "Is he your latest suspect? There's no way. No freaking way."

There's always a way. Greg may know. Greg may be the key.

"Of course not. I've got to go," I say, retreating. "Jayme will kill me if she finds me here."

Dee looks up from stroking the dog. "Call me if you change your mind about the tour," she says. "It'll be worth it, believe me."

24

Long, damp grass grabs my feet as I search the park, trying not to let my eyes alight for long on anyone on this green beside the defunct, pink-gated tracks. Back when Bunker Hill was filled with rat-infested Queen Annes instead of skyscrapers and hotels, Angels Flight ferried people up the hill from their shopping trips at Grand Central Market and its neighboring stores, but the city leaders shut it down when they paved over the slums. The railway reopened in the 1990s, then closed after a runaway car killed someone. Since then Angels Flight has resumed its air of a dusty ruin, someone's small, lost vision of human enterprise among so many surging, anonymous towers.

Greg's not in the park, not unless jail has transformed him into the pale young addict with matted hair and a sooty coat, one shoe falling off, another gone entirely, his blackened toes flattened and splayed like fingers. Nearby a middle-aged, brown-skinned gent is lying on a bench, trembling and sleeping, but I recognize his disintegrating blue binder and baseball cap. By noon he'll become a friendly "lost UCLA student" who "just needs the bus fare to get back to campus." No one believes him, but his ruse is so absurd that most people pay him to go away.

And he's one of the easier ones to look at on this steep green, where the hill spills down toward Skid Row. I catch sight of a hump under blankets, shifting and sliding, close to the bushes. Four feet, two heads.

There's a pressure on my shoulder. I jump and yelp.

A familiar voice says my name. I am turning to look now, and my first impression of Greg is of the weird radiance in his eyes, the look people get when they stare into an aquarium. He's here. It's him. My body doesn't know whether to recoil or throw itself against him, but he's already reaching for me. The moment we collide, it's worse. Greg is putting his arms around my back, but there are too many of them, stringy and tight, and his mouth feels like it's suctioning my hair. Is he kissing me? I freeze, letting it happen, but my insides knot. New heat bakes the backs of my bare legs. The Los Angeles sun is climbing the sky.

Greg murmurs into my scalp something about being sorry and forever, and I let him, because awful as this is, I know it will be harder to look him in the face. Finally he releases me and we just stand there, my eyes on his scuffed blue shoes.

I don't know what I imagined this reunion to be like, but it wasn't this awful squeeze and then me, taking a big step back, digging in my purse and holding up the flash drive. "She was taking pictures of Brent Patrick's wife," I say, finally meeting Greg's eyes. "Do you know why? We need to give this to the police."

"Brent Patrick's *wife*?" Greg staggers sideways, as if seeing the flash drive has knocked him off-balance.

We're attracting attention now, no doubt because I mentioned the police. A blanket hatches and a woman sits up, eying us warily, her blond hair hanging in her face. She could be our age or she could be forty-five. Others are stirring.

"Let's get you something to eat," I say, tucking the drive back in my purse and steering Greg toward the stairs.

He follows without protest, still unsteady on his feet. He totters and grips the rail as we take the long flights down to Grand Central Market, a block-length edifice broken by columns and porticos. The dark caverns inside are crowded with food stalls and merchandise, lit overhead by neon signs. Outside, I spy a few empty tables at a small, dirty patio. They border the counter of Tropical Time, Yegina's favorite establishment, a long silver wall with black spouts and colorful placards advertising dozens of juices: papaya, boysenberry, apple, mango, cherry, coconut. All can be ordered separately or combined. I have stood beside Yegina many times, simultaneously overwhelmed by Tropical Time's lavish offerings and doubting that any of it can be true. "You thirsty?" I say to Greg, because I have already switched into mothering mode.

He is still descending carefully, frowning and shaking his head, as if trying to loosen a memory. "How did you find out it was his wife?" he asks me.

Egg sandwiches and juices procured, we find a perch at a patio table so caked with street grit that we have to hold our breakfast above it, hovering like we might bolt. Our conversation is jumpy and disordered, too, interrupted by trucks rumbling by. First topic: Brent Patrick's wife's appearance on the flash drive. Greg blanches as I explain that I spotted her photo on Brent's desk, that she has been in an institution for months for her illness.

"Jesus," he says. "Why didn't Kim say? She could have told me that's why she was meeting him."

"Brent's just disappeared," I say. "He went on 'vacation.'"

"Jesus," Greg says again. A pigeon flutters heavily down for a half-eaten piece of pizza near us, its iridescent body lunging. "And they still haven't gone after him?"

I lose my appetite as Greg starts harping on the investigation and all the new information that makes no sense to him. The medical examination added several new wrinkles to the case: Not only did the body's state of decomposition shift the time of death to Friday, but it appeared that Kim had struggled in some confined space—some kind of wooden box—for hours or perhaps days before she perished. Splinters of wood were found beneath her bloody, cracked fingernails. And preliminary toxicology on a couple of tiny wounds in her waist suggested that her murderer had injected her with a tranquilizer.

I set my sandwich down on the dirty table and drop my napkin over it. "What kind of tranquilizer?

"Too early to know. They had a huge list, but it's not like I recognized any of them. Amberbarbital sodium. Nembutal. Sodium therpenal. Pentobarbituate something." He drops his own sandwich on top of mine.

"Those don't all sound like drug names."

Greg shakes his head. "I had a hard time listening to Cherie," he confesses, and then tells me how unnerving it was to be riding in her car, outside in the open air, to see sunlight and billboards and molting palm trees, all while hearing the grisly facts of Kim's examination. "My mind kept blinking in and out. Finally I just told her to stop." Now he hunches over our pile of uneaten food. "How could someone . . . hate her so much?" he mumbles, and then his whole body starts quaking with silent sobs.

I don't comfort him. I let the gap of air between us stay open. In the mounting heat of the day, I feel a cool energy thread through me. Anyone watching would think I am delivering bad news or breaking up with the man weeping beside me. Anyone watching would pity him, and wonder at the young woman sitting immobile nearby, shadows under both of their eyes.

But I'm not actually here. I'm not seeing Greg's pain. My mind is traveling too fast over all the facts. A blow to the head. A tranquilizer. A coffin. So many stages to kill her. Not an expert, then. Or maybe someone who couldn't kill her all at once. My concentration separates me from Greg, from everything around me: the grind and dust of traffic; the ugly, insistent birds; the eggy smell of the barely touched sandwiches. I have to know who did this. I've spent too much time on the *what*. I recall Jay Eastman's words again: *Never look for the what. Find the who. Who gets hurt. Who gains. Whose life will never be the same.*

"I'm sorry," I say finally. "About the baby, too."

Greg's head whips up. His face flashes with surprise, then fresh grief.

"What happened with you two on Tuesday?" I press him. "Were you fighting about Brent Patrick?"

Greg looks toward one of the stunted trees beside us, also grayed with soot. Without meeting my eyes, he tells me that on Tuesday Kim flipped out after her positive pregnancy test and wanted time to herself. "I thought she meant time with him."

"You thought they were having an affair?"

"I didn't know," he says. "She insisted she was working on a show idea with him. About mentally ill women. It fits that she'd take a picture of his wife."

It does fit. It also fits that Kim was ultra-private about her artistic process, but that she wasn't sleeping with Brent. So what is Brent running away from? There's a missing piece to this equation, some variable I haven't figured out. Greg. Kim. Brent. Barbara. Four players. One possessive, one secretive, one aggressive, one utterly vulnerable. They could add up to a murder, but I am not seeing a clear chain of events. Unless Greg himself was the killer. Which I don't think is possible. Although he sure made himself look guilty.

"When you thought Kim was breaking up with you," I say, "you texted her seventy times?" I can't help the ring of anger in my voice.

Greg looks ill but doesn't answer.

Why was Kim working on her next show when *Still Lives* hadn't even opened? Because she was scared of going broke? Maybe Greg was right to be suspicious. But not to stalk her.

"I could have suspected you," he says accusingly, shading his eyes. "That note. *You'd better watch out for Maggie.*"

The statement hits me like a blow. "Yeah. Not to mention my expertise with coffins and sodium therpenal," I say.

As I utter the words, I feel something unlatch in my mind, not an answer, just a flash of warning to pay attention to what I'm saying. Coffins. Or maybe not coffins. And not therpenal. Thiopental. Black text on a white background. I've seen it before.

I ask Greg if I can borrow his phone. He pushes it across the table. I take Hendricks's card from my purse and call him.

"Maggie," Hendricks says. "Where are you?"

I tell him.

"Good. Stay with him. I'm almost to your apartment."

"In the medical examiner's report," I ask, "was one of the drugs sodium thiopental?" I know I've seen this name, and I've seen it at the Rocque.

Greg's hand slides from his eyes.

"He told you about the medical examiner's report?" says Hendricks.

I turn away from Greg. "The names of the tranquilizers," I say. "Do you know what they were?"

"Who are you talking to?" Greg says, grabbing for my arm. Sweat and tears have soaked his forehead and temples.

"What else did Shaw tell you?" Hendricks's voice demands.

I leap up from the table, out of reach. "I've seen sodium thiopental on something. I can picture it in my mind, like I copyedited it."

"That's just one of many possibilities. The full report won't be back for weeks," Hendricks says. "But just stay put, okay?"

Greg's voice is rising, but I can't focus on him. As I end the call, I'm still seeing the words. *Sodium thiopental.* The second word doesn't look correctly spelled, so my mind stutters over it every time.

"I don't understand you," Greg is saying. "This horrible thing happens to me and you're the first person I try to see, and you call somebody else to talk about brands of tranquilizers? Do my feelings not even matter to you?"

"I'm really sorry," I say, and hand the phone back to Greg. "But I have to go."

Although the words don't sound like mine, although part of me cannot believe how cold I'm being, I leave him and walk down Broadway, into the rising heat.

"Go where?" he shouts after me.

I walk faster. Greg doesn't follow, but I don't feel like I've really left him until I turn a corner and pass a whole block of grimy buildings, with their ancient arches and crates of cheap plastic sunglasses, piñatas, hats, and socks. Even then I can still feel the print of this morning's embrace on my sweat-stained shirt, and the kiss Greg left in my hair. Inside the shell of my body, however, the rest of me is finally retreating, condensing into a hard core, untouchable. I feel sad for myself, and for Greg, that I held on to the dream of us so long. Maybe if he had felt freer, he wouldn't have gotten so upset over Kim's flight from him. Maybe she would have gone home to him last Tuesday instead of vanishing forever.

A child's laugh tumbles from an upstairs window. I hear a radio tuned to country music.

Sodium thiopental. It hovers big and dark, on an empty field, like a title. A caption.

Find the who. Who gets hurt. Who gains. Whose life will never be the same.

As I turn back to Bunker Hill and climb the stairs to the Rocque, a curtain rises in my mind. The shadows of characters start to gather. The characters are vivid and real, but they're far away; I don't hear their words. All I see is silhouettes moving across a stage, talking, fighting, and embracing in silence. There are two of them. Then four. Then five. The actors have grotesque proportions: hulking shoulders, hands like talons, serpentine necks, as if their human natures are slowly being exchanged with savage animals, and they are battling this, too. In fact, they are battling their own savagery more than each other.

My thighs ache with the ascent. Sweat starts trickling down my forehead and spine. Ten steps from the top, I stop and look back down at Grand Central Market, the dusty table where I sat with Greg. He's gone. It's occupied now by another couple, young and brown, sitting so close they would barely have to lean to kiss.

I have trampled on a grieving man's heart, my best friend hates me, I may lose my job, my apartment is unsafe, a killer may be stalking me. And what am I doing? I am standing still again, frozen, and looking back.

I scan the sidewalk for Greg anyway, and the market entrance, peering into the gloom of food stalls where I wandered, aimless, the day after Brent Patrick put us all to death in *Executed.* But Greg has really vanished this time, and I have the feeling I will never search a crowd for him again. An old blue Mercedes glides across my vision, low as a boat, anonymous, hinting of days of forgotten glamour. I surge up the last steps to the plaza, into its brightness and fountains, suddenly thirsty again, wishing I had kept my cup. And then I remember where I saw the words *sodium thiopental.*

Jason Rains worked hard to obtain real execution drugs for *Executed.* A compounding pharmacy provided him sodium thiopental on the condition that, when the exhibition was over, the museum registrar would dispose of it at a hazardous waste site.

Who would ever know if Evie kept the syringes instead? Everyone trusted her to do her job.

Four players: Greg, Kim, Brent, Barbara. Enter Evie. A fifth figure set in motion by the other four. One possessive, one secretive, one aggressive, one utterly vulnerable. And one driven by her obsession to the threshold of murder.

Evie monitored the comings and goings of the art crates, too. Rothkos and Pollocks to the airport. Permanent-collection works to off-site storage. All of them in the same big pine boxes, stuck with labels. Who would ever guess if she shipped something else—a human being—inside? Everyone trusted her to do her job.

Everyone trusted Evie. Diligent, private, always-working-late Evie, down in her basement office. Theater-buff Evie, who was dazzled by Brent's genius. They all were dazzled by him downstairs. But Evie, who idealized fame and competed for everything, would want to be the one who got Brent. Secretly or openly. Nothing would mean more to her than possessing a star. Until Kim Lord came along and threatened to steal him away.

The last time I saw Kim Lord, she was hurrying down the street, and she jumped like something bit her, and then she kept running. The image stuck in my mind because Kim Lord wasn't the jumpy type. The image stuck in my mind because the woman hurrying wasn't Kim Lord.

But everyone, including me, trusted that she was.

25

Before I round the corner to the loading dock, I stop to catch my breath. Against a spray-painted concrete wall, I smooth my rumpled skirt and pull my damp hair back from my neck. I run my tongue over my fuzzy teeth and spit. By night, a few people crawl down to this underpass to sleep, but by day the asphalt is empty except for guardrails, dumpsters, and the steady rumble of traffic overhead. It's hard to believe that the Gala happened here only a week ago, but it did, flooding this grime with its lights and diamonds and spotless tablecloths. That night was a beginning for the rest of us, but for Kim—for Evie—it was an ending.

Once at the lake near my childhood home, I cut my foot badly on a beach shell. I've forgotten the pain, but I remember the feeling of the shell slicing into my foot. That awful, eerie feeling of my skin being entered and opened—it's stuck with me all these years. The truth—or what I think is the truth—feels like that now. A gash. Impossible to believe.

Memories whir through my mind. I see Evie in her first weeks at the museum, shrugging when I asked where she was from.

"All over California. My mom moved us around a lot, depending on the guy." And then later, telling me about her stepfather Al, declaring his love to her. "He was sure I would run away with him." But Evie didn't. She ran away alone. Something about that story always seemed off to me: the way Evie cast herself as both the victim and the romantic lead.

I see Brent at the Jason Rains opening, and Evie plucking a champagne bottle from his hands. She drank a sip, then threw it away almost full. I remember the heavy clunk it made in the trash. I remember thinking she was protecting a colleague from embarrassing himself, but now the gesture seems so proprietary. Almost wifely.

I see the crew's rooftop party on the night of the Gala. I see Evie watching Brent ranting to the sky about how Kim was the best artist he'd ever seen. The crew looked mostly surprised and alarmed to see Brent's outburst. Only Evie looked betrayed.

"I wonder how long it took her to die," Evie said when she handed me back the *Still Lives* photographs of Judy Ann Dull, bound and gagged in the Melrose apartment. That day I'd chalked Evie's question up to a certain professional detachment—museum registrars are always interested in the effects of time—but when I said, "Not long, I hope," she looked at me curiously, as if she didn't understand what I meant.

Evie, who was strong. Evie at the gym, pedaling faster than anyone.

Evie, who lived alone and had no close friends.

Evie, who'd reminded me so much of Nikki Bolio when we'd first met, with her self-conscious air and the yearnings she so thinly hid to live a bigger, more interesting life.

Evie would have hated Brent's closeness with Kim Lord: Kim photographing his wife, Kim changing clothes in his office. Their secrecy might have driven Evie mad with jealousy. And yet—mad enough to murder? I still don't get the motive, quite. It's the facts that point to Evie. She had access to all the means of the act: the saws to cover the noise, the hammer or mallet to strike the blow, the sodium thiopental, the crate. She had the same body size as Kim Lord, to wear her clothes and hurry away from the museum. She possessed the insider knowledge to text Greg and Lynne, to make them think the artist was still alive. She knew about Greg and me. It wouldn't be hard to frame us, one at a time. Which means she'd have to hate me, too.

If this is the truth, I want to be wrong this time. And I am probably too late anyway. Just in case, I hitch my purse higher on my shoulder and slip a hand in to find my recorder, the first button on the right. Press it down.

I recite a line from Daisy in *Gatsby*, rewind the tape, and play it back. A voice emerges, tinny and not my own.

Beautiful little fool.

"You coming on the grand adventure after all?" Dee says. She's leaning on a big crate with Yegina in the loading dock. She looks jittery, and she's freshened her face with uncharacteristic lipstick and blush.

Lipstick and blush. Wait. Her girlfriend works for Janis Rocque?

I look to Yegina for some confirmation, but she folds her arms and stares at her feet. A frilly sleeveless shirt hugs her tight around the neck.

"How's Don?" I say cautiously. Yegina is so private, I don't know if she's told Dee anything.

"He's doing fine," Yegina says with a meaningful emphasis. "I thought you were out sick."

"Officially I am. But I wanted to see you." I try to keep my voice steady. "Where's Evie?"

"Getting her car," says Dee. "She's probably going to have to drop us off."

"Why?" Fear slices through me. I feel Yegina's eyes flick to my face.

Dee shrugs. "She has to fly to Amsterdam tonight."

I'll bet she does. And I bet she's not coming back.

The sight of the crates sickens me. Blond plywood boxes, the small ones stacked on the wall twenty feet high, the big ones the size of doghouses and garden sheds, parked alone on dollies. All bear their stenciled arrows and warnings. The crates have always reminded me of giant birthday presents, each one full of mystery and splendor, carrying paintings from a Venice studio, or sculptures from a museum in Queens—or objects with a luxury provenance, shipped from a famous actress's second home, or taken down from a wall in a castle in Italy, where they were owned by a real count. But now the boxes look like instruments of torture, and their wooden scent tastes false in my mouth, like air freshener covering the smell of rot.

Yegina is still staring at her feet. I need her. She'll never believe me.

"I'm really sorry. I lost my phone," I say again, hoping Yegina is in a forgiving mood.

She sniffs. In the half-light of the open loading-dock door, she appears aged, an older sister to the self that she's always been. Her hair is darker and heavier, her mouth harder. Her arms are crossed so tightly, her fingers are pressing circles into her biceps. With a chill, I remember the straps tightening on my arms in the lethal injection chair in *Executed*, the capped syringes nearby loaded with the drugs that might have helped to kill Kim Lord.

"How long ago did Evie leave?" I ask, impatient.

"Just a minute ago." Dee looks at her watch. "Don't worry. We should be right on time. Janis might even show us around personally."

The possessive way she says *Janis*, the lipstick and blush—Yegina darts another glance at me and I finally meet her gaze (old habit, this way we have of registering news together)—J. Ro and Dee: a *couple*? Normally we'd fight back delighted grins, but this time Yegina's gray-brown eyes wince and she knits her lips. *I'm sorry about Don*, I want to shout at her. *And I don't care what you did with Bas.*

Instead, I chat politely with Dee about the sculptures we're going to see, a Richard Serra and a Mark di Suvero, some arte povera pieces from Italy, and a giant lifelike horse made of driftwood that's actually brass.

"And there's a real surprise for you," Dee adds, jutting her chin at me. "Or maybe it's not surprising. With Janis's tastes being so eclectic, it's possible she owns something by every contemporary artist who's ever been worth collecting."

The supercollector. My old suspect. I've been wrong before. I need more proof now. Was the scene of the crime Brent's office? If it was, it looks clean; besides, I'm no forensics team. I excuse myself to use the restroom and sneak into Evie's dark alcove instead.

I flip a switch. White light stains the walls and shelves. Evie hasn't left an item out of place—huge blue binders lined up straight, pens standing erect in a cup, keyboard and mouse at exact angles to the computer—and yet there's nothing here to soften all the hard lines. No photographs or stained mugs. She makes Juanita look like a slob. And human. Still, a murderer? Shy, quiet Evie?

Flipping through neat files of yellow carbon invoices, I find three outgoing deliveries last Wednesday, two to the airport and one to our off-site collection facility. Maybe I am staring at the ticket for the crate that held Kim Lord's body, but why would a killer keep a record?

Evie is cleverer than that. She wouldn't send the crate to the facility the Rocque usually used. What about that second one in Van Nuys that she was checking out?

I peek out the doorway, spot Dee and Yegina still waiting by the crates, and flip through another binder. There's a delivery of a sculpture a few weeks ago in the *D*s: Diamond Storage, Van Nuys, California. She had already set up a contract with them. I grab Evie's black office phone and dial.

When the receptionist picks up, I introduce myself as Evie. "I was calling to inquire about an item we had delivered last Wednesday," I say. "I'm sorry, but I lost the tracking number and we actually need to bring it back to the museum for restoration."

"Please hold," the receptionist says in an annoyed tone. I pull the phone as far as I can to check on Evie's arrival. Yegina is tapping her foot. She glances back and I duck out of sight. How much time do I have? I open another line on the phone and dig in my bag for Hendricks's card. And dig. Past the recorder, the wallet, the receipts, the lipstick. The card is gone. I must have dropped it at Grand Central Market. I have no way to reach him.

The storage facility line starts playing Vivaldi. I put the soaring strings on speaker and search Evie's windowless office.

The computer is locked. I open drawers, find nothing but paper clips. On a low shelf behind the desk, all art catalogs—except one textbook, in worn dark-green cloth, *Introduction to Drama and Stage*. I open it, shake it. Nothing falls out. But inscribed on the first page, right-hand corner, is a name in girlish handwriting. Evie Long.

I'm sliding it back when I see a familiar shape, hidden behind the volumes. I pull it out, flip it open. The screen and keypad are dead. The SIM card is gone, but all the scratches and dents are mine. My cell.

The Vivaldi stops.

"We had an escorted delivery from the Rocque on Wednesday, but your staff member rerouted it almost as soon as it arrived," the receptionist says. "We're working out the charge."

Someone grabs my elbow and I nearly jump out of my skin.

"Evie's waiting," Yegina says, and stalks away before I have a chance to respond.

I apologize to the receptionist, hang up, throw my phone in my purse, and run after my friend. A beige sedan has pulled up, Evie silhouetted inside. We hurry toward her through the canyon of crates, Dee first. Watching Evie's profile, I can suddenly picture it: the cold, focused look she must have had when she killed Kim Lord. I picture Brent's tiny office, Kim Lord changing clothes in front of his desk, by the door. Evie must have opened the door fast, brought the mallet down. One blow. One blow only? What about the blood? She could have shut and locked the door, cleaned it up. Changed clothes.

Shock tastes like soap on my tongue. I still don't have physical proof. I should get Hendricks's number from Yegina, go back upstairs, involve him and the police. Instead, I'm still walking through the loading dock to Evie's car. If I don't get into it now, she will escape. She will board the plane to Amsterdam tonight, never to be seen again. I'm sure of it. Yet as I pass beyond the massive doors, the day's heat rolls over me and I halt, afraid.

Dee opens the passenger side, hops in. Yegina bumps against my arm, brushing past, to take one of the back seats. I usually think of Yegina as solid as granite—but not today. No one is safe today. That high white shirt. Her neck appears encased in bandages.

Evie glances over her shoulder when I get in. Her face is a smooth, pale bowl. "Maggie," she says, raising her sculpted eyebrows. "I didn't know you were here today."

Evie can't stay for the entire tour. She had to reschedule the whole Judd shipment last night because the Amsterdam museum is freaking out about timing. She's so sorry. Really. This was going to be the highlight of her week. Her month.

"Well, except that it's such a sad day," she says, with a glance back at me. "It's terrible news. I mean, not about Shaw, but about . . ." She trails off.

"It's terrible all around," I say. "Somebody obviously tried to frame him."

If Evie is guilty of the crime, I can't believe the smoothness of her delivery, the loose grip of her hands on the wheel. I can't believe the warm light in her eyes when she showed me the provenance of Kim's work. She must have been thrilled to set me on the wrong investigation. She must have taken me for such an idiot.

Yegina sighs. "Let's just talk about anything but Kim Lord."

We are on the 101, merging into a steady four-lane stream that will take us to Hollywood. I sit in the back seat, behind Dee riding shotgun. Dee is bent forward, fiddling with the radio. Yegina has scuttled as far away from me as possible, and stares east into the receding downtown skyline. The air conditioner threads a cold wind through the car, but the windows and doors radiate heat. I still don't believe it. Did Evie intend to kill me, too, in my apartment, when I blundered in, home early from my supposed night at Bootleg? Instead, she took my phone and let me go. Because I'm her friend? I doubt it. She must need me alive, to take the blame. Now that Greg is in the clear, she needs someone else to frame.

If Evie's act of murder and cover-up was so meticulous, I can't imagine the flawlessness of her getaway today. I have to delay her as long as possible, and meanwhile get a message to Hendricks. But how can I make her stay with us?

I mull over various scenarios. Direct confrontation. No, then she might just bolt. Dark hints. Only if she's not entirely sure of my intentions.

"Evie, I was hoping I could interview you for the next members' magazine," I say to the back of her head.

There's an awkward silence.

"The theme for the issue is behind-the-scenes," I say.

"Oh. I don't think anyone will be interested. In me," Evie says slowly, as if it's difficult to enunciate each word.

"Of course they will," I say. "People love to know about the art, the crates, how everything comes and goes." I pause. "Dee—you build the crates. Do you always build them for specific works?"

"Mostly," says Dee. "Sometimes I make extras so Brent can give me the hours." She gives a little laugh. "We say it's the Rocque's other permanent collection."

We are nearing the Hollywood exit now, a gray concrete wall beneath a small burst of trees. Bougainvilleas bloom in magenta profusion, as if they know they're running out of time. The spring rains have greened everything in L.A., but by midsummer every flourishing spot like this will fade and wither beneath a glaze of smog.

"I promise I won't print that," I tell Dee. "Say, did anyone ever play a prank with the spare crates? I bet you could smuggle some funny stuff in there."

"There was a keg for the Chris Branson performance," says Dee.

I force a chuckle. "It seems like you could fit an actual person in there."

"Not much air for a person, unfortunately," Dee says.

Evie turns sharply onto the exit, throwing Yegina against me. As our bodies collide, I smell my own rank odor and cringe. "Sorry," I say in an abject tone. Yegina's frown softens.

"Do you think Janis secretly hates us all?" she asks Dee. "For not keeping her father's museum afloat?"

Dee snorts. "What do you mean 'secretly'?" Then she glances back, unsmiling. "Nah. She hates that she can't figure out a way to keep his vision alive either."

"Maybe we have to change the vision," Yegina says. "Insider cachet isn't enough anymore. We need tourists."

As interested as I am in speculation about the Rocque's future—and Yegina's sudden eagerness to alter it, her words sounding more like Bas's than her own—I hunker in my seat while they talk, thinking about my next move. Storefronts on Hollywood Boulevard sail by: stiletto boots for drag queens, a few decrepit bars, pawn shops, taquerias.

We pass the golden dragon and superheroes of Grauman's Chinese Theatre, and we're through the big commercial district and into neighborhoods again. Then we're coasting onto Sunset Boulevard, below the hills. Janis Rocque lives on a Bel Air road that meanders through mansion estates, all gated, all so far back from the street they are only a dream of habitation. Luxury pools, terraced patios, a private bath for every bedroom. From these massive palaces, you can see the whole city, but they are invisible to everyone but their own neighbors. Or so I was told once by Greg, who'd loved visiting them on his last job.

They seem like traps to me. Once we get to Janis Rocque's, we'll be stuck behind some huge fence, down some winding road. Yet if I can convince Evie to stay, then she'll be trapped, too.

"I hate to be gauche here, but aren't our attendance numbers huge this week?" I say. "What if the police find out the murderer was someone at the Rocque? Our budget would be made for years."

"That is really gross," Yegina says, but I am watching Evie for a reaction. With incredible slowness, she reaches back and touches the bare place where her blond hair curls against her neck.

"I know," I say. "I would hate for it to be true."

Evie's hand falls back to the wheel. The light goes green and the car surges forward again.

"We're getting close," says Dee. "There's a right turn soon."

"Can I use your phone for a second?" I say to Yegina. "I've got to text Jayme something."

Yegina hands it over reluctantly. I switch off the ringer and type a message to her instead:

> Get away from us and get J. Ro to call Hendricks. Tell him I'm here with Evie. Tell him that Evie had the drug from the Jason Rains show and put Kim's body in an art crate. Tell him to call Diamond Storage about a recalled delivery last Weds. Say exactly that. You have to believe me.

Then I hand it back. She slides it in her pocket without glancing at it as we turn past some hedges, down a private drive into the hills.

26

J anis Rocque's gatehouse is barely larger than a toll booth, but when a gray-haired attendant slides open the window, I feel the cool gust of its air-conditioning and hear the murmur of a TV.

"Dee here," Dee says, and leans over to wave.

The attendant gives her a knowing smile, and the two green-painted gates to Janis Rocque's estate open inward.

Slowly a narrow road appears before us, flanked by blue-headed bird-of-paradise flowers. Tall hedges make second and third perimeters, but, between them, lawns extend like primeval savannas for dozing dinosaurs of iron, stone, and steel. I see Yegina mouthing the names of the artists she recognizes, her hand drifting to her high white collar like a Victorian in an opera-induced swoon. Here and there, a winglike edifice soars over the hedges that conceal it.

"There are open gardens and hidden gardens," says Dee. "It's designed to make the viewer feel lost and found at the same time."

"Where do I go?" Evie murmurs, though the road twists in one direction, toward a surprisingly small house with a solar-paneled roof, rising above the trees. After all the magnificence and spread of the sculptures, the actual Rocque home seems modest by comparison.

"Is that the servants' quarters?" Yegina asks in a wondering voice.

"Janis tore the old mansion down to make more room for the outdoor installations," says Dee. "It's all about the art."

The road ends in a white gravel parking lot big enough for a dozen cars, its perimeter also marked by trimmed shrubs. We slide to a halt beside a beat-up Toyota and two sporty sedans. Dust shimmers in the heat. Dee and Yegina leap out of the vehicle. I wait in my seat, paralyzed, the air going stale and sweltering as soon as the doors shut. I watch the back of Evie's motionless blond head.

"Coming?" I say. "You'll regret it if you don't."

"Will I?" she mutters, staring out the windshield. She doesn't glance at me and I don't look at her. I force myself to breathe the stuffy heat. She unclips her belt, opens her door. I wait until she's almost out of the car before leaping out after her. We slam our doors in tandem.

Yegina is already staring hungrily around, her phone dropped into her purse without a second glance. She roams to the edge of the parking lot, peeking through cracks in the green walls to see a hulking ellipse beyond. It's a curving metal wall, the height of a garage, the color of wet chocolate.

"Hello! We're here," says Dee, holding her phone to her ear. "Okay." Her face falls. "Sure. You do that."

She pockets her phone and gives a sharp shrug.

"So! Want to see the Richard Serra?" she says with determined glee. "We should stick together, at least at the start. We're still installing works, and there are some holes and sharp edges." Without waiting for an answer, she bounds off after Yegina, leaving Evie and me alone.

I still can't bring myself to look at Evie's face, but I take in her slim legs and her little blue pumps, the same shoes she was wearing the night of the Gala, when I talked to her in the bathroom stall. She must have been hiding then. She was hiding herself away to text Lynne with Kim Lord's phone. Announcing the artist's arrival at seven o'clock. While I was rattling on about parties, Evie was pretending to be the woman she murdered. Was murdering. Kim wasn't dead yet. Kim was bleeding and suffocating in an art crate, her body dying around the child inside her.

"This might take too long," Evie says.

I finally meet her eyes and they're as bright as dimes.

"It's right there," I say.

She slides her sunglasses on, blanking her gaze. "You first," she says.

"No, you first," I say with fake enthusiasm. "You're the one who has to rush." And I wait until she struts ahead of me, feeling that I will survive today only if I keep playing the ingenue, and actually that I'm not playing at all.

When we catch up with Yegina and Dee, they're in the middle of the Richard Serra ellipse, laughing and stepping in and out of the sharp quadrants of shadow and light. "Almost crushed a guy when they put this one in," Dee chirps. "It weighs almost thirty tons."

For me, Serra's sculptures always invoke a feeling of sacred space, and standing inside one now is like being in a labyrinth with one path in, its center an open eye to the clouds. The metal wall is as warm as a burner on low. The steel curves are so smooth and massive that they contort the earth and sky. We're each angled by the artwork, tipped and diminished, and for one tiny instant I forget what Evie has done and succumb to my awe.

But then Dee does a giant cartwheel and almost hits Evie when she lands. Evie jumps back with a shriek; the sculpture amplifies the sound to a long, harsh call.

"You all right, then?" Dee asks, brushing herself off. "Did I hit you?"

Evie shakes her head no, but her face is mottled; her self-control has slipped.

"You seem jumpy," I say, grinning hard at her.

Evie smiles back at me, her lips closed, but one tooth shows over her bottom lip. Behind her, Yegina strokes the wall of the sculpture.

"Let's keep going," Dee says, and nudges me. "Your special surprise is coming up soon."

As we wind our way out of the ellipse, ducking to see around the tilted sides, I tail Yegina.

"I think your phone is buzzing," I say. "Might be Jayme for me."

She hands her whole bag to me without turning around. "Just let me enjoy myself for five minutes, okay?"

I pretend to check the phone, hand it back. "Actually it's for you."

We emerge from the Serra onto the open lawn. Yegina snaps up the screen, reads my message, snaps it back again, but she only hurries after Dee, who is skipping her way down a slope to a giant scrap-metal figure. It's a David Smith, humanoid and reptilian, tall but flat-headed, the two-legged body made of broken scales and loops and shapes. It reminds me of the newspaper game where the letters in a word are scrambled and you have to stare at it to put them in the right order. One of the sculpture's limbs has a long, serrated edge.

I wait for Evie again, then follow her. I am squinting so hard in the sun that my forehead aches. Everything that can reflect light is shining: the last drops of dew in the grass, the buckles on our purses, the vast shapes of metal, the little gold loops in Yegina's ears. Dee and Yegina erupt into *wows* about seeing the David Smith up close, standing in its broken shadow. I hang back, afraid of the glinting, jagged blade.

I wonder where Hendricks is, what he knows. Was he watching Evie all along?

Evie's flipping open her phone every two minutes now, glancing over her shoulder back to the parking lot. She's going to bolt. I want to bolt. I want to knock on the door of Janis Rocque's solar home and hide in some clean, modernist parlor until Evie escapes and someone else chases her. My purse—stuffed with the recorder—is dragging on my shoulder like a stone. I could make an excuse and run to the gatehouse, tell the old guy to let no one out. Maybe there's even a phone in there. I could call the LAPD right now.

Dee's voice interrupts my thoughts. "And through this hedge is your special surprise, Maggie." She bows to me and points to a path snaking into a bower of trees. "I stumbled on it yesterday," she says. "Janis said she bought it years and years ago—but she didn't trust anyone to install it properly until she met Brent Patrick. He did this and a couple of other tricky installations for her last year." She takes a breath and shakes her head. "He's kind of clueless, really. I don't think he knew about your connection, or he would have told you it was here."

At the mention of Brent, Evie stays expressionless, but I see her hand tighten on her phone.

I walk through first, keeping a cushion between me and Evie. As the green branches close around me, I hear Yegina call out, "Hey, I have to make a quick call." And then, "There's no reception. I'm going closer to the house."

Her departure sends needles of fear into me. I wanted her to go for help, but I also need her here.

Dark limbs stretch overhead. Although the path is clear and level, the grove seems jumbled compared to the open fields. A pleasurable coolness seeps up from the earth. The ground here is deep grass, broken by a hole in the earth, long as a schooner and about six feet across. They must have dug it out with shovels. You couldn't get an excavator in here, not with the thick ring of trees that surround the clearing, not with this lush, trackless grass. How far down did they go? The hole looks like a miniature version of the fault lines I have seen out in the desert, but its depth seems dark and forbidding.

Dee bumps into me and I fight back a squawk. She's urging me to step closer, read the plaque.

Instead I look back at Evie, whose face glows with curiosity.

"Read it," Dee says.

I drift sideways, out of Evie's reach, and bend down to see the bold brass lettering:

THERESA FERGUSON
CLEFT, 1970

"Must be a different artist," I say. "Greg's mother sculpted in glass."

"Look closer," Dee says. I keep an arm's length from Evie as I tiptoe to the edge of the rift. The ground is firm up to the last step, and then I feel its looseness, a spongy, crumbly edge where the grass roots cannot hold it. The air smells of soil and dampness.

"The main trick was getting the sun and shade right," says Dee as I crane my neck and see them fifteen feet below: dozens—no, hundreds—of glass apples piled on either side of a long, gleaming blade, sharp as a guillotine. "So you could discover them all at just the moment you might fall in."

The blade runs the entire length of the hole, as high as my knee, its edge slightly beveled. Heaped around it, each glass apple is curvy, fleshy. And each is severed cleanly in half.

I step back, suddenly choked by an emotion I cannot name. When I look over, Evie is also stepping back, gingerly, like her footsteps might crush the grass.

A beeping fills the glade. Dee claws at her hip and pulls out her slim blue flip. "It's Janis," she says in a complicated tone. She waves at the far end of the clearing. "Just go that way. You won't be disappointed."

And she sprints off through the same gap in the trees, leaving me and Evie alone.

For a moment neither of us speaks. We just circle the hole, peering in, moving back. I slide a hand into my purse and turn my cassette tape on. How many minutes are left on it? Do I really expect a confession? No, but she will speak. I will get her to speak.

In the dappled shade, Evie's gaze has softened, and she seems incapable of hurting anyone. I step closer to her anyway, because I have to, because I have put myself here. Out of the corner of my eye, I catch sight of the apples piled on either side of the blade. They look lush. And amputated. I remember Kevin's notes: *Symbol of female sexuality. Cleft apple = woman's reproductive parts. Also, implied violence.*

One of the last pieces in the puzzle comes to me.

"You thought I'd never figure it out." My voice is low but sure. "I almost didn't. I was looking for *why*, not *how*. And I couldn't see the why for you. Jealousy wasn't enough, though you were jealous of Kim. I know I was." I step toward Evie.

She is backing up, cradling her phone.

"I hated her," I say. "I hated the way she could just step in and absorb every last bit of Greg until there was nothing—and never would be any-thing—left for me."

I move closer. Evie holds her ground. She stares at me with such in-tensity that it burns. My skin feels loose and hot on my face.

"But I couldn't have killed her for that," I say. "And neither could you. Until you heard Kim tell Brent about the baby. A baby meant it was all true." I pause. Anger swells my voice; it's my own anger. The bower is drawing closer with its black-gold-green light, and Evie's rapid blinking tells me I'm right, but she's as silent as a statue. "It meant he never really loved you."

As I'm talking, the murder plays again like a movie in my mind, only I don't see Evie doing it, I see myself: flicking the table saws on, and walking in on Kim alone, changing her clothes in Brent's office. I bring the mallet down on the back of her head in one heavy, awkward blow. The body falls. The blood spurts and flows. I wrap the body in one of the painting tarps. Stab Kim's belly with the Jason Rains syringes. Roll a crate in from the carpentry room, load it, and order a storage delivery. Clean the room and dump the clothes and gloves in the crate.

"You're her size," I tell Evie. "You could wear her disguise out of the museum. If you went fast enough, no one would know."

A wind from somewhere shifts the trees, freckling the glade with fresh light. Inside the hole, the glass apples shine and darken.

"I should go," Evie finally says in a remote voice.

"You took the elevator so people would see you," I say, my mind racing ahead. I see myself departing the museum in Kim's clothes, wig, and sunglasses, hurrying down to Pershing Square. "And then you changed somewhere, maybe your car, and came back through the loading dock, and escorted the crate to the storage facility. Then rerouted it again somewhere. Your loft."

It was barely possible. Evie's loft rose in a warehouse neighborhood of brick and rust and emptiness. No one would hear Kim dying there. And the burial in the Angeles National Forest? She might have dug the grave at night. Buried the body on the weekend. What terrible, exhausting, lonely tasks, in a city filled with them. I can't reconcile the slight figure in front of me with the dread and struggle of what she's done. Was it really Evie who struck the blow? Was it really Evie who closed her ears to Kim's muffled screams? Was it really Evie in my apartment last night? It's easier to still picture a strange man, a nameless perpetrator. Then I remember Evie in the mirror of the gym studio, the determination that can flush her strong and rigid. Stronger than anyone I know.

In the distance, the dull roar of a mower. Evie shakes her head, presses her lips together. I'm losing her. I'm losing the connection I made with her over hating Kim Lord.

"You did it for Brent's sake. He didn't want a baby," I say.

Evie almost nods.

"It wasn't his, though," I say. "It was Greg's. Greg's baby is dead. And now Brent is leaving—with you or with Barbara?"

With Barbara. It has to be.

But I can tell from her face that Evie can't hear me now, not after what I said about the baby. She's written her reasons in blood, and she cannot erase them. She glances over her shoulder. When she turns back to me, the tightness is gone, and she looks troubled and sympathetic, as if I've just announced I've got the flu.

"Maggie," she says in a cold, lucid voice. "Do you really believe all of this? Because no one else does. When Dee said you might show up today, I had to stop Yegina from calling Fritz and having you barred from re-entering the museum. You're making it hard for the rest of us to do our jobs. I spent a whole day on that provenance stuff because I took pity on you." She pauses. "Shaw is free. And some twisted creep killed Kim Lord, but the police will catch him. Now I've got to get some sculptures to the airport, okay?"

Evie is lying, but I can't find the falsehood in her face.

"Okay," I say.

She turns away, still clutching her phone. I can't let her go.

"Wait," I say. "I'm sorry Brent hurt you."

She hesitates, gazing at the dark rift in the ground.

"You're sweet," she says. "You know they call you Maple Muffin down in crew."

At that moment, a loud click tells me my recorder has switched off. Before I can fully register this, a man's voice calls from the far side of the clearing.

"Maggie!" He sounds alarmed. And more awake than ever. But how is he already here?

Something hurtles at me so hard I only see it in parts—smooth white arms, swinging blond hair, a fury-distorted mouth—before I stagger two steps and slip on the springy soft earth at the edge of the hole. I hear my raspy, surprised cry. Then Evie's final push, full of senseless strength, flings my head so hard it snaps, and I fall.

27

S ounds: glass shifting and breaking against itself, like the crashing of surf onto small round rocks. The dull crack of my purse hitting the blade and my body after it, thudding to its side. I scramble up, cutting my knees and palms before I notice the wetness spreading over my belly, and a great wind rising through my skull, making it hard to see the sky above me. Evie's gone. The man's voice has stopped calling me. He must not know where I am. He must not know I'm here. I cry out, the effort blacking my eyes. I sink to my knees. The blood keeps spreading like silence. I call again, but the sound is too weak. My fingers fumble in the purse for the recorder. I press the rewind button on the cassette player and turn the volume dial high, blasting what I said to Evie into the clearing.

I hated her.

Footsteps, fainter then louder. The crack of sticks. My name bursts over the stretch of sky, and then there is Hendricks's face peering over, measuring the distance for less than an instant before he leaps.

THURSDAY

28

The room swims in and out, and I am inside it, lying on a bed, my arms taped with tubes, a rubbery taste in my throat. My belly enormous and strained, a beach ball of flesh. White walls blister with light. Women in blue masks lean over me. Then another room, another bed, same tubes, an IV machine blinking. Yegina is sitting with me. Then no one. Then a cluster of doctors who talk about my concussion, broken ribs, and damaged right kidney, the fluids that are filling my body because the organ isn't working properly.

Then Yegina's back, announcing, "They got her, and they found Brent, too. He was in New York. He said he didn't have any idea about Evie, said he was just tired of L.A. But I think he knew. It's so messed up."

I blink away tears, unable to speak.

She looks at me, her lips trembling. "You're going to recover. I won't let you alone until you do."

I struggle to say Yegina's brother's name, but my mouth still won't make a sound.

Yegina's eyes fill. "Don's okay. It's just going to take some time. For all of us."

Later Hendricks comes, sits in a chair by my bed. He looks like he's washed his whole person in darkness: the edges of him are gritty and

247

indistinct. It must be twilight. I don't know how long I have been here, in the hospital. Hendricks raises his closed hands to his mouth; they are lunar, bandaged, and he leans into them like a man in prayer.

When I make a noise, he glances over at me, eyes traveling over the hump of my midsection. His lips tighten.

It's me. The sight of me bloated and bruised makes him flinch.

But instead of looking away, his gaze is steady; he puts his palm over my hand, covering it, his fingers warm, the cotton bandages rough and cool, until I fall asleep again.

In the morning, I waken to the swelling and the sensation of the catheter winding from my legs into a bag, and the heaviness of a blanket. I don't feel pain so much as an overwhelming fullness, as if someone has poured liquid into every hollow of my body. When the nurse comes in, I ask her how long I've been here and she says "Two days," but I have a hard time believing her because it feels like much longer and where is my family?

"Your mom's on the way," she says, standing close to me. "There was bad weather in Chicago and a few flight delays. She's dying to get here, though." She touches my rank hair. "Want me to fix you up later? We could give you a shampoo."

As soon as she leaves, doctors and residents flood in, yanking the curtain around my bed and examining me with clinical eagerness. Their voices volley around me like gunfire. After they quiet, the oldest doctor, a wrinkled woman with eyes the color of dates, tells me gently that I may be able to recover without surgery, and this is good news. She says the swelling will go down with rest and diuretics. I fall asleep again after they leave. The nurse wakes me; she is carrying a blue plastic basin with a tiny bottle of shampoo and a small brick of soap.

"There's still a risk of infection, so we'll do a sponge bath," she says. Her movements are deft, and the warm water feels good on my face and scalp, but when I ask for a mirror, I see the warning in her eyes and I want to cry.

"Let's wait a couple of days," she says. "The swelling should go down."

Then she gently combs my hair and gives me my pills and I gratefully fall asleep again. When I wake, it must be late afternoon: Detective Ruiz is shaking my shoulder, and Hendricks is leaning against the wall, arms folded, hands still in bandages, eyes on his black canvas shoes.

Detective Ruiz reintroduces herself. She keeps her eyes on me, but they clench at the corners, as if she is forcing herself not to look away.

I say I remember her visiting my office.

"Good. I'm sorry to disturb your rest. We just need a brief statement from you about the events that occurred at Janis Rocque's estate."

"Did Evie confess?" I whisper.

"I'm afraid I can't answer that," says Detective Ruiz, but behind her, I see Hendricks shake his head no. How did he get to the sculpture garden so fast? I thought he was almost at my apartment in Hollywood. Gratitude floods me. I could have died if Yegina hadn't found him, if he hadn't found me.

"Maggie, I'm going to ask you some questions and I want you to answer as honestly as possible. You arrived at the sculpture garden at what time?" Detective Ruiz has a little recorder in her hand, proper-sized and digital. The doctors said that the big clunky machine inside my purse actually broke my fall, so the blade only cut my belly after I rolled.

I tell Ruiz everything I can remember about the morning, including calling the storage facility, including the heat and the drive through Hollywood, including the coolness of the bower where Theresa Ferguson's art opened the ground. I keep talking until I get to the part where Evie pushed me and then the words abruptly stop. I can't say it, can't describe the look in her face when she shoved me: *She wanted me dead.* The force of that feeling: it's like a steel wall slamming into my nose and skull. I don't want to experience it again.

"And then?" Detective Ruiz rubs her temple.

I shake my head, still unable to speak. My hair is still damp from the bath. It drags on my cheeks like fingers.

Ruiz glances up at Hendricks, as if soliciting his advice.

Explain what happened, I think. *You saw it. You saw me in the hole, bleeding. You know.*

Hendricks watches me for a moment and then he shrugs, slow and elaborate, as if we're talking not about an attempted murder but about some sloppy habit of mine to which he has resigned himself.

"My guess is that the victim fell," he says finally. "Ground's slippery. Nothing fencing the artwork."

I make a noise and Ruiz looks suddenly puzzled.

"Did you fall?"

Hendricks nods behind her. *Say yes*, he mouths.

Ruiz spins on Hendricks. "Describe again what you found when you got the scene."

"She was lying in the glass at the bottom of the hole, turned on her side." His voice is casual, almost resentful, as if he's told the same version of the story many times. "The suspect was nowhere in sight. I jumped down, cut up my hands"—he holds up one bandaged fist—"stopped the victim's bleeding, and called for help."

"Suppose you start a little earlier," Ruiz says sharply. "You said you were on the estate already—why was that again?"

Hendricks tells her that Janis Rocque had asked him to attend a meeting between herself, Nelson de Wilde, and Bas Terrant to help determine the future ownership of the twelve paintings in *Still Lives* and other, earlier works by Kim Lord. Hendricks had just arrived at the parking lot when a friend of Maggie's spotted him and said that Maggie had an urgent message for him. "And then I heard her scream," he says, his eyes hard on mine. "I ran toward the sound and found her there, as I've described."

"And you never saw the suspect emerge from the woods," says Ruiz.

"No."

"And you did not know the suspect was on the estate"—Ruiz extends every syllable to show her disbelief—"at the point you entered the sculpture garden."

"Again, I guessed as much. I confirmed it with Maggie, at which point I called the unit."

"Maggie, do you remember telling Detective Hendricks that you were pushed by Evie Long?" Ruiz asks me.

I shake my head. "I didn't—"

"Did you fall or did someone push you?" she asks.

I stare back at Hendricks, shocked that this is the same man who gripped my hand last night. I see the new shadows in his face, the studied slouch that cloaks a fierce desperation. He's not in Los Angeles to be a private investigator for rich ladies. He's looking for something else here, and I, with my bumbling attempts to find the truth and save Greg, have been distracting him.

Now he wants me to lie. He knows Evie tried to kill me. Why does he want me to lie? So that he can get the credit for catching her? I did it. I stopped her. This is my story. Not his.

But he's not taking the credit either.

My body feels bubbled, like I am a hot-water bottle filled to the brim, ready to pop.

"Did you fall or did someone push you?" Ruiz says again.

I did it. I stopped Evie. I want to shout this.

As soon as they leave together, the room expands. The window and walls are miles away, and my throat is so dry that I can't swallow. I'm dying for water, though I am drowning in water. The capacity inside me to rise and get a cup, or to press the nurse's button for help, has entirely disappeared. I close my eyes.

I don't know why Hendricks asked me to lie.

I don't know why, when I finally said *I fell*, it felt true.

Maybe I did fall. Maybe I goaded Evie to push me because I wanted to feel what her rage was like. To feel, face-to-face, a rage strong enough to kill so that I could finally understand it. I thought if I could slip inside the skin of a victim and emerge again, I might be able to explain why it happens. Wasn't that the reason Kim Lord made *Still Lives*?

I lie on the hospital bed, motionless, under the weight of my own swollen flesh. I fell. I lived. I am nothing like Kim.

For the first time, a dark idea spreads in my mind: *What if Kim didn't choose this subject? What if it found her because she sensed, deep down, that she was about to die?* She might have felt it somehow, when she caked her blond hair in fake blood, and painted her own slumped body, face down, the red gore pouring out of her. Nicole Brown Simpson was the first painting she made in the series. It took a year, according to Kim, until she "knew what to do with all the blood." She shaped a tree with it, upside down, bearing its tiny fruit. A life-bringing image in the midst of a slaughter. Meaning in the darkest horror of human nature.

Did she believe in that herself? We'll never know.

But I think it's what she wanted us to see.

SUNDAY

29

My mother, Lillian, perches in the vinyl chair by my bedside from eight in the morning until seven at night, leaving tactfully and resentfully when the nurses come to change my dressing. She brings her yarn and needles, a British mystery novel, and ham sandwiches that she made in my kitchen; she brings her practical clipped-back blond hair, the graceful way her neck arches when she knits, and the little hisses she makes when she drops a stitch.

Against the backdrop of this busy urban hospital, my mother looks pale, lovely, and slightly stiff, as if she's been washed on the delicate cycle and gently flattened to dry. She broadcasts a friendly voice at the nurses, but her eyes are glinty and watchful until all medical personnel leave the room. She doesn't trust them. When she knows they're gone, a rush of tenderness softens her features and she takes my hand and holds it tight.

I'm grateful for the tenderness. It keeps me from thinking about Hendricks or Evie or the dreams of falling that wake me every night for the last four nights here. My mother refuses to discuss the case or what happened to me in the bower.

"You need to move on so you can heal," she says.

So instead of being pushed into a pit by a murderer, it's as if I've contracted some terrible disease that has swollen my midsection and made me too dizzy to walk. Once I get over this illness, I will go back to being the Maggie she knew, the good daughter, instead of the clumsy, wannabe reporter who helped get a girl killed, traveled the world, and then moved far away.

"We could fix up the old homestead for you, if you want your own place," she says. "Your father's dying for a new project."

My mother has decided that I'm coming home with her. I'm going on disability leave from the Rocque, and bit by bit, she is packing up my bungalow. I want to ask her if she found any evidence, something Evie planted to frame me, but I can't. It now sounds crazy, even to me.

"Don't throw away anything without asking me," I tell her instead.

"Your furniture's not worth keeping," my mother says.

"I mean small things, Mom."

"Small things add up," she says.

"Just in case, ask me."

But she doesn't ask. Instead, we talk about boxes, temporary storage until I decide what's next.

What we both don't utter aloud: I might not come back to Los Angeles at all.

There is, of course, one formidable opponent to this plan. My mother, recognizing a sophisticated adversary when she meets one, won't budge from her chair whenever Yegina comes.

"Oh I'll just knit over here in the corner while you chat," she says.

So we can't talk about real stuff—not about Don or Bas or the case—but Yegina, not to be outflanked, brings a plethora of temptations to stay: dark chocolate laced with raspberry; honeybush tea; wrapped and be-ribboned macaroons from an overpriced bakery. The more exotic the edible, the more convinced Yegina is that it will heal me. She thinks people in hospitals suffer from the lack of sensory stimulation, so she's also made me CD mixes, pasted reproductions of Kahlo and Matta paintings up on my walls, and scattered lemongrass sachets in my drawers.

"It's so *international* in here," my mother marvels, and pats my hand.

Today the doctors have come by with news about my discharge—a few more tests and I can go.

I ask my mother if she minds returning to the apartment to finish packing. "The sooner we're done, the sooner we can get home," I say.

She brightens at the word *home*, but inside I feel the discernible prick of a lie. I picture Vermont in May, mud season giving way to crocuses and the delicate gold-green that explodes all over the woods. It's still mine, but it's also very far away.

"I'll go for a couple of hours," my mother says. She stands and regards me. "You're looking better now." She puts both hands to both her cheeks, and, for a moment, her resolutely cheerful manner slips. "I didn't even recognize you when I first came," she admits in a quavering voice.

"Oh, Mom."

I let her hug me too tight. She leaves her knitting lumped on the chair, needles poking up, as if to prevent anyone else from occupying it.

As soon as she's gone, I call Yegina.

"Just bring yourself," I say. "And hurry."

I'm so relieved to finally have time alone with Yegina that it surprises me when she walks in the room and I don't know what to say. There she is, with her beautiful, alert face, laden with bags under her arms, my friend and rescuer. My memory flashes to the open door at her house, the anger in her eyes, Bas behind her on the couch—and then to Don, tumbling from his bike. I want to thank her with my whole heart, I want to beg her forgiveness, or to cry, or just to pretend nothing happened, but not knowing where to begin with her is terrible. It paralyzes me.

"I brought magazines," she says awkwardly. "You want to know about the case, right?"

"Definitely," I say. "It's all I've been thinking about since I fell." I emphasize the last word, and Yegina nods. She doesn't say *What happened with Evie? How'd you slip?* Doesn't wait for me to lie. She just nods.

"And I brought mochi," she says, and sets a Japantown box on my bedside table.

Then she looks warily at my mother's knitting needles and sits on my bed instead. The jostling sends a wave of discomfort through me.

"Where should we start," she murmurs, and spreads the magazines and newspapers out on my white blankets, cover stories with pictures of Evie in an orange jumpsuit, of the glass-and-steel front of the Rocque with photoshopped blood running down it.

Nothing squalid. Nothing cop-show. This is supposed to be high art. Lynne must be shattered and impossible now, I say.

"She got herself a third cat," says Yegina. "It seems to be helping her cope."

"How about Jayme—did she quit?" I received a card from her, wishing me a speedy recovery, but I'm surprised she hasn't visited. I've been here almost a week.

"Jayme's on vacation in Hawaii," says Yegina. "She actually sat Bas and me down last week and told us that she was stalked as a teenager, and that Kim Lord's disappearance and death have been extremely upsetting to her." Her eyes rest on me. "She said she didn't want this public, but she'd already told you, and it made her realize she needed to tell us, too." She adds, "I always wondered."

"Yeah, me too," I say, grateful that Jayme has finally stopped bearing her pain alone. "I'm glad she left all this behind for a while."

I finger the cool, smooth pages spread around me. The "museum murderess" is huge news, both the grisly homicide and the quick reprisal by the LAPD, which gets all the credit for solving the case. Hendricks is absent from the story. I am absent from it, too, and Evie's flight through the sculpture garden is reduced to a simple arrest. Instead, reporters have sunk their teeth into every other aspect of the murder. Yegina shows me "Dimensions of Death" in one magazine, a timeline that chronicles Kim Lord's alleged killing, hour by hour. A dotted line shows a figure in a wig and a trench coat entering the museum through the loading dock, passing the guard station, then proceeding into the carpentry room and into Brent's office. It also shows a second blond figure in a blue pantsuit in the registrar's room, and a dotted line leading to the same office. The police found traces of Kim Lord's blood on Brent's floor and on one of the mallets. They never found the syringes holding the sodium thiopental.

"Any ordinary day, and this murder could never have occurred," wrote one journalist. "But on Wednesday, the entire exhibition crew was upstairs in the galleries, installing the opening show, and Evie Long was alone for hours. She turned on the saws in the carpentry room, grabbed a mallet, and crept to the door of Brent Patrick's office."

"How an Art Crate Became a Coffin" follows how Evie shipped the unconscious and dying Kim Lord out of the museum to the Van Nuys storage facility, and then retrieved the crate two hours later and relocated it to her loft. The Diamond Storage shipment is key to the police case, because the second truck driver, the one who picked up the crate, remembers rolling it into Evie's loft. The crate itself has vanished, but dirt on Evie's sneakers matches dirt from the burial site. Enough puzzle pieces will finish the picture for the jury, even if key ones are missing. Yet Evie's cruelty will never be completely explicable. Did she assume Kim Lord was dead? Did she ever hear her cry for help? No one knows. While Evie played business as usual at the Rocque, and stayed out late at the Gala in Kim Lord's honor, the artist was clawing at her coffin, dying from suffocation and thirst.

"The Gallerist, the Artist, the Murderer, and Her Lover" focuses on Brent Patrick, the "Leonardo of stagecraft" who relocated to L.A., watched his marriage collapse with his wife's mental illness, and got involved with an obsessive young woman who later murdered her supposed rival. Tawdry stuff. I can't believe I sat through dozens of thumb-twiddling meetings with these people. Brent claimed he had no relationship to Kim Lord beyond a professional one. He did know Kim was pregnant because she'd told him in his office earlier that week. He also admitted to a few months' affair with Evie Long last year, which he ended when Evie began appearing at his apartment without his invitation. "I'm not proud of it, but I broke it off," he told the reporter. "To be honest, I partly wanted to move back east to get away from her."

"Dee knew about him and Evie," says Yegina, leaning over my shoulder. "She thought it ended last fall."

In my mind's eye, I see Dee and her hurt but obstinate face. "She was being so secretive about Brent last week, though," I say. "Do you think she suspected something anyway?"

"Brent begged her not to tell about him being hired in New York. He was double-billing his two health insurances. For his wife's care," Yegina says, and taps a paragraph where Brent claims his "insanely busy" schedule kept him "utterly unaware" of Evie's actions. "I believe Dee. She was all lovesick about Janis. She was absent the days it happened. But I don't buy Brent. He must have known something. His office must have stunk of disinfectant. There was a crate missing. Tarps missing. Why wouldn't he tell the police?"

It's a logical question, and the logical answer would be: He's telling the truth. He simply didn't know.

But I don't believe that's it exactly. Brent let himself go blind. I think of the momentary fire in his eyes after the Jason Rains preview, how even my small burst of admiration affected him. What if such adulation were magnified a thousand times by the big theater company orchestrating his Broadway comeback? Why would he care about anything else? I relay my thoughts to Yegina.

"But Kim told him she was pregnant," she says. "It seems like they were really close."

"Maybe." I muse aloud that Kim was panicking about the responsibility of a child, and how it might ruin her art career. She might have thought Brent would understand. Because of Barbara.

"So Evie overheard the pregnant part and she went nuts," says Yegina. "But she was so calculated, too. I feel like I never knew her."

"I agree." I grab an article and read aloud about Evie's childhood in small towns in the Imperial Valley and Northern California. She moved often with her single mother, who had a drug habit, and for several years was placed in foster care by the state for neglect. Evie's biological mother declined to be interviewed, but the foster mother characterized Evie as the "prettiest little psychopath" she'd ever met.

"One thing we do know: it was dangerous to be close to her," I say. *It was dangerous to know her at all*, I add internally, wanting to confess to my stolen phone, my hunch that Evie sent the warning note to Greg, that she was scoping out my house to figure out how to frame me next and ran out of time. I wait again for Yegina to say something about my fall in the sculpture garden, but again, she doesn't. She is looking down, pressing a finger into her forearm until the skin whitens.

I ask about her brother. She tells me Don is living at home, but the whole family is seeing a great therapist, and Don's saving money to bike up the coast to San Francisco. Yegina says she might go with him.

"Work is so busy, though," she adds. "With you and Jayme gone. And Bas is fund-raising like crazy in Kim's name, which I know you'll think is crass, but people want to do something, they feel so sad . . ." She trails off.

"How is Bas?" I say. "I mean, how are Bas and you?"

Yegina heaves a giant sigh. "The day Don tried to . . . Bas was with me in my office," she says. "And yes, we'd been flirting, in this silly, sinking-ship sort of way, because his career was going down and his marriage was breaking up and Kim Lord was missing and my best friend was lying to me and we might all lose our jobs if the Rocque couldn't balance its budget." She absently stacks the magazines as she talks, periodically pausing to tuck her black hair behind her ear. "And then I get a call from my mom saying she's bringing Don back from the hospital because he tried to hang himself. I can't drive, I'm too upset. And you're totally unreachable. So Bas just dumped everything and drove me." Bas told her that his older sister had committed suicide when he was a teenager, and that he'd never recovered from it. "We both realized we came from these pressure-cooker families, where you have to stay on track or you've failed forever."

That day, Bas stayed in the car for two hours while Yegina went inside with her family, and then he escorted her home.

"And if you must know, we decided not to sleep together," she adds. "He's only an okay kisser, anyway." Her tone is light, but her eyes, locked on mine, are hurt. "So you didn't really interrupt anything, and you didn't have to take off like that."

"I was in shock," I say. "And there you were with him. I felt like an intruder . . . What was I supposed to do?"

"You could have trusted me," Yegina says.

I did trust her. I might have died if Yegina hadn't believed my text in J. Ro's garden. It hurts how much I trust her, and she rescued me. But I don't want to start bawling now because I don't know when I'd stop.

The bustle of the ward fills the silence: the custodian rattles her mop bucket, rolling it down the hall. There's a burst of conversation at the nurse's station.

"Ray Hendricks was in the office today," Yegina says. "He said he left something for you."

"Strange," I say, my stomach dropping. Hendricks hasn't been back to the hospital since we lied to Detective Ruiz. "Why was he there?"

Yegina says that Hendricks came for the legal sorting out of the *Still Lives* paintings. J. Ro insisted he take part in the dialogue because he was the one who identified Kim Lord's alleged stalker. "It was this big collector who was trying to own everything Kim Lord ever made. Really creepy."

"Sounds it," I say.

"Anyway, J. Ro is buying them, on the condition that Nelson give Kim's percentage of the proceeds to Kim's family, and Nelson's percentage to nonprofits for women artists. And then Janis is loaning the paintings to the Rocque indefinitely."

I try to show enthusiasm, though I am having a hard time processing the news. *Still Lives* will belong to the Rocque, as Kim wanted, but what will happen with the rest of her paintings—all her early work in *The Flesh* and *Noir*? Now that Steve Goetz and his supercollector scheme are known, will he continue with it?

"How did you figure out that Evie did it?" says Yegina, watching my face.

"I don't know." I don't meet her eyes. "I just pieced things together."

"You should have gotten credit."

"So I could put it on my résumé?" I ask.

"Hendricks said you would make a great investigator if you weren't such a decent person," she says.

"It sounds like you two talked for a while," I say.

"Not really. He didn't want to talk to me," Yegina says, now smiling. "But I knew something was up between you, so I got nosy."

My mind flashes to Hendricks jumping into the pit of glass, smashing down with his knees bent, then swimming over to me, his hands cut on the broken pieces. His red-streaked palms reaching. I don't remember what happened next, but he must remember. He must have done something to stop me from bleeding to death. He must also have taken the cassette in my recorder. And then he made me lie. Made me look like a clumsy idiot to Detective Ruiz. And never apologized. I mumble something and flip through the magazines. A masthead catches my eye.

"Check this out," I say, grabbing the issue of *ArtNoise*, which shows a blurry picture of the crew party on the roof on the night of the Gala. Evie is circled in bright-red ink. "Kevin's article." There I am in a full-page photo, standing at the threshold of the third gallery, my head bowed, blond hair falling in my face. Jayme's green dress curves tight around me; her high-heeled boots extend my legs to spikes. I look good. A little dangerous. Unpredictable.

But I also look like someone has just slapped me hard, and I am afraid to raise my head.

I close the magazine and sink back to my pillows, suddenly exhausted. "I'll read it later. I'm sorry. I'm so tired."

Yegina sits there a moment, and then starts sliding the magazines back into her bag. "I'll hold on to them," she promises. "Do you want me to bring whatever Hendricks left you?"

"No," I say, closing my eyes. "Leave it in my office. I'll be back."

"Good," Yegina says softly, and strokes my forehead. "I'll swamp your inbox and take you to lunch at the new shabu-shabu place on Sunset. It'll be old times."

"Can't wait," I say.

I wish we both believed it was true.

A MONTH LATER

30

The swelling is down all over my body, thanks to walks to the creek with my parents' collies and deep sleeps in the starry northern quiet, but my face still looks unbalanced to me. Not bigger or puffier, just not mine. Every morning I pull my T-shirts over it, open my mouth for hearty breakfasts, whistle as I wander down cool dirt rows, helping my parents plant tomato seedlings. Every day I try to look pleased to hear (again) about the neighbor's grown-up doctor son, who runs marathons and works at the local hospital, and I smirk at stories of the town's crazy libertarian, who recently hung the governor in effigy from his plumbing sign.

Yet every evening I stare at my face in my mother's mahogany mirror, and try to find what's different.

"Mirror, mirror," my mother says from the threshold one day. "You look like my daughter again."

"Thanks to you," I say. Every day I ricochet between gladness and dread at my mother's homemade bread, her clean, crisp sheets, at my father's ebullient teasing, the solid weight of his arm around my shoulders. I wish I could belong to them again.

My mother steps into the room and straightens the already straight pillows on the bed. Then she shakes the gauzy curtains so that the evening light spills through them. It's spring light, frail and silver-gold.

"There are some new graduate programs at the university," she says. "Your father and I want you to live here. If you find a degree you like."

I don't know what to say. Behind every delicious meal and chat about the new bike path has been this unspoken question: *Why don't you stay here?*

Why don't I?

A fly buzzes out from the window, huge for this time of year, and we both watch it. The black body loops and settles back against the pane. Ever since I arrived home, Kim Lord's death has receded behind the avalanche of a new homicide. Laci Peterson, a missing and pregnant California woman, washed ashore in Richmond in April, within miles of the beached body of her unborn son. Picture after picture of her life layers the media now: pretty at Christmas, holding her belly. Handsome husband with his strong chin, his arm squeezing his wife.

Meanwhile, Kim is not forgotten, not replaced. She has simply faded as another victim takes the spotlight. Before long, another lovely murdered face will rise beside Laci's, and Laci, too, will move to the background with the other victims of homicide. We'll talk about her case as *solved* or *unsolved*, as if knowing who killed her and dumped her body explains anything about why her life had to end. Eventually the reason she died will frame her whole existence—and not the infinite reasons she deserved to live.

My mother sighs at my silence. "I'm afraid there's something back there that won't let you go," she says. "I don't think it's Greg anymore."

"It's not Greg," I say.

"Then what is it?" She's almost in tears. "Why do you get involved in this stuff? You don't have to."

I shake my head, wishing I could explain. Instead, my dry eyes follow the fly, imagining slapping it, and the way its grotesque body would open, spilling its guts, smearing the glass. It crawls up the window until it reaches a ledge, then pauses, tenderly rubbing its legs together.

•

The next morning even our distant Vermont newspaper is covering the Laci Peterson case. The husband's lawyers are floating the idea that a Satanic cult kidnapped and killed her, which of course has spawned a juicy headline to make people once again wince over her story, her curving belly, her huge, happy smile.

I go outside to help my mother spread compost on her future strawberry garden before she plants. The work is tedious and a bit smelly, but the softness of the soil promises that summer is coming and takes my mind away from the image of another mutilated female body. It's also good to labor alongside my mom, who becomes so intent on her gardening, bending and plucking, it's like she's having a private conversation with the earth. I could learn from this. I could heal.

When it starts to drizzle, I go inside and call Yegina. We gossip about the explosion of visitors to the Rocque, and Jayme's return from Hawaii, her stories of swimming with dolphins. As we talk, I can feel Yegina's L.A. filling my childhood bedroom: her favorite Korean barbecue place, her date with Hiro to the silent-movie theater, the Chilean singer that the public radio station is playing. I can see Yegina's yellow Mazda in a long line of cars streaming to downtown, the sunlight already glaring off her windshield, as she passes signs for wide avenues that run for miles.

"But the big news is that J. Ro strong-armed that big collector into donating all of Kim Lord's paintings from her first shows," says Yegina. "So the Rocque now owns her entire collection and we're building a special gallery in his name. Steve Goetz."

"It should be in Kim's name," I snap.

Yegina makes a surprised noise. "You ended up admiring her, didn't you?"

There's a sinking sensation in my gut, like I've arrived at an important occasion far too late, and everyone is already there, staring at me. I was so focused on my own shame at losing Greg to Kim that she became a specter of my own self-loathing, and I couldn't acknowledge the real Kim Lord. I wish I could have met her again, in a different year, and that we had become friends. I might have liked to see her and Greg's child, even if it hurt. But most likely, I would have been happy to stay a stranger, to know her through her paintings alone, to appreciate the next stunning work she made. "I'm grateful Janis does," I say. "It's great news for the museum."

"The press release had typos," Yegina informs me. "When are you coming back?"

"Soon," I say.

"They'll stop asking you," says Yegina. "I'll never stop, but others will."

My mother is standing in my doorway, holding a large padded envelope, a dubious look on her face.

"It's from someone named Ray in L.A.," she says when I hang up the phone. "Didn't he visit you at the hospital?"

"He was working on Kim Lord's case," I say.

"Well, what does he want now?" She continues to clutch the package and I have to grab it from her. It feels light, like there's very little inside.

"We were sort of friends, too," I mumble.

I wait until she's gone, and tear the envelope open. A black object spills out. A digital recorder, like the one Jay Eastman had, Detective Ruiz had. The size that could fit in my fist.

A piece of tape is attached to it, a note in a man's handwriting:

> Got this for you, but they said you're not back. Sending
> it along in case.

A gift to replace my old broken one. In case I don't return. In case I never see him again.

A meter indicates that there's a short recording on it already.

I shut my bedroom door, press play, and hear Hendricks's voice:

> You want to know why we lied. You might have found
> your own reasons by now, but I owe you mine. You
> accuse a famous killer of trying to murder you, and you
> can never be yourself again. You'll be in the trial, the
> newspapers, TV, you'll be the one who escaped, but your
> life won't be yours. It'll be hers.
>   Don't let her have it. Make your life about the

things and the people that matter to you, the ones worth saving. Keep them well, and let the dead go. The dead already know their ending.

And then nothing for a long moment, and the recording stops.

Hard as I listen, the words don't sink in. I play it again, trying to understand if it's an apology or warning. Or both. Finally I rewind to the end of Hendricks's speech and just listen to his silence. It makes me remember my first night in the hospital. I can see it clearly now: Hendricks sitting by my bedside, his bandaged hand on my hand, his eyes on my damaged face. How the closeness would have ended if either of us had spoken. How in that moment there was nothing to say, no words that could explain yet how we felt. How we both were waiting.

31

When the rain stops, I go down to the kitchen to ask my mother if I can take a drive with her station wagon. It's gotten warm today, almost sixty-five, and I can't stay inside anymore, but I don't want to wander my parents' land either.

"Need company?" she says, handing me the keys.

"Not this time," I say.

"Where are you going?" she asks, trying to sound casual.

I tell her I don't know. She grips the counter. I hug her until her shoulders relax. "I won't be long," I say.

She nods.

When I reach the end of our road, I have the choice to drive west to Burlington, the lakefront city where I used to meet Nikki, or east, deeper into the country, where Nikki lived. I turn east. I've only visited her hometown once, when I was younger, to hike the cliffs above it, but when I get there, it is exactly as I remember: a gas station, a village of white wooden houses set too close to the road, a volunteer fire department, and a couple of churches. Blink and you miss it, this little center. Most people in the town live on long woodsy roads that wind off in either direction. Exactly like my hometown. I don't know which house Nikki grew up in, or where her killer lives, but I bet the houses are close. I bet in the winter they are visible to each other through the bare trees and snow, and if not the houses, then their woodsmoke, winding skyward, mingling in the gray air.

I could stay here and find out who killed her. It might take a while, but I could do it. Is that what Nikki would have wanted? To bring down her neighbors?

At Luster's, Hendricks told me that Nikki had bragged to everyone in town that she was talking to a reporter. Even before that, she knew she was in danger for squealing on people, and she made it worse. She made herself a target, and she didn't run away. I never understood why, until I witnessed Evie also hesitate.

Evie was so meticulous at first. Killing Kim and getting her out of the museum was nearly impossible, and she pulled it off. All the way through the Gala and into the next day she'd kept her cool, going about her usual business while Kim died slowly in the crate. Evie could have left L.A. safely and easily after she buried Kim, but she didn't. She waited. She stalled. Was she hoping Brent would pick up where they'd left off? She would have known by then that he'd reject her, but still she lingered.

Like Nikki, Evie stayed. She must have been waiting to be caught. To be recognized. Spotlighted for all to see. Finally, this daughter of no one and nowhere: a household name. When Evie started researching the photographs of murdered women for *Still Lives*, something had clicked. Instead of pitying the victims, she began envying each murderer his power, his gaze, his ability to position himself, godlike and merciless. When Brent broke things off with her, seemingly to pursue Kim, Evie began to describe to herself a killing that would make her seen. She studied the images; she studied Kim's career and began plotting her own brutal work. After all, to her, Kim was hardly human, just an idol to be sacrificed.

I wonder how long it took her to die, Evie had said about the photograph of Judy Ann Dull at her own crucifixion. I thought it was a question about the magnitude of suffering. Now I see that Evie was measuring time.

I swerve up the road to the cliffs and crack my window, the scent of spring thaw and greenness flooding the car. It's not nowhere here, the breeze seems to say as it rolls across the dash; it's the most beautiful place there is. A white-flowering tree dips and sways by the bend; the serviceberry is in bloom. Fiddleheads unfurl their tight, hairy coils by a steep-spilling stream. My love for my home comes slamming through me. The rivulets of water glint and slide. Moss carpets the rocks by a fragile, ghostly clump of mushrooms.

The path up the back of the cliffs is muddy and narrow, and my heavy, weak body begins floundering thirty steps from the parking lot. I gasp and push myself higher. I remember the view up there, the broad, patched valley, the far horizons of more hills. I need to get there. I need to stand on the brink of it, and find out why I am here and if I am meant to stay. Three times I stop and almost collapse. I wish I'd brought water. I wish I'd brought my mother to tell me to turn around right now and get back down to the car. The woods are wet and still, the rust-colored pine needles slipping beneath my boots. I couldn't be farther from the desert, from the Pacific, from L.A.'s huge metal ribbons of traffic. Silence and footfall.

I double over, my head spinning and shimmering with the memory of Evie-as-Kim hurrying from the Rocque. If only I had recognized the angry, lonely, invisible woman inside the disguise, Kim might not have died.

I grip thin tree trunks, pulling myself up. I keep staggering until I see the clearing in the trees. The white, clouded sky.

The cliff is a burst of emptiness and cold wind. Trees, trees, then nothing. Not even a branch before me. It's such a long way down to the tidy cluster of the town below. The buildings are smaller than my fingertips. They sit alongside a slender road that winds to another village, more rumpled hills, and eventually the flat silver curve of Lake Champlain.

I take another step, then I feel it, deep in my breastbone, Evie's shove, what has been pushing at me ever since I woke in the hospital. How fast she moved. She *flew* at me. And behind me the ground gave way and the black pit rose. Since then, I've startled awake, many times, from the dream of falling backward.

This time, I am facing the abyss. It yawns straight ahead, a lethal fifty-foot drop to the pines below, the gray rock rough with age but high and sheer. And Evie's still here, with her flat face and furious palms, pressing me away from the edge. She won't let me get within a step of it. She won't let me get past her rage to the place where I might feel the great gaping blankness, *why live*, where I might let it lift me until I plummeted.

She won't let me go forward at all. This whole month she has been holding me back, and I cannot go on now except by passing through her.

I don't know how to do this, but the answer isn't here.

I once saw a painted map of Los Angeles circa 1880. It took up half a wall at an exhibition, and was drawn in 3-D from the distance of a short peak, like this one on which I now stand. The map showed rising green hills, orange groves, a low, delicate grid of streets, the pale-blue ocean. The dream of a city in a valley of paradise, flanked by the sea. It was the mapmaker's gift to render both the existence of L.A. and its possibility, at the end of our continent, our last and greatest destination.

Over a century later, immense, overcrowded, and corrupted, that's still the Los Angeles that people fall in love with, the Los Angeles that drew Greg and me, and Kim and her paintings, and even Evie. It's also the city where monstrous appetites meet private hopes, again and again, and devour them. Where ambition is savaged and changed to devastation, where a brilliant artist can be beaten, stabbed, and locked away to die while her party goes on, cups are raised, and bright beats begin to play.

Los Angeles hangs before me now, though I am looking at my own familiar, humble slopes of pines, my own jags of granite, and it's what I breathe though I am gulping the sweet, sharp scent of hemlock and wild raspberry. It gathers in my ears, L.A., like the harsh wind up here that won't stop blowing, though I have ducked my chin and tucked my head into my jacket collar, and am turning away, down the hill.

I'll be back, I promise inside to so many people. It's hard to see my destination, or who I'll find there. I only know that I'm going.

Acknowledgments

My deepest thanks to the following friends and mentors, who were all instrumental in realizing this novel: Rita Mae Reese, Sarah Frisch, Melanie Abrams, Sara Houghteling, Malena Watrous, Robin Ekiss, Glori Simmons, Kasie Carlisle, Karen Lofgren, Eavan Boland, Tobias Wolff, Ken Fields, Adam Johnson, and Tom Kealey. I am indebted to Stanford University, the Jones lecturers, and my former coworkers at the Museum of Contemporary Art. I would also like to thank the University of Vermont, UVM's Office of the Vice President for Research, and my dear colleagues for supporting the book in a myriad of ways.

Thank you to Dan Smetanka, an editor of unparalleled dedication and brilliance, for deepening this story page by page. Thank you to my wonderful agent, Gail Hochman, for many times setting me straight on mystery writing, and to Megan Fishmann, Jennifer Kovitz, Sarah Baline, and the whole crew at Counterpoint and Catapult for bringing this book to readers.

My loving family cannot be thanked enough. My everlasting gratitude goes to all the Hummels, Parmelees, Greenfields, Ochiais, Shettys, Hallans, Cohens, and Creasons, and especially to Bowie, Bruce, and Kyle.

MARIA HUMMEL is the author of *Motherland*, a *San Francisco Chronicle* Book of the Year; *House and Fire*; and *Wilderness Run*. Her fiction, nonfiction, and poetry have appeared in numerous magazines and anthologies, including *The Pushcart Prize*, *Narrative*, *The Sun*, and *The Open Door: 100 Poems, 100 Years of Poetry Magazine*. She worked as a writer/editor at MOCA in Los Angeles, then received a Stegner Fellowship at Stanford University and taught there for many years. She is currently an assistant professor at the University of Vermont, and lives in Vermont with her husband and sons.